Love is a River

Laurel Houck

Love is a River
Copyright © 2020 Laurel Houck

ISBN: (ebook) 978-1-949931-52-5
(print) 978-1-949931-53-2

Inkspell Publishing
207 Moonglow Circle #101
Murrells Inlet, SC 29576

Edited By Yezanira Venecia
Cover art By Najla Qamber
Photograph By Sky Williams

THIS IS DEDICATED

to

Harry, who stands by and lets my light shine

LAUREL HOUCK

THIS IS DEDICATED

to

Harry, who stands by and lets my light shine

LAUREL HOUCK

ONE

"Where else am I supposed to go?"

Not expecting an answer, Abby inhaled a lingering hint of her father's citrus sweetness that hovered over the persistent stench of his death. Her wandering gaze took in the things he had loved—Civil War mementos crowded on the mantel, shelf, and curio cabinet.

"I get it." Her mother put her hands on her hips. "You don't want to move. But your grandmother went back to Florida. Fifteen is too young to stay here alone. That leaves *us* together."

Her words were bullets—quick, brutal, and painful.

Sorrow and fear wound through Abby's heart like laces in an old boot. She glanced at the date on her phone. Could this be her mother's lame attempt at an April Fools' Day joke? "Dad's only been … gone … for two months."

"It must have been hell watching your father suffer." Her mother sighed. "But I'm back. You have to trust me."

Abby considered the thin stranger across the room. Obviously, she was serious. Should she give her a chance? Did she have a choice? She forced words around the tightness in her chest. "I miss him so much. Living here is what helps the most. Seeing his garden, sleeping in the

5

room we painted together—pieces of him that are part of this house. I need more time."

Her mother looked at the floor. "Staying here isn't an option. We had a serious buyer come through the house this morning; I accepted their offer. They put down hand money. Their loan has already been approved." She stared at the floor. "Consider this place sold."

Abby gasped, total disbelief ballooning into white-hot anger. "Sold? What happened to trust, to sharing, to your little 'take all the time you need to heal' crap? Dad would *never* have done this to me if you had died." The poison of her mother's twelve absent years roiled at the bottom of her stomach.

Racing to the bathroom, Abby held her long blonde hair back with her right hand while she threw up in the toilet. She flushed the residue of her peanut butter and jelly sandwich, wet the corner of the hand towel, and wiped her face. The bright red zit on her forehead and the smeared mascara under her blue eyes brought out a frown.

Her mother walked in, brushed a lock of flaxen hair out of Abby's face, and grazed the soft flesh on Abby's cheek. "A new start will be good for us. I *am* your mother."

Abby flinched. "Seriously, Lisa? You haven't been my mother for way too long."

Her mother frowned. "I prefer to be called Mom, if you don't mind."

"'*I prefer.*'" Abby grimaced. "It is all about you, isn't it? Turns out I do mind."

Abby crossed her arms and waited. After too many years of wishing for a mom, the time to welcome this one back had passed.

Lisa sighed. "Okay. I won't fight that battle with you right now. It's more important to focus on finding our way back to each other."

"It's going to be a long trip. You don't know me."

"Of course I do. You're my daughter."

"Right." Abby pulled the phone from the back pocket

of her jeans. "What's my favorite music?"

Lisa paused. "I'm guessing Disney princess songs would be wrong."

"Ya think?" Abby took a deep breath. "My best friend, my only friend, moved to Oregon in January. You never met her. Can you make my favorite dinner? Nope, because you have no clue what I eat. I hate exercise, math, ghost stories—and you. Now you know something about me. Feel connected?"

Lisa's voice caught. "I love you. It's him I left."

"Funny thing about that. When you left him, I got left behind, too. No calls, no visits, no nothing." Abby stalked to the kitchen, shuddering at the anger pulsating through her but unable to make it stop. Pulling a bottle of water from the refrigerator she downed half of it, choking when her mother followed.

Abby swiped dribbles of water off her chin with her fist. "After twelve years, I'm over you. But even when Dad got sick you stayed away." She jabbed a chewed fingernail at Lisa. "You—stayed—away."

Lisa ran trembling fingers through her already-tousled bob. "You have to believe me. I had a good reason to leave."

"What's your 'good reason' for dumping us?"

Lisa pulled a kitchen chair away from the table, sat down, folded her hands, and lowered her head. "It doesn't matter anymore."

Abby longed to tell her that everything would be fine and to accept a big mom-hug. Instead, she wrapped her own arms around her body, fingertips pressing into bony ribs. "Did you ever wonder about me, even once? If I liked ballet or baseball? If I was short or tall? If I lived or died?"

Lisa opened her mouth and then shut it.

"You already decided to move back to Pittsburgh." Abby tamped down her anger and went for reasonable. "If we stay in *this* house we can bond here."

In the moment of silence that followed, a brief twitch

of hope tickled Abby's gut.

"I can't live here," Lisa said at last. "Memories that are precious to you are ghosts that keep me tied to the past. I know you loved your dad. I'm sorry he died. But my life isn't inside these four walls anymore. Neither is yours."

Abby's stomach gurgled, as if begging to hug the toilet bowl again. The cool porcelain would almost be a relief next to her burning cheeks. "It's hard to believe how understanding you are, *Mother*. I won't let go of my dad."

"Let go? It's not like I'm asking you to forget him. Just take a step back and loosen your grip, that's all." Lisa shrugged. "It may even help you to get over it."

A raging heat crept over Abby. "*If?* I'm not getting over *him* like some virus."

She turned away and ran her hand across the butcher-block kitchen counter, ending at the stove. Plucking a griddle off the shelf, she banged it on the burner. "This is where Dad made chocolate-chip pancakes, every Saturday morning." She closed her eyes. With very little effort, the sizzle of batter, the mingled aromas of chocolate and butter, and the light flap of a turned pancake drifted through her mind.

Leaving the kitchen, Abby stalked across the great-room past the stone fireplace, Lisa following. "I remember being four years old. Dad built a fire and danced with me during a thunderstorm; storms never scared me again."

She gestured up the stairs. "Dad's bedroom is up there. He died in that room, holding my hand, not yours." Silent tears coursed down Abby's pale cheeks, as she realized leaving his house would be as if she were losing him all over again.

"I refuse to play the guilt game." Lisa once again put her hands on her hips. "I've been more than patient. When your grandmother left in March, I came to help you work things out. When that didn't happen, I gave you space. I'm not sure where you thought things were heading, but I guess I didn't explain myself clearly enough. What part of 'you're moving' don't you understand?"

Silence stretched between them, broken only by the ticking of the antique mantle clock. They stared at each other; Abby's mother looked away first.

"Lisa?"

Silence.

"Mom?"

More silence.

Screw her. "Are we moving to a cardboard box under the Liberty Bridge or a homeless shelter?"

Lisa stared at a point above Abby's head. "I already bought an old house on the bike trail by the Youghiogheny River, in Boston—Pennsylvania, not Massachusetts, of course. It's only forty-five minutes away. We'll remodel it and open an inn for people riding their bicycles long-distance from the Canadian border to Washington, D.C. I'll drive you to your old school until the end of the year."

"So, let me get this straight. We move to a total dump in a tiny town no one ever heard of, slap on some paint, heat up microwave pancakes, and make a fortune from people on bicycles?"

Abby's anger seeped away like murky dishwater oozing down the kitchen drain; the sludge of grief and disappointment remained. "It's a done deal?"

Lisa nodded and reached out to hug her. "Abby—please ..."

Abby pushed her mother away. "Fine. Whatever. Leave me alone."

She retreated to the kitchen once more and waited until Lisa's footsteps faded, cringing at even the murmur of her shoes on the carpeted stairs. "Why did you do this to me, Dad? What am I supposed to do without you?"

The blue gingham curtain rustled in a sudden draft of cool air that wafted through the partially open window above the sink.

"Abigail ..."

Abby thought she heard someone whispering her

name, carried by a breeze that smelled like campfires and coffee. "Dad?" But he always called her Abby. Were things different in heaven?

Rubbing the goose bumps on her arms, she took a few halting steps and looked out the window. No one was there. The sound should have been frightening, ghostly, freaky to the max. Instead, she found it oddly calming, as if her name had been murmured with love. Blinking her burning eyes, she gazed out at her father's garden. The birds still chirped, and the pansies remained fragrant. In the clear, cerulean sky, the sun shone bright, warm, perfect.

How could everything outside be so predictable and normal, while everything inside spun out of control? A stray cirrus cloud drifted across the sun. Abby pressed her palm against the warm glass. Nothing would ever be the same. Ever.

TWO

Lisa's strident voice echoed, amplified by the almost-empty house. "*Abby*. Get busy up there. It's Wednesday, moving day—so you better get it together."

Abby blinked back the familiar press of hot tears behind her eyes as the thought of a different Wednesday took shape in her mind. Back then it seemed like an ordinary day—school, homework, Campbell's tomato soup, Dad's grateful wink as he drifted off.

Setting down the box she'd been packing, Abby sank onto the mattress, caressing the brass headboard with her fingers. Today the open window let in a late-April breeze. Four weeks since the house sold. Twelve weeks since the bleak, icy, cold February afternoon forever frozen in Abby's mind.

"ABBY. Are you done yet? I want to finish loading the truck. It's supposed to rain."

Abby ignored Lisa. Her gaze swept the room, taking in the rocking chair where she would watch her father sleep. She got to her feet and placed her father's cherished items one by one into a carton; she lingered on each precious piece. Civil War books they'd read together, bike gloves, an old snapshot of them in the garden, captioned "Daddy loves Abby" in his bold, slanted cursive—bits and pieces of an abandoned life.

The ache in her heart grew at the sight of the faded quilt still folded at the end of his bed. Everything had remained in its proper place, as if February's grand finale never happened at all.

Lisa stood at the door of the room. "It's almost time."

Her soft tone almost pushed Abby over the edge into tears, but she clung to her anger, the only thing that had never left her in all these months.

"Yeah, okay." Abby shook her head, remembering the snowdrifts getting deeper as her father's breathing became shallower. Then silent as snow, he had slipped away to another place. Now she'd be in another place, too. But not with him.

A refreshing chill crept up her arms and wound around her shoulders, accompanied by the subtle scent of coffee. Somehow the odd caress strengthened her. "Can't wait."

As she closed the door on her old life, the cool embrace returned, lingering until the click of the latch. Not the tiniest scrap of fear accompanied it. She knew ghosts didn't exist, couldn't possibly be real. But somehow this sensation spoke of pure, celestial love. Abby felt, more than heard, her name being whispered … again.

"*Abigail … Come to me …*"

From deep in her gut she wondered if her dad had found a way to say good-bye. How could she go to him? She ached for his presence with a pain so sharp she could imagine a butcher knife sinking into her heart hilt-deep.

The ride to the unknown house seemed to take forever, the silence in the truck thick enough to smother. Abby's neck ached from staring out the side window, avoiding even a glimpse of her mother behind the wheel. She imagined a bright blue ribbon stretching from the home left behind to the one waiting by the bike trail. A connection that could tie her to the love in her past. But did it lead to new love in her future?

Lisa's fake-chirpy voice broke into her musings. "We're here."

Speechless, Abby got out of the truck, leaving the door open as if she could jump back in and drive away. She fought the urge to rub her eyes as she stared at the monstrosity up the slope from the bike trail. The ancient house, topped with a tin roof and boasting an arrow-shaped weather vane, could be a movie set for a horror film. Dark windows, peeling paint, and a sinister atmosphere surrounded the place.

"Isn't it amazing?" Lisa threw one arm around Abby and squeezed. "So much potential for so little money. The realtor said it dates back to Civil War days. Can you believe that? It's perfect for us. That's why I wanted it to be a surprise."

"Yeah, serendipity." Abby slipped out of Lisa's embrace and nibbled on a fingernail.

Budding leaves rustled as the temperature suddenly dropped. Abby turned her head to a faint murmur.

"Abigail ..."

Lisa was pulling a bag from inside the truck, and Abby saw no one in the deserted yard around the isolated house. Her nostrils twitched at a faint tang; the outdoors with a tinge of coffee? Her heart lurched in a crazy, pre-teen crush kind of way. No doubt it was nothing more than the local Starbucks sending her heart soaring.

For almost two seconds Abby wondered if she had lost her mind, if it was Lisa's fault, or if the blame belonged to Dad for dying. She rejected the latter; it made no sense to be mad at her father or his cancer. But nothing made sense anymore. Resentment tugged at her like a bobber being pulled by an unseen fish.

"My life sucks." Saying it out loud made her life an official failure.

As she scanned the façade of the house she noticed a hexagonal window on the third floor. Abby thought she glimpsed a face, distorted by the wavy panes of old glass.

She squinted, shielded her eyes against the backdrop of sun and stared. Nothing. Her heart did a hop-skip-jump, and spidery tingles ran up her arms.

Behind the house stood a large barn attached to an ivy-covered silo. Spotlights of sun shone through holes in the barn roof. She started toward the outbuilding to escape her mother at least for a few moments.

"No, honey, come see the house first." Lisa's voice held a note of pleading excitement. "Doesn't it have so much potential?"

"'Potential.' The P word." Abby trudged back to the house.

Lisa stood on the derelict front porch, opening the shell of a screen door with a flourish. "Ta-da." She patted Abby's back, ushering her inside.

Abby stepped into the foyer, gagging on a mixture of mildew, grease, and sour milk permeating the area. She brushed a cobweb off her face. "You're kidding, right?"

Random leaves congregated in the corners. A small black mouse scurried into a hole in the baseboard. Strips of yellowed wallpaper embossed with faded roses hung in shreds from the walls.

Lisa sighed. "Abby, please. Give this a chance, okay? I would've had it cleaned before we moved, but things happened too fast." Her voice brightened. "We can do it together."

"Sure. I love to clean." A twinge of guilt zinged through Abby when her mother's smile froze in place and then faded.

"Pick a room for yourself on the third floor." Lisa's dull monotone matched the flat look in her eyes. Her mouth opened and closed, she gestured around the room in silence, and then plodded outside.

The squeal of the truck door sounded to Abby like the cry of a tortured soul, as if saying, *"Welcome to hell, Abigail Whitney. Looks like you'll be here for eternity."*

She rolled her eyes and ascended the curving stairs to

the second floor. Six doors opened off a central area; one of them, smaller and arched, opened to another set of steps. She headed for the doorway. A second mouse skittered in front of her before running into an empty room. "Our guests will love sharing the crumbs—and their rooms—with you. Wait until I tell Dad about this place …"

As grief roiled to the surface, Abby made an effort to take deep breaths and push it away. "He's not in pain; he's in a better place. He's not in pain; he's in a better place."

She recited the mantra she'd practiced for months. Dad had been a Civil War buff; a civil war between grief and healing went on inside her every day. Grief seemed to be winning.

After tromping up the paint-splotched wooded stairs, she explored the top level. She gave a cursory glance into one space draped in cobwebs, with shadowed nooks, warped floorboards, sloping rafters, and someone else's junk. The other two rooms were finished with plaster and paint, and she chose the one that included a view of the bike trail and the barn. She rubbed a clean spot on the glass with her sleeve and looked outside, catching a glimpse of the river threaded between a profusion of trees.

She imagined her dad riding his Cannondale on the bike trail. In her mental image he rode away from her, his face already starting to slip from her recall. As she walked downstairs something crunched under her sneaker. Two M&M candies, one bright blue and one orange, were pulverized on the step.

A floorboard creaked over her head, and she stopped, her senses on high alert. Ghosts? Serial killer? She pressed her fingertips against the rough plaster wall, her ears tuned into every nuance of sound, her eyes scanning the stairwell. Stale air clogged her lungs, and the metallic taste of fear drenched her mouth. She had read about murdered girls in abandoned houses. Thick old walls didn't let screams—or people—escape.

A door squeaked, a slow, deliberate sound followed by a stealthy footstep.

Abby waited in the curve of the stairs, back pressed against the wall. Her thin black sweater clung to her suddenly damp skin, and the urge to pee made her squirm. Footsteps came closer. She sniffed a sudden whiff of chocolate. The hair on her arms stood straight up, threaded between the goose bumps raised there. Her heart labored harder, a painful drumbeat in her chest. A dust mote floated through the air, tickling her nose with the threat of a sneeze. She held her breath, fight or flight vying for her attention. But if she didn't handle this, Lisa might get hurt, too.

Taking a deep breath, she peered around the corner.

A piercing shriek split her eardrums. "Ahhhhh."

THREE

Abby put one hand over her pounding heart and leaned against the wall for support. The echo of that scream reverberated in her ears. She waited for her body's functions to get back to normal while studying the intruder.

A boy stood on the stairs above her. Unkempt red hair curled at the edges, plastered to his sweaty forehead. Round, wire-framed glasses enlarged surprisingly intense brown eyes. His mouth, open and panting, caused his chest to heave and his pudgy stomach to rise and fall. Cobwebs decorated his worn T-shirt, a gossamer line across an embroidered logo, *Boston, PA: Not Just Baked Beans*. A smudge of dirt slashed across one flushed cheek.

Abby took a deep breath and put her hands on her hips. "For a serial killer you're not very scary."

"I wouldn't kill anything."

"Ya think?"

He wiped a grubby hand on his equally-grimy jeans, then extended it to Abby. "Hi. I'm Morton. Morton Sabrosky. I'm more of a cereal killer—get it? I like cereal?" He chuckled. "Your name must be Blondie."

Abby avoided his hand and his joke. She flipped her

17

hair to the side. "I'm Abby. What're you doing in my house?"

"*Your* house? But I thought—I mean, everyone knows—this house is abandoned, at least since Old Man Corson died, like, centuries ago." Morton sneezed and wiped his nose on the back of his forearm, smearing a glistening snail-trail line of snot onto his skin.

Abby wrinkled her nose. She pulled a mostly-clean tissue from her pocket and handed it to him. "It won't be empty anymore. My mother bought it, and we're moving in today. So, what are you doing here?"

"You're moving in? Wait. What? But there isn't even electricity."

The hall light above Morton's head flicked on, as if on cue.

"It looks like we do have electricity, doesn't it? And you're here because …?"

"I'm just hanging out." Morton shrugged. "You know, something to do." He shuffled his feet. "I'm kind of an amateur ghost hunter, and this seems like the best place around here to hunt for spirits—except for the cemetery, of course. That's the coolest; it's real ancient, and because old soldiers are buried there, guys from the Civil War, I figure there must be supernatural activity in the vicinity."

He stared at Abby.

She fidgeted in the sudden silence, pulled her sweater over her hips, and ran one hand through her bangs. "What? Do I have three eyes or something? Quit staring at me."

Morton frowned. "No … not three eyes, but you do have a weird kind of aura."

"Yeah, okay. What's an aura?"

"It's hard to explain to someone who isn't sensitive—you know—into the supernatural world around us." Morton gazed at the ceiling as if the answer could be found in the strips of wood. "I've been doing this all my life, so I know what to look for."

Abby laughed. "Uh-huh, and how long is 'all my life?' You're what, maybe twelve years old?"

Morton pulled himself up straight. "I'm thirteen— almost fourteen, well, in ten months. And for your information, an aura is like a force, almost a kind of light that's around a ghost or someone who's, uh ..." He took two steps away from Abby. "You aren't a ghost, right? I mean, if you are, that's cool and all, but this would be the first time I've really talked to a supernatural being." He raised his voice. "HELLO."

"Seriously?" Abby shook her head. "You need to find something else to do around here. It's hardly ghost central."

"Yeah, well, here's the thing, and I hate to tell you on your first day in Loserville, aka Boston, PA." Morton sighed. "There isn't much else going on in a small town like this one, except the bike trail. And I'm not too athletic." He looked down at his bulging abdomen. "You might have guessed that already."

"The M&M's are yours?"

Morton nodded. "They're perfect, ya know? Small enough to fit in my pocket, melt in my mouth, not in my hand, and I can eat a little or a lot. Kind of a chocolate security blanket. And FYI, I didn't know someone bought this property or I wouldn't be here, honest. Trespassing is against the law, and I'm real careful to follow the rules."

"It's hard to believe you didn't hear us downstairs. The doors squeak, and we walked all around the first floor."

Morton gestured to the hexagonal window. "Yeah, okay. I saw the truck but didn't have time to get out before you came up here. I thought I'd hide until you left, but you aren't leaving, I guess, since you live here now." He paused for a breath.

Abby stared at him, hoping he would soon be the one to leave.

Morton scuffed the toe of his sneaker on the step and ran the back of his hand under his nose again. "Guess I'll go now. So ... see ya." He clomped down the stairs, glancing back at Abby over his shoulder.

Abby watched him. Maybe he had an older brother, someone cute, in better shape. She held up one hand. "You can help us move in and fix up the house if you want."

Morton smiled. "Sure. Great. If it's okay with your mom and dad."

Abby frowned. "Just Lisa."

"Oh, she an aunt or something? Auntie Lisa, I like it."

"You ask a lot of questions. And no, not an aunt; she's my mother, sort of."

"Yeah, I know how it is. My parents are divorced, too. My mom's, um, busy a lot, and my dad, well, I never knew him. What a total loser. You know how it is. It's the mom who takes care of the kid, and the dad who skips out."

A slow burn started in Abby's stomach and traveled up her throat. "I have no idea how it is. I wish my parents were only divorced. *My* dad is dead, departed, buried, crossed over, gone into the light, whatever you want to call it. He disappeared in February. He's not even *in* my world."

Morton pulled a crumpled brown package of candies from his pocket, struggling to release it from the tight denim. "Oh, sorry; everyone I know has divorced parents. Here, have some M&M's. These little babies are miracle workers."

Abby snorted. The myth of chocolate. As if candy could make it all better.

"Hey—where'd you go? Zoned out on me, huh? You got attention problems? PMS?" Morton waved a hand in front of Abby's eyes. "Maybe you should see a doctor or something."

Abby longed to put both hands over her ears and hum to block out Morton's annoying chatter. "I don't think we need help moving in after all. Thanks anyway."

Morton shrugged. He lumbered down the steps.

She followed him to the first floor.

Morton lingered in the doorway. "You sure? I have more muscles than you might think. And I'm real good company. No one's ever lonely when I'm around."

"Thanks, but we're almost done. And I'm not lonely. So …" She gestured to the front door.

"Gee, it doesn't look like you even got started moving in." Morton nodded his head and pursed his lips. "You don't have to be embarrassed to admit you're lonesome. Happens to me a lot."

"I'm trying to be nice," Abby said. "But you need to go. Okay?"

Morton nodded. "I'll come back some other time. When you're in a better mood." He jumped down the front steps and ambled out of sight around the barn.

Abby sighed and held the door open as her mother entered, carrying three stacked cardboard boxes that teetered as she maneuvered them through the entrance.

"Who's that? We could use some help."

"Forget it. I'll carry the stuff from the truck." Abby let the screen door slam behind her. For better or for worse, she lived in this house now. With Lisa.

The day dragged on until the soft shadows of dusk began to soften the harsh reality of the old house. By the time the truck sat empty, Abby's arms ached, and her damp cotton sweater stuck to her back. She wiped a paper towel across her forehead as a white car with a Vocelli's logo on the side pulled up to the house.

Lisa paid the driver then opened the cooler and pulled out two cherry Cokes. She handed one drink to Abby, then sat down on the front steps and opened the cardboard box. "Mushroom—your favorite, right? See, I remembered."

"Great. Thanks." Abby sandwiched two slices of pizza together, cheese to cheese, on a napkin. With her soda balanced on the other hand, she retreated to the kitchen. Her thoughts bounced around in her head as she mechanically chewed and swallowed. She jumped when Lisa plopped the pizza box on the counter. "Oh. I thought you were outside."

Lisa opened the lid of the container and lifted a fragrant slice onto a paper napkin.

The aroma of garlic and tomato wafted through the kitchen. Abby's stomach growled, and she extracted another cheesy piece loaded with fresh mushroom from the box. She knew she should thank Lisa again—even *wanted* to thank her for remembering the mushrooms—but the words stuck in her throat.

Lisa seemed to be waiting, then gave a small shake of her head and pursed her lips. "After we eat we'll sweep up, clean the bathrooms, and make the beds, okay?"

Abby shrugged. "Whatever."

While she worked, Abby wondered if Morton really did know anything about ghosts, auras, and things she always thought were ridiculous ... and if the voice that had whispered her name was something he could explain.

By the time she crawled under her sheets in the third-floor bedroom, the home she had occupied all her life seemed like a distant memory. The imagined blue ribbon connecting her from there to here didn't exist. Her dad no longer did either.

FOUR

Time blurred for Abby as the weeks passed. The day-to-day effort of traveling to and from school with Lisa, followed by helping with the house every evening, became an anesthetic; numbness replaced anger, tiredness replaced grief.

Abby watched the battered red truck pull into the circular driveway of Milton Fritch Senior High, as the church bell across the street chimed twelve times. Lisa reached across the seat and opened the door. "Hey there. Summer vacation, here we come."

Abby climbed in, slammed the door, and slouched in the seat. "Can't wait."

Lisa peered around at other kids spilling out the doors, down the sidewalks, and onto busses at the curb. "You're welcome to have some friends over. We could have a barbecue, play some badminton, ride bikes, that kind of thing."

"You've got to be kidding." Abby gestured to the bodies that passed by without a glance, most of them smiling, waving to each other, getting in cars together. "See any friends out there? I like being by myself. And please, *badminton*? What, next you'll be all 'Where's the shuttle*cock*?' That would so boost my popularity."

They drove home in silence. The rhythm of the tires on the asphalt lulled Abby into a fitful doze, where one by one she watched everyone she knew drop out of her life. Dad's pain-filled face, urging her, "Go do something with your pals," didn't work in her dreams, any more than it had in reality. She'd shut out the world, except for him, until no one remembered she existed. Which, by then, she didn't, not really. When he died, he'd taken along the feeling part of her heart. She didn't have the energy to mourn for him or for herself.

Abby woke with a start when the truck stopped. Lisa pulled on the emergency brake, then disappeared into the barn without a word. And why not? Not even her mother wanted to deal with the total bitch she had become.

She climbed the wide board steps, crossed the porch, and opened the screen door. Tossing her backpack in the cubbyhole under the stairs, she wandered from room to room, as if seeing the place for the first time. Through the pounding of nails, the swish of a paintbrush, and the addition of personal items, the house had become beautiful. In the living room, soft lace curtains framed the bay window. Sunlight shone through the dining room casements, illuminating the strips of stained glass above them.

Abby wandered into the kitchen, sniffing the aroma of cinnamon and apples that lingered in the air from the warm pie on the counter. A pleasant sense of hunger moved through her belly for apple pie with chocolate ice cream. Most people ate pie with vanilla; her dad had said that was "only for wimps." She ran from the aroma—and the memory—and stumbled onto the front porch to get some fresh air.

At the bottom of the steps Lisa struggled with a long board, dark blue with a hand-painted border of flowers entwined in a bright blue ribbon. In script it read: Bikers' Rest.

"Help me hang this, Abby. You do the honors."

It occurred to Abby in a flash that the still, quiet comfort in her belly resonated as an almost-happy feeling. And she owed it to Lisa. "This is all about you. You had the idea, you planned it, you named it—it's all yours." When she smiled her muscles felt stiff, unused, almost painful.

"No, it's ours." Lisa leaned the sign against the porch railing and placed a ladder against the gutter. She didn't look at Abby. "Your father and I talked about opening a place like this when we first got married. We had dreams—then."

Abby surveyed the orange daylilies, purple wild geranium, and red poppies peeking through the slats of the picket fence. Along the porch steps, tightly closed buds peppered the dark foliage of two deep red rose bushes. Turning, she caught a glimpse of the river flowing endlessly through the trees, murky umber against a profusion of pale green. Had her dad really dreamed of a day like this? How could Lisa know so much about him?

"Okay, I'll do it." Abby climbed the aluminum ladder, hung the sign on twin brass chains from the gingerbread trim under the eaves, and re-joined her mother.

Conflicting emotions raged through her brain. She realized her mother waited for a response. "Great, good, love it. I … um … I have some things to do." She chewed a ragged fingernail.

"Like gnaw on your nails? Why not take the Cannondale for a spin? The pie will wait until you get back, and then we'll celebrate." Lisa clapped her hands together, like a small child. "I even got ice cream—French vanilla, the best."

"I know you don't understand—I can't expect you to get it—but I just can't ride his bike." She escaped as tears gathered in the corners of her eyes, trying to ignore the sound of Lisa's big sigh.

"Wear a bike helmet if you change your mind!"

Lisa wanted her to be safe. Abby smiled all the way to the barn. She looked around the dim space, and her eyes fell on her old purple bike in the corner of the front horse stall.

"No, I won't." Abby shook her head but reached over to squeeze the front tire. "You need air. I'm not riding you, but I can do some bicycle CPR." Abby inflated both tires with a hand pump and wiped dust off the seat. She pushed up the kickstand and rode in a small circle inside the barn. "I guess it's true; you never forget how to ride a bike." She glanced at the bike helmet on a hook but left it hanging there.

Moments later she glided down the path from the house onto the gravel trail surface, passing a small sign: Youghiogheny River Trail. The breeze blew her hair straight back in a cool, cleansing rush, even through the mid-day heat.

The chirping of insects accompanied the crunch of bike tires on limestone. Both were drowned out when a train passed by on the other side of the river, wheels clacking, whistle blowing. Abby lost track of time, weaving between dappled shade and sun-drenched sky.

The smell of wildflowers tickled her nose, and she sneezed. She recognized a patch of Queen Anne's lace, braked, and got off the bike. The huge blossoms, comprised of multiple, tiny white buds, grew in profusion. She searched through them; hidden in the center of one flower she found a single, bright red bud.

"I remember you." Abby ran her index finger over the velvety flowers that some called weeds, but her dad saw as beautiful. Queen Anne's lace grew in the meadow at home.

Ages ago she'd taken a walk with her dad and picked a bouquet. "I love them, Daddy," she told him that day. "They're like princesses and weddings and happily-ever-after."

Her dad found one with a red center. "These are very special. I call them Queen Abby's Lace. The red center is the heart of the flower. When you see one, always remember you're my heart, little princess. I know you'll live happily-ever-after. I promise."

Abby sniffled and blinked back hot tears. She picked the red-centered flower from its stem and tucked it in the pocket of her denim shorts, even though she couldn't imagine the promise of "happily-ever-after" working out. She got back on the bike and pushed off, her fair cheeks and shoulders burning in the hot sun. A cramping ache spread from her thighs, to her knees, to her ankles as out-of-shape muscles protested.

Pop.

She veered across the trail as the front tire deflated. Struggling to maintain control she braked too hard and skidded. The bike hit a rock, plunged into a ditch, and flipped over, knocking her off.

The rough gravel, rammed into Abby's knees, brought pinpoint jabs of pain. A sharp, hot gash traveled across her cheek. She bounced onto her back, landing in damp weeds that reeked of onion. With a loud whoosh, her lungs emptied; she gasped for breath. Her head smacked into something hard and unyielding, with a loud crack of bone on stone. She lay still for several minutes, afraid to move until it became obvious something had to change.

With great care, she stretched each limb, relieved to find her body responding the way it should. Craning her neck back, she searched for what her head hit. She saw a weathered gray tombstone, rounded at the top with straight sides. The granite appeared to be moving. Hundreds of bugs covered the surface, their bodies bright red like blood, wings black, heads quivering with antennae.

Abby rolled over, scrambled to her feet, and brushed a squirming insect off her forehead. "I'm in a freaking cemetery with a skinned knee, bug bites, and rotting corpses." Every image she'd ever seen of putrefied, decaying bodies came into her mind. Each one had the face of her father.

Abby gagged and vomited into the weeds, until dry heaves took over. Finally she took a deep, shuddering breath and waited until her heart stopped pounding. Wiping her lips with the back of one hand, she grimaced at the sour taste in her mouth and wished for a tall, frosty glass of water. The gurgling of real water brought her head up. From her vantage point on a small rise, she caught a glimpse of the Youghiogheny as it rippled around a fallen tree at water's edge.

She limped toward the river to splash her face then stopped, realizing it meant walking through the cemetery. It would be her first time in such a place since her father had been buried. She had to think he rested in peace, rather than rotted in pieces. She took several tentative steps through the overgrown brush and around a tilting headstone. A huge shadow appeared against the trunk of a gnarled tree, looming over her.

Abby ducked and screamed.

FIVE

"Abby?"

Abby jumped, heart thumping, adrenaline shooting through her veins. Whipping around, she almost expected to see her father, magically resurrected.

What she saw made her shoulders slump forward. "Morton. What are you doing here? This is, after all, a graveyard, and you're not dead. Not yet."

Morton stood, contemplating his untied sneakers in silence.

"Hello? Who's the one with attention problems now?"

"Look, I know you don't want anything to do with me," Morton said. "At your own house, you got a right. But this is public property." He stopped, put his hands in the pockets of his khaki shorts, and studied his black high-tops again. His chubby cheeks flushed in two bright red spots, his nostrils flared, and his breath snorted in short, asthmatic gulps as if drowning.

Abby picked at a scabbed-over zit on her forehead, under her bangs. "Sorry. Really."

"I get it." Morton nodded. "You got issues, your dad and moving and stuff."

"Where'd you get that idea?"

Morton considered the question. "Who doesn't have issues?"

"Yeah, okay." Abby took a step, wincing as she moved.

"Hey, you're hurt." Morton reached to steady her. "Sit down."

"I'll live." Abby pulled away from him, but she limped to a tree stump and rested on the uneven surface. She rubbed the back of her head. "Just a little lump." Flinching, she touched her cheek then brushed gritty limestone dust from her legs.

Morton examined her knees. "Road rash. And you should've worn a bike helmet. That's what they're for, you know. It's not responsible to ride without one."

"You sound like Lisa."

Morton shrugged. "She's right. I'll take care of the cuts. I have antiseptic wipes in my backpack. Wait here." He trotted across the cemetery, shoelaces flapping, and returned with an orange backpack.

Abby took out her ponytail and ran a hand through her tangled hair, finger-combing out bits of leaves and grit. She winced when her fingers brushed against her sore scalp. "What are you, some kind of Boy Scout?"

"Yeah, you know, always prepared." Morton started to clean Abby's cheek.

"*Ouch.*"

"Don't be such a baby. Actually, you look more like a raccoon, with that black make-up stuff under your eyes. Your cheek's okay, but I have to get the gravel out of your knees. Infection is a big problem with injuries like this. Hold still. I got a merit badge in first aid. I know how to clean it without making it worse."

Abby jerked her leg away at the sting of antiseptic. "Why *are* you hanging out in a cemetery?"

Morton gently pulled her leg back. "The Boy Scout troop I belonged to fixed up a campsite down by the river." Morton tucked the soiled wipe in his pocket and pulled out a fresh one. "It's called Dravo Landing; there's a sign and everything. It's pretty awesome. And Civil War soldiers are buried here. I read some of the inscriptions on their headstones; they tell stories, you know—the stones, not the dead guys. That's the ones you can still read. A lot of them are worn away from the weather. It happens after almost 150 years."

"My Dad was into the Civil War," Abby said. "One time we went to Gettysburg and he made me tour the battlefield on horseback. I didn't want to; it seemed stupid so I refused at first, but he made me. Then we had to ride bikes up some major hills he called 'long grades.' I whined the whole way. I wish I hadn't been such a pain in the ass." Abby sighed and made an effort to re-focus. "Why's this cemetery in the middle of nowhere?"

"Dravo Methodist Church used to be here." Morton gestured to the area beside the cemetery. "It burned down, like, a hundred years ago from a train engine spark—they used burning wood or coal to make the engine run. Weird, huh?"

"But the train tracks are on the other side of the river."

Morton shook his head. "The bike trail used to be a train track. That's why they call it rails-to-trails, get it? The trains back then came right past the church and the cemetery."

Abby looked at the towering trees surrounding the cemetery, the river below, and the wildflowers here and there. "It's beautiful, but you have to admit it's weird to hang out in a graveyard. What if you skidded in on your bike during a funeral?"

"Not likely." Morton covered Abby's knee with a gauze pad and taped it in place. "There hasn't been a burial here since 1942. But no one knows too much about these old graves. The church records got burned up in the fire."

"You know a lot about it." Abby groaned as he patted her knee, right on top of the torn skin. She pulled her leg away.

Morton stuffed his supplies in his pack. "You're a total

girl, you know that? Just put some antibiotic ointment on this tonight and a clean Band-Aid. No charge."

"I'll take that as a compliment, I think. But seriously, it's kind of cool that you know so much about this place."

Morton blinked rapidly, eyes magnified by his glasses. "I like history, and there's tons of neat stuff around here. Maybe even a stop on the Underground Railroad. Down in West Newton there's one for sure."

"Our house is supposed to be from the Civil War era," Abby said. "But it's nothing special."

Morton beckoned to Abby. "Come on, I'll show you around."

Abby meandered through the small, unkempt cemetery behind Morton.

Grass and weeds surrounded the graves. Headstones tilted this way and that as the ground sloped toward the river. Old-growth trees cast gloomy shadows, perfect for ancient spirits and decay. The fragrance of wildflowers perfumed the air, a sickly-sweet aroma reminiscent of a funeral home. It brought back memories of the long day spent by her father's coffin, mumbling mechanical "thank-you's" while people mouthed their repetitive condolences.

The breeze picked up, swirling the humid, sticky air. A rumble of thunder rolled through the accumulating clouds. Little swirls of twigs and leaves raced through the cemetery, and Abby's hair blew into her face.

Morton studied the sky, wet his index finger, and put it to the air. "I'm out of here."

Abby's eyebrows went up. "It's just a little rain. It won't hurt you."

"I, uh, I'm—I don't like storms, okay?" Morton jogged toward his bike. "Make fun of me if you want, but I have to go, right now."

Abby followed him. Images of dancing with her dad waltzed through her mind, flickers of memory like flames in the fireplace. She shook her head and raised her voice to compete with the wind. "Everyone's afraid of something. I used to be terrified of storms, too. Sometimes you just have to suck it up. But I hate heights, so we're even. You go ahead. My bike is destroyed, so I'll have to walk."

Morton swallowed hard and scanned the darkening sky and tree branches rustling in wind gusts. "Let me see. Maybe I can get it going. It'll take you forever to walk back."

Abby pulled her mangled bike out of the ditch and wheeled it to the trail.

"The front fender's bent, and the tire's flat." Morton pulled a portable pump off his bike and put air in the tire, then straightened the fender. "Try that."

Although it wobbled and the tire still rubbed, it worked.

"Thanks," Abby said. "Come on, before the rain starts, and you have a panic attack."

A bolt of lightning cut across the sky above the trees. A fireworks-style clap of thunder boomed. Morton whimpered, then shot past Abby on his bike. He disappeared through the mist.

The wind picked up even more, bending tree branches over the trail. Slow at first, then with increased intensity the rain began. Abby rode with her head down as much as possible, wet strings of hair dripping into her eyes. Her leaden feet fought both the impaired bike and sodden shoes. Sore and tight, her skinned knees flexed, pumping the pedals. The rain-soaked tape over her bandages let go; the gauze disappeared on the trail. Damp foliage gave off a pungent odor—of rotting brush and something even more foul, maybe a dead animal.

Finally, the old house materialized through the curtain of rain and fog. Electric candles in the windows emanated a soft glow. Her mother peered out the screen door, waving in welcome.

Abby blinked the water out of her eyes, and an unbidden smile blossomed on her lips.

She rode to the barn, stored her bike, and stomped into

the mudroom where Lisa waited with a towel still warm from the dryer. It surrounded her with comfort and the smell of a fresh summer day.

"Honey, I'm so glad you're back," Lisa said. "I worry about you." She stopped and frowned. "What were you thinking, being out in a storm like that? What happened to your cheek—and your knees? And where's your bike helmet?"

"I had a little bike problem," Abby avoided the helmet question. "I'll just take a hot bath and get changed." She trudged upstairs to the relative peace of the claw-foot tub, filling it almost to the brim. Leaving her wet clothes in a heap, she slipped into the water, cringing as her skinned knees submerged.

She reclined in the steaming bath until only her face floated above the surface. The scent of lilac bath salts combined with the rain's staccato drumbeats on the tin roof, a combination that should have been relaxing. But her thoughts refused to rest. They bounced from Civil War soldiers at the cemetery, to Lisa, to her dad.

As if in slow motion, Abby's eyelids drifted closed and she fell asleep. Her head sunk below the water, a line of bubbles ascending to the surface.

She dreamed of her father, laughing as his bike skidded into the Dravo Cemetery. "Hurry up, slowpoke." He disappeared in a ray of bright sun behind a tombstone.

"Dad, wait for me." Abby dashed through the cemetery, dodging tombstones. "Where are you?"

A clap of thunder pierced the sunny afternoon. The humid air made it impossible to breathe, but Abby's feet wouldn't move. "*Dad.* I can't breathe."

Then she saw it—him?—floating above the grave where she had hit her head. His translucent face and neck extended from a tattered Union Army uniform. Dark brown hair peeked out from under his cap, a curl dipping over one hazel eye highlighted with gold flecks. His morose visage brightened as he smiled, revealing bright white teeth; a deep dimple opened in his right cheek.

She had the crazy thought that she loved him at first sight.

"*Abigail ... it ain't your time. Go back.*"

She choked trying to get words out, and no matter how hard she tried, she couldn't force any air into her lungs. Willing her leaden feet to move she walked toward the specter, drawn as if by a magnet. As she got closer, he drifted away into the storm clouds.

Abby's heart shriveled as he disappeared. She feared, from a place she had never explored deep inside, that he had left her forever and taken the best part of her away with him. "I can't breathe ..."

The line of bubbles in the tub ceased, the surface of the water unbroken. It became still in the small bathroom, the only sound a drip-drip-drip from the old faucet.

LAUREL HOUCK

SIX

"Abigail ... Git up!"

Like a surfacing dolphin, but less graceful, Abby's body arced out of the tub toward the sound of her name. She coughed, fierce and hard, leaning over the edge of the smooth porcelain. Nothing came out of her empty stomach. Lilac-scented water overflowed, soaking the blue rug and spilling onto the white tile floor. Her head pounded, and dark spots danced in front of her eyes. She gulped in the steamy air—redolent with a strange hint of coffee—then retched again.

Flinging one slippery, wet leg over the tub rim, she pulled her body out of the remaining water and onto the soggy mat. Dragging herself into a sitting position, she leaned her head against the side of the tub. Tears and bathwater dripped down her face as she sat there in a puddle, arms wrapped around her wet, naked body.

"Abby, what's going on? Let me in." Lisa rattled the doorknob, but the old lock held firm. "I heard a *thump*. Are you hurt?"

"No, I'm ... fine." Abby cleared her bullfrog throat. "I just tripped getting out of the tub."

"If you're sure." Lisa lowered her voice. "We have our

first guests. They stopped because of the storm, and I need to get them settled. Come down if you feel like it, or I'll be up a little later. I'm making tea. I'll bring you a cup of Kenyan black with raw sugar, just the way you like it." Her footsteps faded down the stairs, dull thuds against the oak boards.

Abby shivered. She got up, noticed a blue bruise on her left breast from the bike accident, carefully patted dry, and put on a pair of old pajamas. Grabbing extra towels from the closet, she mopped up the floor, then dumped them in the hamper; they could wait for tomorrow, even if they did stink by then.

She went to her room and collapsed on the bed, shivering in spite of the heat. After tucking her feet under the quilt, she stared at the ceiling and tried to make sense of what just happened. She hadn't seen a ghost, of course. No way. Not possible. It seemed *so real.* But in what universe did a ghost soldier know her name? It had been just a dream, fatigue, or pure stupidity. And love at first sight? Lame.

Yawning, Abby burrowed under the multi-colored quilt her great-grandmother had made. In the misty moments right before sleep claimed her, she envisioned the tombstone from her bike accident, the same one she dreamed about in the tub.

"Dreams," she murmured as she dozed off. "Weird."

Voices and squealing barn door hinges awoke her early the next morning. She rolled over and groaned; stiff knees, tender cheek, pounding head, sore throat. She peered out her window as three strangers rode away on their bikes, down the hill and out of sight on the bike trail.

Still in her pajamas, Abby descended to the first floor and found her mother in the kitchen. "Hi. I saw our guests taking off. Sorry I fell asleep early and didn't get up in time to help."

Leaving the sink full of dishes, Lisa hurried over and hugged Abby. Her arms dropped to her sides when Abby flinched. "I came up to your room last night with some tea. You were asleep, but restless—tossing and turning, moaning. Are you sure you're as fine as you say you are? I remember your dad giving me the same song-and-dance; he always said he felt fine even when he was anything but."

"I'm fine. Not Dad-fine, truly fine. If you don't need me, I'm going to take my bike into town. It blew a tire yesterday and needs some work."

Lisa went to the sink and kept her back to Abby. "I'm so glad you're riding again. You can help get the guest rooms in shape later." She paused, started to speak, then became silent.

"What?"

"Maybe that purple bike is getting a little small for you. If the tire needs replaced, it might be time to consider another one."

"You mean I can buy a new bike?"

"No, but why not use your dad's Cannondale? I noticed it's still in good shape. He used to be so obsessive about his precious bike, even when we were dating. It's out in the barn, in the rear stall. You said he loved that bike, and he loved you; he'd be happy if you use it."

Abby stared at her mother. "You can't be serious. How 'happy' can he be about anything? He's dead. My bike, my purple bike, the bike *he* bought for me on one of the many birthdays you missed, that's the one I'm going to use. Personally, I think *that* would make him happy."

Lisa grabbed a towel to dry her hands and turned around. "Abby, wait. There's something I need to tell you. Something important."

Abby turned away and took two steps.

Lisa's voice went up a notch. "Come back here. Right now."

A moment's hesitation froze her in place, then Abby stomped out the side door of the house, over to the barn, and into the back stall. Finding the Cannondale, she ran her hand across the blue center bar. She wiped dust off the black leather seat with her sleeve. Ready to go, just like always: tool kit attached under the seat, Mt. Zefal air pump on the bar, utility rack complete with bungee cord and water bottle. Even the canister of dog repellent her dad always carried still clipped on the handlebars. She found it hard to imagine a big, strong guy like that being afraid of dogs. Afraid of dogs but not of death.

She hugged the bike, laying her cheek on the seat. It smelled of leather, saddle soap, Dad. Her eyes filled with silent tears that turned to quiet sniffles, then gut-wrenching sobs.

"Um, excuse me." A deep, unfamiliar voice interrupted.

Abby kept her head down, noting a pair of blue and white leather bike shoes firmly planted on the barn floor. A spicy-woodsy aroma filled the air, clean, not over-powering. She wiped tears from her cheeks with the dust-covered sleeve of her striped pajama top, realizing she wasn't wearing a bra under the thin material.

She crossed her arms over her chest and maintained eye contact with the shoes. "Who are you, and what do you think you're doing in my barn?" Heat infused her face, overriding any fear of the stranger or desire to look at him.

"Sorry. I got a room at the house, and Lisa said I could put my bike out here. I didn't know I'd be interrupting your … whatever."

Abby mumbled, "Oh, well, okay, gotta go," and fled.

She ran into her mother at the foot of the third-floor steps. "Could you at least warn me when we have company?"

"I tried to tell you about our surprise visitor, but you didn't want to hear it," Lisa said. "Remember, we're running a business here. You'll have to get used to people coming and going. The time for running around in your cute little pj's is over."

Abby tightened the drawstring on her pants and ran upstairs, tempted to say, "I hate you." But she knew that as much as she wanted to detest Lisa, it was becoming harder to do so. And that she felt like the real bitch.

After dressing and washing her face, Abby stared at herself in the mirror. Dark smudges underlined powder blue eyes rimmed with nearly colorless lashes. She applied cover-up, blue eyeliner, and mascara. Two new zits had appeared on her chin; she applied acne cream before covering them with make-up. She escaped from the house without seeing anyone and entered the barn, pleased to find it empty.

She pulled her bike out and walked it to the road before climbing on. It took forever to coax the battered metal frame along the narrow road to town. Cars beeped their horns and swerved around her, someone gave her the finger, and a kid in a convertible shouted, "Wear a helmet, you stupid idiot."

The guy at Sweet Rides agreed to do some basic repairs. "This here your little sister's bike, Honey Bun?" he said.

Abby frowned at him. "Can you fix it now or not?"

"Yeah, give me a couple hours and check back." He coughed, spit, wiped his hands on a greasy rag, and wheeled the bike into the repair shop. "You know we got some sweet *new* rides up front if you want to take a look-see while you wait."

"I'll be back."

Twenty minutes later she had glanced in the old-house-turned-cutesy-gift-shop and the salvage-pretending-to-be-antiques shop. At the drug store she bought a bright duo-pack bronzer; the package said it would give her cheeks a healthy glow, something that had been missing for months. She picked up and rejected several shades of nail polish, none of which would help her ragged nails. That left an hour and forty minutes to waste until her bike would be fixed.

Then she saw a boy crossing the street from Sweet Rides. He looked as if the sun had decided to live right on him. Golden hair and tanned skin topped a compact, muscular body encased in ripped jeans and a blue T-shirt that said: RIDE ON.

Abby's chin dropped. She pulled her long hair forward so it cascaded over her shoulders and wished she had sampled the new bronzer at the store.

While she tried to think of some reason to meet him, he crossed the street and walked right over to her. "Hi, how are you?"

Abby dragged her line of vision from his biceps to his face—the voice somehow familiar.

Mesmerizing, morning-sky blue eyes rimmed in pale lashes stared back at her.

She tried out a smile on him, realizing it had been quite a while since she had truly smiled at anyone. Looking right into his eyes she said, "I'm great. Do you live around here?"

He seemed puzzled. "No. You're all right, eh?"

Then she looked down at his blue and white leather bike shoes, breathed in his woodsy scent, and knew. "You're the guy from this morning, the one in my barn."

"Guilty." He smiled, revealing even, white teeth. "My name's Jack. I thought you recognized me, but I guess I looked different through all those tears."

Abby's face heated up; she knew it would now match her red tank top. Her face burned even more at the thought of him seeing her in old pajamas, boobs hanging out and bawling like a baby.

They stood in silence, and then both spoke at the same time. "You first," Abby said.

Jack gestured across the street. "I have to check on my bike. The guy at the repair shop is installing a part for me. But since I'm staying at your place, maybe we could talk later."

"Sure, okay."

He waved and hurried away.

A few tentative drops of rain splattered on the sidewalk then increased to a drenching shower. Abby imagined Jack must have taken the sun with him. When they were together again, would that be the start of a new beginning in her life? Even though he had only stopped at Bikers' Rest for a visit, it might be a good omen of better things ahead.

SEVEN

Peering through the downpour, Abby saw an old house across the street, weathered white wood with a slate roof. The sign in front read: Elizabeth Township Historical Society. She sprinted for the building, scanning the sign on her way past: Open Tuesday, Wednesday, Saturday 10:00 a.m. to 3:00 p.m. Research Librarian available.

The crumbling stepping stone path led to a front porch. Half of the area had been glassed in to display an old carriage. She leaned forward and rung out her soaked hair, making a dark, wet spot on the worn greenish-blue indoor-outdoor carpeting.

The Civil War tombstone from yesterday's bike accident popped into her mind, and she checked her watch. Maybe they would have some information about the cemetery or the graves. Which might help make sense of the strange dream-soldier. For some unknown reason, he had invaded her heart, as crazy as it seemed.

A bell jingled when she entered the building, but no one appeared in response. Except for the ticking of an unseen clock, silence hung over the house. Period furniture filled the front room, along with mementos of bygone years. Abby looked up as she passed a curved oak staircase, loosely barred with an orange ribbon, and continued to a doorway on the left leading downstairs. She descended the tread-covered steps.

The walls of the stairwell were covered with vintage black and white photographs. One depicted several elderly men standing at attention, dressed in old military uniforms. Their caps sat askew on their heads, buttons straining over abdomens that must have seen slimmer days. They stared at the unseen photographer with blank, unblinking eyes. A small square of white paper taped to the wall identified them as Civil War veterans.

At the bottom of the steps, Abby glanced to the right and uttered a yelp. A skull sat on a shelf in front of her face, empty eye sockets staring. She took a step back, noting antique medical equipment in a glass case below the skull. A hand-lettered sign stated: Dr. Prescott, circa 1910.

She giggled. Did the equipment or the skull belong to good old Dr. Prescott?

Antique lanterns and a jumbled storage room yielded nothing of further interest, and she went back upstairs. A whiff of Estee Lauder Youth Dew perfume hovered at the top, reminding Abby of her grandmother.

A very short, gray-haired lady stepped out from a back room, exuding the fragrance. Thick-soled white sneakers, fastened with Velcro, squeaked as she walked. Rimless glasses sat lopsided on her well-powdered nose. She sneezed into a handkerchief embroidered with yellow daisies. A hand-made pink cardigan sweater, miss-buttoned, covered a pair of flowered slacks in garish hues. On her right wrist a silver charm bracelet clanged with every movement. Her tiny eyes darted this way and that. She reminded Abby of a scrawny, colorful bird.

She gave Abby a pleasant smile and tucked a lock of white hair behind her ear, setting off a screech from the hearing aid lodged there. "May I help you, dear? I'm Mrs. Thurman. I don't believe you've been in before."

"Hi. I'm waiting for my bike to be repaired and

thought I'd check things out."

"Feel free to look around in the display rooms. We have quite an assortment of local items, furniture, clothes and such. Just do be careful, dear." Mrs. Thurman gazed around as if perplexed. "Oh yes, and of course we have over three thousand volumes dealing with local history in our library."

Abby pulled her wallet from her backpack. "Do you charge a fee to help with research? And do you have time now? I'm interested in something specific, a local gravestone."

Mrs. Thurman shook her head. "Oh my, I'm so sorry. Mr. Holcomb, our research librarian, retired. I can point you in the right direction and give you some general information, but after that, you're on your own."

Abby got oriented to the small room designated as the library, then Mrs. Thurman left her alone. It seemed very quiet after the squeaking shoes and clanging jewelry. High shelves lined the walls, stacked with books and periodicals in all shapes and sizes. Some were old and dusty, others more recent. The musty smell of aged paper permeated the space.

She leafed through copies of the "Western Pennsylvania Genealogical Society Quarterly," *Pennsylvania History Magazine*, and a "Township Cemetery Listing of Graves," scanning names of people long deceased and the location of their final resting places.

After searching through several other titles, Abby had to admit Morton had been right; no useful records on the old cemetery seemed to exist, just dry lists of little interest.

She stepped to the window to check the weather. The rain had stopped. A chocolate milkshake at Dairy Delicious would be perfect for an early lunch. Old tombstone research or ice cream—no contest.

On her way out of the reading room she spotted an orange plastic milk crate behind a partially closed closet door that read: Employees Only. She glanced around; no

Mrs. Thurman. It would be easy enough to hear her coming. What could be so special that only employees had access in a small place like this one?

She opened the door, cringing as the hinges protested, and slid the crate forward. Only two books, but huge ones. The top volume turned out to be a dictionary, way out-of-date; she set it aside. A Bible rested below it. Abby heaved it out of the crate. She hauled it over to a table, dropping it with a thud; still no Mrs. Thurman. Maybe she blew a battery in her hearing aid.

The worn cover of the Bible felt like quilted leather, thick and padded, with the words *Holy Bible* and a dove embossed in gold. It closed with two tarnished brass hasps. Although it may have locked long ago, it popped open easily when Abby pressed the mechanism. She scanned the first page, an ornate, multi-colored scene of Bible figures.

The heading, in elaborate lettering, stated, "Pictorial Family Bible."

The only personal information appeared in the form of a hand-written entry at the top of the next page, in spidery, faded ink: "Presented to Mrs. Leticia Jean Munroe on the occasion of the birth of her son Silas Jacob Munroe, June 9, in the year of our Lord 1843; Ladies' Guild, Dravo Methodist Church." A dried rose, pressed between the parchment pages, crumbled into powdery dust as Abby touched the fragile flower.

Gently she turned the pages, fascinated by the archaic language and drawings. Halfway through a handful of old photographs fell out. Faded prints—heads only—of people in old-fashioned clothing, gave no clue to their identity. An advertisement on the back of one stated, "Photographed by Harbaugh & Green, No. 43 Federal Street, Allegheny."

In the center of the Bible she found pages for Marriages, Births, Deaths, & Memoranda; they were ripped, the entries missing. Closing the book, Abby noticed something sticking out at an odd angle. A folded piece of thin, yellowed paper protruded.

She extracted the document, opened it, and walked to the window to see it better. Pale gray cursive script crossed the paper in uneven lines.

"*New Store, May 1862,*" Abby whispered into the empty room. "*Dear Daughter, Your parcel received last night and very much obliged to you. I am mush better this morning, as I have been for some time. I eat yesterday, some kind of beef tea, wich done me so much good. I have not so much pain at the stomagh, and I feel mush relieved. Hope is will continue. Know our Silas, rest in peace, sleeps with the angels after what he did for Mr. Lincoln. This gives me peace, mor than tea. Wish coud share with all, know secret must be kept. Greaves me, he lies in shame when shud be hero. Remember Gene III. William visits agin about Friday. Do not tell him nothing. My love to you all, Leticia Jean Munroe, your Mother.*"

Abby became aware of her heart echoing in her ears as she rescanned the note. The name *Silas* seemed to jump off the page. Her finger traced the letters.

"*Abigail …*"

Abby whipped around; no one else seemed to be nearby. Clearly, her brain must be on overload because of … what? Whatever. She wished she'd paid more attention to her dad or to history class. Mr. Lincoln as in the Civil War president? What did this guy Silas do? How could she find out? Because—for some reason—she had the unshakable thought, *I have to clear his name.*

"I'm sorry, dear, but I'm closing up for lunch," Mrs. Thurman said as she entered the room. She looked at the Bible, open on the table. "Now where did you find that old musty-dusty thing?"

Heat rose in Abby's cheeks. "It just, um, I saw this milk crate and there were some books …"

"Of course." Mrs. Thurman shook her head, sending her hot pink earrings into a spin. "Those are set for the antique store down the way. Our library has several other historic Bibles that are in excellent shape. We can't keep everything you know."

Abby hesitated. "Could I have it, if you don't need it for the library?"

Mrs. Thurman's stomach growled, loud and insistent. "Well now, I don't think I can give it away to just anyone. It is already promised. You come back again and look at the other Bibles." She shooed Abby out of the room and jingled away toward the foyer.

Abby took one last look at the Bible on the table. She reached out to return the letter to it, then stopped and slid it into her backpack instead. She hurried out the front door, waved at Mrs. Thurman, and left the building, hearing the click of the deadbolt behind her.

The pavement gleamed as the sun peeked out from behind a huge, dark cloud. Abby brushed past a laurel bush, creating a cascade of leftover raindrops that splashed onto her arm. She didn't notice.

At Sweet Rides she paid for her bike at the counter and wheeled it out of the store.

Riding home, questions about the long-dead Munroe family and President Lincoln swirled like a tornado in her brain.

"I'll find out what happened, Silas. You can count on me." Abby's words drifted away in the wind, as a new sense of purpose settled in her heart.

EIGHT

Abby put her bike in the barn. Her dad's Cannondale sat propped against the wall where she left it; no other bikes. Jack must be gone already. She had set a new record for chasing a guy away.

She stepped in a puddle and looked up to see the cloudy sky through the dilapidated roof. After moving her bike to what appeared to be a drier spot, she sighed. Like any serious biker would want to use leaky storage, even for one night. Probably Lisa's lame business would fail. Which would mean moving again. Leaving another place that had started to feel like home.

"Hey—Abs, you in there?" Morton shuffled in the barn lugging his bike. "Got yours fixed, huh? Looks okay to me. Want to try it out?"

Abby craned her neck to see if Jack might be coming. "No, I just got back. Maybe later. Lisa needs some help with the guests."

Morton craned his neck around the empty barn. "What guests?" He started at the sound of footsteps.

Jack wheeled his bike into the barn. He reached out to shake hands with Morton. "I'm a guest—Jack. How's it going?"

Morton attempted to pull himself up taller, sucked in his stomach, and cleared his throat. "Yo. Great. Morton here."

Abby hid a smile. "I'll catch you later, Morton."

Jack watched Morton leave. "Boyfriend, huh?"

"Seriously? I mean, he's a friend, a really good guy, but just a kid. He helped me out yesterday when I wrecked my bike. So, are you getting ready to leave?" Abby crossed her fingers behind her back and held her breath.

"I got lucky," Jack said. "I'm staying for a while. Your mom wants this roof fixed, and I can do it. I'm low on money and need a place to stay. We decided to barter, your new barn roof for my room and board and some spending money. Now I guess we'll have to get to know each other better." His smile lit up the gloomy old barn.

Abby smiled back, until a tiny finger of suspicion wiggled into her mind. Just because a guy had innocent blue eyes and killer muscles, it didn't mean he could be trusted. Had Lisa even checked him out?

Abby left the barn with Jack close behind. She struggled to keep her tone noncommittal. "So, you're not from around here, are you?"

"I live in Canada, Montréal, actually," Jack said. "At least for now."

"You're Canadian? Where's your accent?"

"What, you have something against foreigners, eh?"

"Of course not. But it's just a little weird to have a Canadian so far from home on a bicycle."

Jack laughed. "I'm just teasing you. I'm from the good ole U.S. of A. I go to college in Montréal at McGill University."

"College. Got it."

Abby tossed her damp hair over her shoulder, wishing again that she'd taken more time with her make-up and not been caught in the rain. A college guy around the house would be unbelievable, although she would take it slow until she got to know him better. She dragged her eyes away from his biceps as he spoke.

"I just finished my first year. I'm going for a degree in creative writing."

"And U.S. colleges don't have that as a major?"

"Tell you what." Jack cocked his head and smiled. "You find me a glass of iced tea, and I'll give you my life story, abridged version. Not that it's all that interesting."

"You're bartering again," Abby said. "A roof over your head for a roof over the barn, tea for your story. Don't you ever just do things because you want to or because it's the right thing to do?"

A shutter closed over Jack's open features. He scowled, squinting at Abby so the blue of his eyes almost disappeared. They had lost their glimmer, expressionless and dead.

Abby shivered.

"Believe me, I know what's right and what's not." A flush spread across his face. "You think that a guy like me is itinerant and has no scruples? Try some hardship in your life, and see what happens. Someday I'll be famous, and you'll understand how much you didn't know."

Abby took a step back. "You don't know anything about me. I'll get you the tea, but I don't really care about your 'life story.'" She stalked toward the house, pleased that she had avoided calling him an asshole. Even though he deserved the title.

Jack followed her and smiled, open and friendly once again. "Wait, I'm sorry. Maybe I'm a little intense, okay? But I'm harmless. Meet me on the porch? I could use a friend around here." He paused and once again seemed to be appraising her. "Maybe you could use a friend, too, eh?"

Abby considered. It would be a chance to check him out—his information as well as his obvious attributes. He seemed to be the best scenery in town. "Yeah, okay. I'll be back."

She went to the house, taking the time to duck in the

powder room and brush her hair back into a ponytail, leaving tendrils loose at the sides. It almost looked like a style she had seen in *Epic Hair*. After adjusting her bra and pulling her tank top a little lower in the front, she tried to smooth her full eyebrows with a finger dipped in water. From the medicine cabinet she grabbed Lisa's cologne and spritzed her neck.

A pitcher of iced tea from the refrigerator, complete with a sprig of fresh mint from the garden, a plate of Lisa's homemade chocolate chip cookies, and she had what she needed. She carried it to the porch on a tray and poured Jack a tall, frosty tumbler, dripping with condensation and clinking with ice.

He raised his glass to her. "*À votre santé*. To your health."

Abby pushed the plate of fresh chocolate chip cookies toward him. The aroma of the warm, rich chocolate made her mouth water, but she waited. He ate a cookie in silence, licked his lips, and drained his glass. He set it on the wicker table, careful to place it on a napkin.

"I do believe you've earned the full and complete story of Monsieur Jacques Charpentier. Make yourself comfortable."

"Jacques …?"

"My official name. Here goes. My dad is French Canadian, thus the Jacques, and my mom was American, which is where Jack comes from."

"Your mom isn't American anymore?"

Jack shrugged. "She died a long time ago."

"I guess losing a parent gets easier after a while …"

He gave a dismissive little wave. "It's been years, I barely remember her. After she died we stayed in this country and I grew up in Erie, right along the lake. Dad's a U.S. citizen now; he owns a construction business. We specialize in roofing, so the barn repair is no big deal."

"You have brothers and sisters?"

Jack paused and looked at the floorboards. "That's a

complicated question. The simple answer is one older brother, Etienne—that's French for Steve. After Mom died, Dad took care of the company, and Steve took care of me. He wiped my nose, taught me to tie my shoes, and to drive, he, well, he just …" He stopped talking and played with a loose piece of wicker on the table edge.

"You live in Erie and go to school in Montréal." Abby hoped to sidestep what seemed to be a painful memory. Brother Steve must have totally screwed Jack.

Jack shook his head as if to clear it. "Right, right … my story. There isn't much more to tell. I'm on summer break. Steve used to pick me up when the semester ended. I thought about staying at school; the Beluga and Beer Bike Tour might have been fun. But I decided to go home. I could have rented a car, but the bike seemed like a better idea."

"A better idea? Really? How far is it?"

"It's 624 kilometers from Montréal to Erie; that's around 399 miles. It took me a while, but I needed the time to think and plan, so it all worked out."

"I can't believe you rode your bike all that way."

Jack stretched out his legs. "I ride a lot all year, so I can do around forty miles a day, depending on the terrain. That's just average, nothing special. The important thing is to be prepared. Rule of thumb is three thousand calories and a gallon of water a day to stay healthy on a long-distance cycle trip."

"Why didn't you just stay in Erie? Why come to Pittsburgh of all places? Not even Pittsburgh. Locals call this town Little Boston because it's so small compared to the Boston in Massachusetts; it's not even on all the maps."

"I did spend some time at home," Jack said. "Usually I work with my dad in the summer. But things there are … difficult right now. He's angry and sad all the time. I couldn't stand it for long."

Abby wanted to ask what made his father so upset, but

something in Jack's voice stopped her.

Jack sat quietly for a moment, eyes unfocused, then continued. "The bike trail goes all the way from Erie to Washington, D.C., and it runs right past your door. That's why I'm here; I'm headed to D.C. There's a bike rally on the Fourth of July, and I'm going to ride in it. Even the president will be there. I'm planning to meet him." He paused, lips thinning in what could pass for a smile. "I'm looking forward to lots of fireworks for the holiday."

"You mean President Keller? *The* President Keller?"

"Yeah, President Hartley H. Keller III, in person. Commander-in-chief." Jack gave a mock salute.

Abby rolled her eyes. "Good luck getting close enough. Security is killer around him, no pun intended. If anyone gets protection, it should be him."

"It sounds like you respect him or something."

"Well, of course I respect the president, even if I don't always agree with him."

Jack's eyes narrowed, his breathing quickened, and his face flushed.

"Anyway," she said, eager to change the subject, "you must be in amazing shape, riding all that way." She let her gaze linger on Jack, dropping her eyes when he caught her. "My dad used to bike, a long time ago, but there's no way he could've made it here from Montréal. He did it for fun, a weekend warrior."

"He shouldn't have stopped riding."

A flashpoint of heat rose in her chest. "Dead people don't ride the rail trails, do they?" To her disgust, tears ran down her face and dropped onto her jeans, leaving dark spots like a trail of dribbled tea.

Jack reached into his pocket and pulled a picture from his wallet. A young man smiled into the camera, black hair blowing in the breeze, dark eyes crinkled at the corners. He held it out to Abby.

She wiped her eyes with a napkin, then took the picture and studied it. "Who is this?"

Jack cleared his throat and blinked several times. "My brother, Etienne."

"He doesn't look anything like you. And why show this to me now?"

"Etienne is—was—a Marine, killed in combat. You were right; I don't know what you've been through. But I do know what it feels like to lose someone you love. Someone taken away too soon for all the wrong reasons— someone who means the world to you. It's almost like I died when he did—and now neither of us has any peace."

Abby sniffed and swiped her nose with the back of her hand. She picked up her half-full glass of iced tea.

Jack clinked his empty one against it. "To those we've loved and lost."

Abby nodded but didn't trust her voice. She took a gulp of sweet tea and scrutinized Jack. All concerns about him evaporated in the cocoon of shared loss and grief. She jumped when the screen door banged.

Lisa walked across the porch, patting Jack's shoulder as she passed. "Hi, you two. I'm glad to see you're getting to know each other." She waved and headed for the car.

Abby watched her go. Shouldn't she be worried about leaving her precious daughter alone with a virtual stranger? Not that having Lisa out of the way would be a bad thing.

She turned to Jack. "I don't get her."

"Shh." Jack smiled, friendly once again. "Don't worry about anything. She's being polite, that's all."

He leaned over and touched Abby's hand, just the briefest moment of contact.

She tensed for an instant then relaxed, forgetting about the folded letter in her backpack, Lisa, and everything else. Because at last, someone understood her.

LAUREL HOUCK

NINE

The days began to take on a routine, something Abby had missed since her dad died. A trickle, then a steadier stream of guests stopped at Bikers' Rest. Jack slept on a cot in a stall at the back of the barn to accommodate paying customers. Lisa had taken pains to make it homey, hanging colorful Native American blankets along the railing and putting in a few odd pieces of furniture. She kept a vase filled with fresh flowers on the scarred nightstand, next to a carafe of mineral water.

During the day Jack balanced on the barn roof, removing the rotted wood and shingles. Progress seemed to be slow, and Abby wondered if he really did know how to replace a roof. Lisa swore she checked him out with his father's construction business and got references, but Abby doubted it.

After finishing the breakfast cleanup, Abby called upstairs, "The dishwasher's going, the food's put away." She held her breath, hoping no more chores came her way.

The door banged open, and Morton marched inside. "Hey, Abs. Great day, huh? Can you come, or is it Housework 101 again?"

Abby put one finger to her lips. "Shh. She'll hear you."

She walked to the bottom of the steps and spoke quickly. "I'm going on a ride with Morton." She yanked her pack out of the small cubbyhole beneath the steps and slung it over her shoulder. Grabbing Morton's arm, she pulled him out the door and down the front steps. "Time to escape. Wait here, and I'll get my bike from the barn."

Rounding the porch, Abby noticed an unexpected silence—no hammering, no Jack. A pile of lumber rested in the weeds next to a bin of nails and a palate stacked with shingles. Where did he go in the middle of the day?

Abby opened the barn door and entered the musty space, her footsteps muted on the packed-dirt floor. A few pieces of residual hay drifted through the sun-streaked air. The pungent odor of damp earth mixed with dry hay ticked her nose. She reached for her bike and stuck out her right foot to release the kickstand. A rustling noise came from the left rear stall at the back of the barn—where Jack slept—and broke the silence. She froze. A rabid raccoon or a gnawing rat? Not good.

She snuck toward the sound, curious and repelled at the same time. Instead of finding an animal, Jack sat cross-legged on the floor. He hunched over something, muttering in French, which she didn't understand. His underlying rage came through.

Reaching up, he ran a hand through his already disheveled hair. He crumpled a piece of paper and threw it to the floor, then smacked a closed fist into the exposed side of the stall with one swift movement. A jagged hole appeared like magic. He held the hand close to his chest, nursing it while he rocked back and forth.

Abby's heart tripped like Jack's hammer against the shingles. She eased back and collided with her bike. It crashed to the floor.

Jack darted out of the stall. "Abby, what the hell are you doing?"

Morton came running in. "Abby? Oh, hey, Jack."

Abby studied Jack from under her lashes; he seemed

ordinary, whatever that might be. She wondered if he could hear her heart racing. "I, um, tripped but didn't want to bother you. So, let's go, Morton."

"Sure, I'll take your bike out. Hey, Jack, want some M&M's?"

Jack knocked the candies from Morton's hand. They scattered, multi-colored marbles amidst the dirty straw. "Get lost."

Morton sputtered but stomped outside, dragging Abby's bike.

"You rude bastard." Abby glared at Jack and turned to follow Morton.

"Whoa, hold on." Jack walked between Abby and the door, blocking the light, and put one hand on her forearm. As he tightened his grip the tips of his fingers blanched. "What exactly did you see back there? Tell me. Now."

Abby wrenched away from the rough calluses on his palm. "Nothing. Get away from me." She edged around him.

Jack laughed. "Want to know a secret?"

Abby paused. "I'm not sure." A sudden urge to pee made her bladder ache. She wished Morton hadn't left.

Jack's eyes glittered. "I know it isn't very manly, but I'm keeping a journal. You know, about the bike trip. Maybe I can use the notes for a class or to write a book. You won't tell on me, will you? I want to keep my macho reputation, especially with pretty girls." He winked, and the intense light in his eyes faded from crazed to normal.

Abby took a deep breath and let it out all at once. His excuse rang hollow. "I won't tell about your journal if you tell me something."

Jack raised one eyebrow. "What do you want to know?"

"Am *I* in your journal?"

"A writer never tells."

"That's a magician."

"You got me," Jack said. "Of course you're in it, *Cherie.*

How could I write about this trip and not include you? Go and ride your bike. I need to get to work before your mom fires me." He winked again and went back to his room, as if nothing unusual had happened.

Abby headed for the door, paused, then crept back and peeked around the corner into the stall. She watched as Jack put his binder into a black metal box, locked it, and hid it under a floorboard. Holding her breath she tiptoed outside to join Morton.

Abby's thoughts went around and around like a hamster running on a wheel. A wave of dizziness swept over her, as she tried to balance what she had seen with what she wanted to believe.

TEN

Abby rode away from the house and onto the bike trail, the rhythm of the bike wheels a soothing antidote to Jack's outburst. The satisfying crunch of limestone gravel under the tires made concerns about a college journal seem ridiculous.

After a few minutes she noticed the heavy humidity in the air, making it almost too thick to breathe. Sweat ran down her face, attracting tiny gnats that dive-bombed against her skin. One insect stuck in the corner of her eye, and she swerved, steering with one hand until dislodging it with a dusty finger. A trickle of perspiration itched its way down the center of her back. She pulled into Dravo Cemetery behind Morton.

"You said this would be a great day to ride. Are you kidding? Once I'm sixteen I'm getting my permit and learning to drive. Then I can ride around in my air-conditioned Fiat. Maybe, if you're nice to me, I'll take you along."

Morton grinned and patted his belly. "Ha. This was just a little ride. Maybe I'm in better shape than I thought. And you're improving since we've been on the trail more often, better stamina, you know. This is the first time you've complained in almost two days. That's a record—for you. I like riding. Besides, who's gonna get you a car, even if you can drive, huh? There's insurance and gas and upkeep … all that stuff you can't afford unless you get a job, and then you'll never have time to drive." He took a deep breath.

Abby stuck her tongue out at him and opened her backpack for a bottle of water. "You are officially barred from my car. And think how nice it would've been to have me haul your butt around on rainy days."

Morton picked up a rock and tossed it from hand to hand. "What's the big secret with Jack the Ripper?"

Abby shrugged. "Just some college project. What do you think about him? Not much, I guess, if you call him that."

"I don't like him. And I'm a good judge of character."

"Big surprise; you're just jealous."

"No way. He's old already, and I've got my whole life ahead of me. Besides, anyone who hates M&M's is creepy." Morton pulled something from his bike bag. She watched while he aimed the small device to the left and right, moving at a snail's pace through the cemetery. "What're you doing now?"

Without even turning around or pausing, Morton answered. "Research. I hunt ghosts, remember?"

Abby laughed. "There are no ghosts, genius. Or are you earning your forensic ghostology badge for Scouts?"

Morton held out the device for her to see. "This is an EMF meter I got on eBay. It finds electromagnetic fields. The five buttons light up if there's a signal, like from a power line or something else."

"What kid cares about the location of a power line? You're weird."

"It also detects the energy given off by a *ghost*. And of course the perfect place to find ghosts, *genius,* is a graveyard." Morton smiled in triumph and wandered away.

Abby rolled her eyes and meandered over to a tilted

headstone. "It's a shame so many of them are falling over. They deserve more respect than this. Doesn't anyone care?" She put one hand on either side of the stone to right it. A crater of longing opened up in her being, such that she never wanted to let go.

Morton returned and peered at the stone. "Hey there, Private Munroe."

Abby's head jerked up. "What?"

Morton pointed at the grave. "Look at the inscription: PVT. Silas Jacob Munroe."

"He's the one. I found an old letter in a Bible. His mother wrote it. We have to check this out. The letter said something about Silas helping Mr. Lincoln."

Morton's eyebrows went up. "*President* Lincoln?"

"I don't know. That's what we have to find out. It's meant to be. It can't be a coincidence I found the grave of a soldier who's in a letter I happened to discover in an old Bible." Abby checked out the carved name. Could this be the same grave where the soldier appeared in her dream?

Morton shook his head. "This is no big deal. It's where any local soldier would've been buried in those days. The family Bible would have ended up around here, too, because they obviously lived close by."

"Yeah, whatever, Ghost Boy."

Abby squatted in front of the tombstone on the leaf-covered grave. She studied the old-fashioned outline of the words. The weathered gray granite had been carved with block letters and outlined in a shield-shape:

Silas Jacob Munroe
PVT CO F
103 PA VOL
B: June 9, 1843 D: March 27, 1862

In script, a weathered poem below the personal information read:

When we asunder part,
It gives us inward pain,
But we shall still be joined in heart,
And hope to meet again.

Tears welled in Abby's eyes, the burn of salt stinging. She swiped a hand across her face. "He was only nineteen years old when he died. I wonder what happened. Maybe he got shot in a famous Civil War battle. Leticia must have been so sad. Death cheats everyone. It did then, and it does now. It's so freaking unfair."

"Who's Leticia?"

Abby sighed. "That's his mother's name, the woman who wrote the note I just told you about. It has to be the same one. How many Silas Jacob Munroe's can there be with the same birth date? Read what she had carved on the stone; she felt the same pain losing her son as I felt losing my dad."

She ran her hand over the name on the surface of the cold stone. As her fingers connected with the carved letters, a face wavered in front of her eyes—the face she had seen before. She longed to make the sad eyes brighten, to push the shock of dark hair across his forehead, to kiss the full lips—

"Where's the letter?"

"What?" Abby started and the image disappeared, leaving an emptiness in her heart.

"You said there's a letter." Morton nudged her shoulder.

"Right. Letter." Abby shook her head to clear it, wondering if losing one's mind felt like this. She rummaged through her backpack, pulling the old note from a waterproof inside pocket; she handed it to Morton. "Be careful, it's fragile."

Morton squinted as he read, "She's not much of a speller. But she lived around here. Boston is in Elizabeth Borough, and the borough used to be called New Store."

He finished reading. "Yuck, beef tea? That doesn't sound good, even to me."

Abby leaned over his shoulder. "I wonder what she meant, the part about 'secret must be kept ... he lies in shame.' Did you ever hear about anything like this? If he did something for the president, he should be a local hero, even a national one, not some unknown name in an abandoned cemetery."

Morton studied the paper. "Nah, I never heard of him. Maybe she thinks he's a hero because he's her kid, and the shame is because he did something bad. That makes more sense. If he's a hero, why keep it a secret?"

Abby tapped her foot in the grass. "My point exactly. It makes no sense. And who are Gene and William? I have to look through the antique Bible again. Maybe there's another letter or something I missed the first time." Once again she traced the name Silas with her finger, the indentation faint on the weather-worn stone. A tingle ran up her arm.

"It's just some old story, who cares? She must have been in denial." Morton looked toward the river. "Let's go home and get the inner tubes. We can float down the Yough and cool off after the ride. Or we can make a snack. How about beef tea?" He laughed.

Abby rested both hands on her hips. "Who cares? Me. This is an actual event, not some crazy ghost story. My dad would have tried to solve a Civil War mystery—we would have done it together. Once I start something I can't give up until it's done; strange, right? But I *am* going to figure this out. I want to do it; I *have* to do it." She meant to say she would do it for her dad. But her voice whispered, "For Silas."

Morton rolled his eyes. "You'll never find out the truth, you know. It's not like you can call and ask for an interview or look up a video on YouTube."

"I'm not sure what to do." Abby looked at Morton. "You know a lot of local history. Would you help me?"

"You want *my* help? Really? Cool beans, dudette. This is *awesome*."

"Morton, you'll agree to anything. And then there's the graveyard and all that ghost crap." Abby paused, reconsidered, then started again. "Look, it's none of my business, but you spend a lot of time alone in a cemetery, you don't seem to have any friends your own age, and you and your mother, well, I don't know."

"Is there a question in there?" Morton frowned and ticked off answers. "Because I'm interested in lots of things; I like it here, it's quiet and peaceful; ghosts are my hobby. I have friends and my mother, she's great ..." He trailed off, stared at the ground, and blinked several times.

"Either tell me the truth or to butt out. Either way, it's okay." Abby waited, surprised to feel sorry for someone other than herself for a change.

Morton took a shuddering breath. "Here's the deal. I do like the cemetery—the history, the ghost stuff, you know. That's the true part. And my mom *is* great, but she can't go out or do things with me. She has a disease that makes her muscles jerk around. When I had friends they made fun of her, so I quit them. I don't like to talk about it much." He pulled a small brown bag from his pocket and chomped several M&M's, mouth moving rapidly like a hungry squirrel. "Comfort food."

"We won't talk about any of it unless you want to. And you'll help me solve the mystery about Silas, right?"

Morton looked at her and stuck out his right hand. "Partners?"

Abby shook his hand. "Sure, partners. Maybe Jack can help, too." She ignored Morton's frown. "I know the Historical Society is open tomorrow because I was there a week ago."

Morton shrugged. "Why didn't you go back already if it's so important to you?"

"Because I hadn't made the connection with this grave until now. We'll go after breakfast, see if the Bible gives us any more clues, and then decide what to do next." She checked her watch. "Let's get out of here."

Morton held up his device. "I'm staying for a while. After you leave I want to check out my EMF meter. Ghosts don't come out if there are too many people around, you know."

"Sure. Later." Abby climbed on her bike and steered onto the trail. She watched a fat groundhog waddle out of the switchgrass and cross the path ahead. It would be good to focus on something other than her own problems.

As she rode away from the cemetery, thoughts of Silas absorbed her.

ELEVEN

Lightning flashed across the sky, a jagged tear in the fabric of black, roiling clouds overhead. Sheets of rain cascaded down the window of Abby's attic room, making the landscape outside blur. The downpour, deafening against the tin roof, almost covered Abby's frustrated rambling.

"I know, I know." She held the phone away from her ear for a moment. "Calm down, Morton. We can't go into town in the storm. I get it, but I don't have to like it." She paused. "If it slows down, we can go to the Historical Society later, right? I need you there. You can distract Mrs. Thurman while I search for clues about Silas in the Bible." Another long pause later Abby sighed. "I know the forecast. Yeah, text you later."

She couldn't sit still, ready to forge ahead with research on Silas but stuck in the house. As she peered out the window trying to wish away the rain, a thought took shape. Jack wouldn't work in the rain. He could drive her into town and entertain Mrs. Thurman, and no time would be lost to the crappy all-day Pittsburgh rain.

Abby brushed her hair, pulling her bangs over her forehead. She darkened her lashes with mascara, smacked her full lips together over a fresh layer of lip-gloss, and sprayed a hint of Sexy Spring cologne behind both ears. After trying and discarding three T-shirts, she chose one from Abercrombie with a V-neck in bright yellow, hoping she would look like a ray of sunshine to Jack.

Lisa poked her head in the door. "I need you downstairs, honey. Our guests are staying a while until the storm passes, and I still have breakfast, beds, laundry, well, too much for me." Without waiting for an answer, she hurried back downstairs, calling out a hasty, "Thanks."

"Hey, I had plans."

Lisa's voice accompanied the clatter of her hurrying feet. "Sorry."

Abby bowed to the empty space where her mother stood seconds ago. "Whatever you say. I just love to help here at the ever-popular Bikers' Rest. It's fun to fetch and carry for adults who want to act like kids and ride their little bikes all over the country. Getting up each morning to scrape gross dishes and wash strangers' sheets makes my existence complete. Please, don't let me ever have a life of my own. Unbelievable." She rolled her eyes.

She toyed with the idea of sneaking out the front door to the barn but knew Lisa's wrath would cause too much trouble. Instead she cursed mentally while she gathered dirty sheets and towels and took them to the first-floor laundry room. Glancing out the window, she sighed as Jack drove away in the truck. Mascara and cleavage wasted on dirty sheets.

The clatter of dishes and Lisa's off-key humming came from the kitchen. Abby followed the aroma of bacon in the air; it smelled warm and inviting until she saw the grease congealing on dirty plates in the sink and gagged. Scraping grease. The worst.

"Lisa, could you give me a lift into town? After I help you, of course. Morton and I planned a trip to the Historical Society to, you know, study local history. We can't take our bikes in the storm." She took a deep breath and smiled her most engaging smile.

"Not today. Sorry, honey. With guests here it makes more work," Lisa said. "And since when are you interested in history?"

Abby sniffed. "Yet another little fact you missed in your total absence from my life. FYI, Dad and I talked about the Civil War all the time."

"I seem to recall seeing a Civil War paper you wrote in middle school in a box I unpacked. You got a C."

"So glad you noticed, now that I'm in high school." Abby still remembered that grade and the disappointment it had caused her dad. "Don't forget to mention I didn't want to take Dad's advice on homework, I didn't want to go biking, and I stopped kissing him good-night. As usual, your insight is invaluable. Take care of the guests and don't bother with what your daughter needs. I'll ask Jack to drive me when he gets back."

Lisa threw the dishcloth in the sink; a little plop and splash followed. "I've had my own problems. You don't have the patent on heartache around here. And you need to tone down the sarcasm; I don't deserve it, and I'm tired of putting up with it."

Abby opened her mouth, but Lisa kept talking.

"Now please get this kitchen cleaned up; it *is*, after all, your only job in a summer of doing whatever you want. The 'poor me' routine is getting old. And forget about Jack today. He went into the city for an appointment of some kind. Oh, and keep your busy schedule open to help clean out the attic space. I want to finish it as another bedroom so Jack doesn't have to sleep in the barn."

Abby wanted to ask why Lisa planned to remodel for Jack's short-term stay, but what did it matter? She tried to stay angry at her mother while she did dishes and put away the remains of breakfast, but instead the weight of her own miserable behavior tugged on her heart. The lemony dish detergent reminded her of another morning, a flash of memory from somewhere deep inside and long ago. Her parents were doing pancake dishes, splashing each other with soapsuds and laughing. One of them had put a daub of suds on her nose. Where had the happiness gone? Would it ever return?

Abby stared at the bubbles in the sink, one drifting up to eye level. Like a shimmering prism it caught the overhead light, twinkling in the rain-specked reflection from the window. Then it popped, the fragility of the soap reminding her of how fragile life could be: Dad's life, Jack's brother's life … Silas's life.

Lisa found task after task that had to be done, so that afternoon shadows had deepened before Abby could open her laptop. She Googled "Silas Munroe," finding genealogies with the same name in Texas, Virginia, and Ohio, but nothing in Pennsylvania. She found a website for Dravo Cemetery, but no information on graves seemed to be available because of the fire that destroyed cemetery records. Did Morton always have to be right?

She stood, rolled her shoulders, and walked to the kitchen for a drink. Through the window she noticed Jack returning in the truck, the vehicle a silhouette in the heavy rain. He sat there for several minutes in the gloom, until the truck windows began to fog.

"What are you doing out there, Jack Charpentier? This rain could last all night."

As if he heard her, Jack opened the vehicle door slightly. In the overhead light Abby saw him wrap a red rag around something. He took off his baseball cap, put the wrapped item in it, and shielded the bundle next to his body. Ducking into the heavy rain, he ran into the barn.

Maybe researching Jack would be more important than Silas Munroe's history. Abby returned to the computer but found no Google entries for "Jack Charpentier." Next she typed in McGill University Montreal. Soon she knew their mission statement, address, and website. Lists of subjects, campus facilities, and alumni information popped up. The site even noted something called the Beluga and Bike

Tour, which Jack had mentioned. But he could have looked up the same information online.

Nothing seemed useful, until she found McGill University Student Directory. The simple form asked for student name or email address. Her hands started to sweat, slipping off the keyboard as she typed. She typed in the last name, Charpentier, first name, Jack. No one listed by that name. A keen sense of betrayal pierced her heart. Maybe he made up the dead brother story. And the dead mother, too.

Abby sat back in the chair, pondering. What did this tell her about the person who now lived in her barn? Even his name might be bogus. With a muttered, "His name, right," she entered Charpentier, Jacques on the Student Directory screen. His email address and major, creative writing, appeared. She breathed a sigh of relief. He seemed to be for real, but some of the veracity of Jack remained puzzling at best. What if he stole the entire name and identity off the web site? What if she had totally lost it?

In spite of being distracted by Jack, Abby's heart tugged her back to Silas. "I'm losing my mind. Silas died forever ago. Ghosts aren't real, and even if they are, no one falls in love with a ghost." She couldn't reconcile her confusion about Jack and something—love?—for Silas whether it made sense or not.

She exited the university web site and typed Civil War in the search block on the computer screen. Before anything came up, the empty battery icon flashed on the screen and it went black. Abby got up to plug it in, and the desk lamp blinked out. The house became very quiet—no refrigerator sounds, no fan noises; only the steady rain continued its rhythmic beat. "The electric's out again?" She sat back down in front of the blank computer screen, thoughts drifting.

Crack.

Abby jumped. In the stillness, the abrupt reverberation split the din of the rain; an echo of it lingered even after the initial noise subsided. Turning her head to the side, Abby listened for a repeat of the sound, but only the storm continued unabated. She got up and peered out the window into sheets of rain ... but no thunder.

The pounding of a headache chased away any concerns about strange noises on a rainy afternoon. Abby went in search of Tylenol and downed two capsules but couldn't turn off her brain. Underlying everything else, niggling doubts about Jack and curiosity about Silas kept her company.

She stretched out in her dad's old recliner, face pressed against the soft fabric, seeking the reassuring smell of him. A faint citrus scent remained embedded in the headrest. She reveled in it and drifted off.

The comfort didn't last. Jack invaded her dreams—a handsome face that morphed into a skeleton with dead blue eyes.

And a frantic voice beseeching her, "*Abigail ...*"

TWELVE

Abby awoke in the recliner, cranky and lethargic instead of energized. The desk lamp and computer screen remained dark. The gloom of the afternoon seemed intensified.

She went to the kitchen for a bottle of water and found a note on the refrigerator: Abby—went into town, didn't want to disturb you. Back soon. Lisa (aka Mom)

"Thanks, Lisa aka Mom. I ask for a ride. You say no and then go without me."

After digging under the sink, Abby pulled out the old coffee tin of emergency candles, inserting one into a slit in the plastic lid and lighting it. She looked out the window; the rain continued in torrents. In the barn a beam of light shone through the partially open door.

Jack's silhouette wavered in the glow.

Abby shivered, not certain if from anticipation or a chill. A cool barn in the rain with Jack or an empty house in the rain alone? No contest. And it would be an opportunity to gather more information about the elusive Monsieur Charpentier.

Ignoring her misgivings, she took a yellow slicker from a peg in the mudroom and pulled it on. It had a musty odor and the plastic lining stuck to her bare arms. Before she could open the door, thunder boomed and lightning struck somewhere nearby, with a crash and sizzle.

Abby shivered, took the slicker off, and went back in the kitchen. Now what? No computer, no TV, nothing but books. She realized how little she had read since her dad died. Stormy days used to mean candlelight, her dad studying the Civil war, Abby deep in a mystery. But in a few short months everything had changed. The things she enjoyed no longer enjoyable; the people she loved no longer lovable.

She picked up the candle and walked upstairs, shielding the flame and carrying three more candles. Lisa had stored her father's books in the attic. There were volumes of information on the Civil War, pages his hands had touched, covers he had used as coasters for his tea mug.

Abby stopped on the third-floor landing as the sound of moaning swept past the house. "Ghosts be gone." She laughed, knowing it had to be the wind, and ignored the raised goose bumps on her arms.

Cobwebs hung from the rafters of the unfinished attic room, and Abby heard a distinct scurrying under the pounding of the rain. She held the candle aloft and peered into the dark corners. No visible mice.

Holding the candle away from her body, she peered under the eaves. A reflection came from an ancient, dust-covered lantern. The rusted top had a large iron ring attached. The middle, made of glass, sat in a metal framework. When she looked closer, the surface seemed to bubble and shift, as water boiling on the stove. The extra candles in her hand clattered to the floor and rolled away as a familiar face swam into her line of vision. She saw the same soldier—Silas?—unkempt dark hair, dimpled grin, his worried eyes a stark contrast.

She reached out to caress the pale cheek, longing to light up his eyes. The face disappeared. Her fingers connected with nothing more than cool glass.

Disappointment crashed her yearning to make contact. For several minutes Abby stood still, clutching the sputtering candle in her hand. It would soon go out, leaving her in pitch dark. The extra candles were lying somewhere near the lantern, where she had dropped them.

A tree branch whispered against the side of the house, and with it a voice murmured, "*Abigail ...*"

"Silas?" Abby peered through the murky gloom for the source of that odd, echoing tone. Rather than fear, anticipation coursed through her. "Are you here?" Taking a deep breath, she held her candle nub aloft. The attic space showed nothing more than cobwebs and old boxes.

Placing the coffee can on the floor, Abby reached into the shadows and pulled out the lantern. It sloshed when she moved it, full of oil. The plain glass held no face. She turned a dial on the side, exposing a nub of cotton wick. Using the matches in her pocket, Abby lit the lamp and set it on a crate in the middle of the room, illuminating the area in a soft glow as the candle sputtered out.

Abby tried to refocus to search through the boxes stacked around the perimeter of the area for her father's belongings. A box in the far corner behind a red plastic tub of Christmas decorations caught her attention: Adam's Civil War books: KEEP.

Dragging the heavy carton into the lantern's light, she ran her hand over the name Adam and paused, startled to realize he had been more than just her father. Maybe other people missed him, too. Maybe even Lisa.

The dusty box smelled stale when Abby opened it. She shuddered when a silverfish scurried over the lid and disappeared into the floorboards. One book at a time she emptied the box, leafing through each to get an idea of the contents. Some looked interesting, about spies from Canada, the Underground Railroad, and slavery; others appeared more daunting, with titles appropriate to a reference library.

At the very bottom of the carton she found an old

book that looked promising, *A History of Civil War Regiments of Pennsylvania.* Sitting cross-legged on the floor, she pulled the volume onto her lap and searched through the musty pages. Checking the index in the back she found 103 PA Volunteers, the same group as on Silas' tombstone. "Perfect."

As she turned to the correct page, the flame in the lantern flickered and went out, leaving the attic blanketed in total darkness. A gust of air ruffled the book pages; the door to the third floor had been opened. Footsteps sounded, tentative but heavy, one step at a time coming closer. Abby closed the book and held her breath. The footsteps stopped, just out of her line of vision.

A whispery voice hissed under the drumbeat of rain, too soft to understand.

"Who's there?" Abby's voice cracked.

The door burst fully open. "Abs, I got so freaked just now." Morton stomped in the attic and plopped down beside her. "I didn't know where you were, so I looked all over the house and saw this eerie light coming from up here, and it kept storming, and I didn't know what to do because my ghost meter's at home, and then I heard your voice and thought, like wow, it's gonna be okay." He took a deep breath.

"Morton, chill," Abby re-lit the lantern. "What're you doing here? Don't even tell me you rode your bike in the storm." She didn't mention the face she had seen moments earlier in the lantern glass, or the sound of someone calling her name. Or her belief that Silas might be reaching out to her … from beyond the grave.

"Your mom stopped at my house. She knew my mother had tests scheduled at the hospital all day. She brought me over in the car so I wouldn't be alone."

"Amazing," Abby said. "Just when I think she's a total bitch she does something decent. Go figure. Anyway, check this out. I found one of my dad's books and Silas's regiment is in it." She consulted the index again and turned to page 152. "Listen to this. The soldiers in the 103rd were sent to Camp Orr in Kittanning, wherever that is."

"It's in Armstrong County. About an hour north by car."

"I'm guessing Silas didn't get there in a Jeep," Abby said. "The guys from around here left in 1861, in December. I wonder if Silas left before Christmas. How sad for Leticia. She probably didn't feel like celebrating with him away."

Flashes of past Christmas's played through Abby's head. Chopping down a tree and decorating it with goofy ornaments, warm cider and crumb cake by the glow of colorful tree lights, two stockings hung on the mantel, embroidered Adam and Abby. With effort she tuned back into Morton.

"My family is my mother, and she can't do much celebrating these days. Want an M&M?"

"No. Okay, focus. In February, that means it would be early 1862, the Regiment left Camp Orr by train and went to Harrisburg by way of Pittsburgh. After a stop in Baltimore, they stayed in Washington, D.C. Then in March they were in something called the Peninsula Campaign, near Alexandria, Virginia. I think the inscription said Silas died in March 1862. It must have been in that battle."

"But what about the shame thing?" Morton frowned. "Didn't Leticia's letter say he died in shame? How could that be if he died in the line of duty? Maybe he deserted or shot another soldier or something. You know, friendly fire."

"The letter also said he *should* have been considered a hero. Even his mother wouldn't think of him as a hero if he ran away or shot a friend."

"I've got it." Morton nodded and stroked his chin. "It's a government conspiracy. Has to be, right? Those guys on talk radio always find out about stuff the government does to cover things up."

"We're talking about 1862. All that conspiracy theory

crap is ridiculous." Abby looked at Morton, red-faced and ready to argue. "And even if it's true now, which I doubt, it certainly isn't Civil War-era true."

Footsteps sounded on the stairs and a moment later Jack's voice. "Abby? You up here?" The beam of a flashlight preceded him into the attic.

"Looks like a party, and I didn't get my invitation." Jack glanced around the room. "It's M&M Boy and Biker Chick. Your mom asked me to see if you needed anything. What's all this?"

"Abby found this cool Bi—"

Abby interrupted Morton. "It's nothing. Just some books of my dad's, Civil War stuff. We're reading about the Underground Railroad and looking up info on the Dravo Cemetery. There's nothing better to do." She couldn't figure out why, but she had changed her mind about sharing Leticia and Silas with Jack. It seemed like a good idea an hour ago, but now it didn't. The more she thought about Jack, the less she wanted him to be involved in her life until she knew him better. He made her head hurt and her heart question everything.

"I rode to the cemetery the other day," Jack said. "You were right; the graves are interesting. It looks like the foundation of an old building is there, too. I saw some stones that are the right shape; an archeology class I took last year described how to find evidence of ancient structures. I'll show you sometime, free of charge." He looked at Morton. "You can stay home." He turned to go.

"Why did you go into Pittsburgh? And what were you doing out in the truck earlier?"

Jack tilted his head. "I could make something up, but want the real answer?"

Abby nodded.

"It's none of your business. That's the real answer." Jack marched down the stairs, the sound of his boots on the wooden steps getting fainter.

Abby shook her head and looked at the floor. "He can

be so mean." She wondered why she even cared.

Morton put one hand on Abby's arm. "Hey, he's a loser. Don't waste your time on him, 'cause we have work to do. I'll check out one of these other books."

They read until the words blurred, and Abby's eyes ached from deciphering small print in the dim light. Morton left for home during a break in the rain, and Abby went to her room.

Long after evening shadows slid into murky night, she stared out her window at the light coming from the barn. She heard a car backfire, but otherwise everything except the crickets remained silent.

A profound, vague sense of unease kept her awake for a long time. And the face in the lantern glass swam through her mind. She longed to see it—him—again.

THIRTEEN

Abby parked her purple bike along the side of the Historical Society building, avoiding a large puddle leftover from the storm. Leaning against the white frame siding, the garish violet color looked even more childish than usual, incongruent next to the century-old carriage in the window. Morton pulled in behind her.

"You want to go in there?" he said. "It's not your kind of place."

"How do you know what I like? I don't hang at the mall with my gal pals in the food court all day, giggling about the latest movie star. Jeez. Besides, the Munroe Bible is here, and it's the key to the mystery about Silas. *That's* what I'm into." Abby couldn't resist rolling her eyes.

"Oh yeah? Then why do you wear that gunk on your eyes and face? That's what girly girls do. I saw it on *Makeover Magic*." Morton batted his eyelashes and wiggled his butt.

"If you must know, I wear makeup because it covers my zits."

"Yeah, all two of them. And you don't go to the mall because you don't have any friends, I get it." Morton grinned. "But you got me, and I'm a way better friend than any back-stabbing girl."

"I am *so* lucky." Abby gritted her teeth; somehow Morton knew her too well. "Can we get back to the reason we're here? The museum isn't open all that long."

"We could check with someone in town about the Silas thing. I got people."

Abby shook her head. "Don't you think if someone had discovered an unknown fact about President Lincoln we'd have heard about it? Nothing's a secret in a small town. There would be a plaque somewhere or a statue of Silas. If we get stuck, we can ask around."

Abby grabbed Morton's arm and pulled him into the building. The interior, cool and dim, smelled musty with an overlay of peppermint. "Hello? Anyone here?" A light jingle, accompanied by squeaky footsteps, approached.

"Welcome to the Elizabeth … oh, it's you again," Mrs. Thurman said, coming out of a back room, the charms on her bracelet clanging against each other. "I just had to have my cup of peppermint tea to start the day right. My mother always said, 'A cup of tea to start the day, everything will go your way.' And I see you brought a little friend. How lovely to find young people interested in local history. Now, what can I do for you, dear?" She straightened the white cardigan that hung in limp folds from her narrow shoulders.

"I want to show my 'little friend' the old Bible from my last visit," Abby said. "You know, the heavy one with the brass closures."

Mrs. Thurman frowned, and her eyes darted from side to side.

"The one from the milk crate … we'll just go back and find it ourselves. Thanks."

"Yes, of course, now I remember," Mrs. Thurman said. "We had a Bible and a dictionary all set for the antique store. I forgot about them, but you jogged my memory. Sometimes I need that. Getting older is not a picnic, you know. I took those books over and left them at the shop across the way. Let me show you the other historic Bibles in the back. Some even have family histories." She marched toward the library.

Morton started to follow her, but Abby stopped him. "Maybe some other day. Thanks anyway." They hurried out the front door, Mrs. Thurman muttering behind them about "silly children."

"I can't believe it. That Bible would still be here if I hadn't made a big deal about it. Why didn't I just come back the next day and get it? I'm such an idiot. Now we have to track it down. I just hope it looked ruined enough that even an antique-lover would reject it."

"Look at it this way," Morton said. "If you hadn't seen it in the first place, Silas might never rest in peace. At least now he has a chance. Here, have an M&M."

As he held out a fist-full of candies to her, Abby had a disturbing image of Jack hitting Morton's hand and scattering the bright-colored pieces on the barn floor. She shook her head to clear it. She could almost hear her dad's voice: "Focus on the job at hand, Abby. It's the only way to get things done."

After a short ride through town, Abby pulled to a stop in front of The Boston Shoppes. The old yellow brick structure now housed a gift shop with antiques. Garden decorations were displayed on the wide front porch. A multi-colored whirligig twirled wildly in the breeze, the improbable neon shades glaring in the sun.

"No, not here." Morton clutched his throat. "I hate this stuff, it's for girls, old girls. It's like cutesy hell, that's what it is. Please, no."

"Get a grip. We'll find the Bible, buy it, and we're out of here. You think I like home décor any more than you do? Even if I am a girly girl?"

The signature smell of floral potpourri assailed Abby's nostrils as she entered the establishment. An old bell attached to the doorframe announced their arrival. To the right, behind a polished wooden counter, a middle-aged woman sat reading. She looked up and smiled. "Welcome ..." Her smiled faded as Morton picked up and almost dropped a crystal paperweight. She pointed to a sign on the counter: You break it, you buy it.

"I'll watch him." Abby tried to think of a plausible reason they might want to spend time in a store like this one. "Actually, we're looking for a, um, birthday gift, a surprise."

"A gift? Whose birthday? Huh?" Morton scratched his head.

"Men," Abby said to the woman. "They never listen to us, do they?"

The woman smiled. "Just be careful. We have three floors; I'm sure you'll find the perfect item for that special someone. Whomever it might be."

Abby trudged up the oak staircase, dismayed by the wall-to-wall merchandise. A plethora of candles, stuffed animals, framed prints, and country furnishings competed with assorted small antiques. Each floor, divided into individual shops, looked the same.

Morton's wheeze became audible on the second floor, but he kept going. Reaching the third floor, he took a noisy breath, raced ahead and pounced on a pile of old books. "Abs, over here!"

"At last. I've seen enough frou-frou decorations to last me forever." She searched through the stack. "Not here. It's huge, you can't miss it. We have to ask."

Back downstairs, Abby approached the clerk. "I'm looking for an antique book, a Bible I saw at the Historical Society the other day. Mrs. Thurman said she sent it over here. It's exactly what I want. Any idea where it is? You have so many, um, interesting things, I must have missed it."

"A Bible? I don't recall anything like that. We don't carry many books, although Jeannie on the third floor has a few."

"No, we already looked there," Morton said.

The woman thought for a minute. "Wait, I think I know. Is it a big old thing, falling apart? With brass clasps?"

Abby nodded, fingers crossed. "That's what I'm looking for."

"Sure, I remember now," the woman said. "It looked too disreputable for us, so we sent it to Bill across the street. He has the salvage place, calls it his home for orphaned antiques and tragic furniture." She went back to reading her paperback, then glanced up as they went out the door. "But I think I saw him throw a big book into the trash. The truck came by while you were upstairs. Sorry."

"That's it," Morton said. "Some things aren't meant to be. Maybe it's better to let Silas rest in peace."

Abby gave him a shove out the door. "I refuse to give up."

LAUREL HOUCK

FOURTEEN

Abby tapped one foot against the curb while she waited for traffic turning the corner off the bridge. When the final car went past, she dashed across the street to Bill's. She noticed Morton licking his lips as he gazed at the Dairy Delicious cater-cornered from them. "Don't even think it. If we find the Bible, I promise you ice cream."

"That's a big 'if.' It's probably at the landfill by now."

"If it's not here, I'll need ice cream, too," Abby said. "Chocolate, and lots of it."

"Chocolate's not good for zits." Morton popped a handful of M&M's in his mouth. "You shouldn't even have these, but who can resist?"

"Whatever." Abby grabbed some candy as they dodged an odd assortment of chairs and old clothes on metal racks on their way into Bill's.

No bell, no potpourri, no one greeted them in the dimly lit store. A chaotic hodge-podge of unrelated items covered every surface, from the floor to the leaning shelves lining the walls. Old washing machines rested next to rocking chairs. A set of faux pearls decorated a shade-less floor lamp adorned with a moldering fur coat. Stacks of old books leaned here and there. An oscillating fan whirred in the corner, faded ribbons attached to the front fluttering in the breeze.

Abby wrinkled her nose at the aroma of old linen, oil, and dirty dog. She took a tentative step into the room and jumped as a high-pitched whine pierced the stillness. "What …?"

"You there, girlie, watch out for my pooch." A husky voice filled the space.

Abby stepped back and a mangy hound dog moved out of her way. It stretched, licked Abby's hand, turned in a circle, and plopped onto a ratty braided rug in the middle of the aisle. "Sorry, doggie," she said, looking up as a huge, bearded man approached. She took another step back as he towered over her.

"Hey, Bill, how's it goin'?" Morton said.

Abby looked at Morton and back to the man. "You know him?"

Bill laughed. "Sure, honey. Me and Morty go way back. We're what you call the unofficial local historical society, right, son?"

"This is the old guy. Sorry, Bill. I mean the guy I told you knows some things about the area. Ask him about the Bible."

"Well now, I do love the Good Book." Bill folded his hands as if in prayer. "You new in town? Lookin' for a church?"

"No, I mean yes, I'm new in town, but I'm searching for a *specific* Bible." Abby glanced at Morton who was too busy petting the dog to help her. "The *real* Historical Society had it. They gave it to The Boston Shoppes, and the lady there said she gave it to you. I need it; I want to buy it."

Bill's eyes narrowed. "What do you want with an old tore-up Bible?"

"So you do have it," Abby said. "Otherwise you wouldn't know it looked torn and old. Can I see it? I know it's not worth much, but it has sentimental value to me."

"Hmm, sentimental are you Miss Munroe?" Bill said.

"My last name's Whitney, not Munroe," Abby said. Seeing Bill's raised eyebrows she realized her mistake. "I know what you're thinking, but it's a different kind of sentiment. I saw it and thought it looked interesting, that's all. So, can you get it for me? I have cash."

"Well now, that all depends." Bill pursed his lips. "Seems to me you went to a powerful lot of trouble to find something you think is kinda 'interesting.' If it's all that exciting, you'll have to work a little harder to get it."

Abby sighed. "What's your bottom line? How much? This might be your one chance to unload it."

Bill laughed and nodded to Morton. "I like her, son. She's a keeper, even if she don't trust no one." He turned to Abby. "Sorry, honey, I don't have that ole Bible anymore. A bunch of folks came by on bikes, they was from down in Confluence, some church group. One of the gals wanted it, and I gave it to her. They took off down the bike trail not too long ago, heading for Pittsburgh I think."

Abby charged out the door, shouting "Thanks." She got on her bike and headed down the hill to the trailhead parking lot. "Maybe we can catch up with them," she called over her shoulder to Morton. She put her head down, raced past the parking lot and onto the trail to the city.

Ten minutes later Abby's knees ached as she pounded the pedals. She looked around for Morton, stopping when she couldn't see him. What if he'd fallen and needed her? She gritted her teeth and got back on the bike.

"Damn you, Morton." Another fifty feet and she turned around at a wide place in the gravel. She retraced her route and reached the edge of the field by the trailhead parking lot where she had started.

"Hey, Abs, over here."

Morton sat in the grass. "I met these great people. They stopped me to get directions."

Abby glared at him. "We really have to go, okay? Nice

to meet you." She nodded at the group seated by Morton. As she started to ride away she passed an older teenage girl on a burgundy cruiser with a wicker bike basket. She caught a glimpse of something big and dark in the basket and skidded to a stop. "Hey. Wait up."

The girl stopped and dismounted; her bike fell. "I can't ride with this," she said to her friends. "I don't know why I brought it along, or what to do with it now."

Abby walked over, and laying in the grass she saw the Munroe Bible. Morton saw it at the same time.

"Hey, is that …"

Abby raised a hand to silence him and walked over to the girl. "If you don't want that, I'll take it home with me. I just live a couple miles away."

The young woman appraised Abby. "Why do you want it?"

"It looks like a piece of history."

"How do you know?"

Abby felt her frustration level building. "It's obviously old, and old things are historical."

"Hey, Kel," one of her friends shouted. "Maybe it's valuable, like the things on Antiques Road Show. Some of those people get thousands for old stuff they just happened to find."

"Kel, right?" Abby said. When the girl nodded, she continued, "I know you got this from the junk dealer in town because I went there looking for it. I'm sure if it's valuable he wouldn't have given it to you. I'm just trying to help."

Kel shook her head. "I'm going to keep it and have it appraised. Thanks anyway." She picked up her bike, tied the Bible to the back of it with a bungee cord a friend supplied, and rode away.

"I can't believe that just happened." Abby's shoulders slumped. "We might as well give up right now."

"I thought you never give up." Morton snorted.

Abby thought about her dad calling her "a bulldog with

a bone." The old pull of adrenaline and ambition he always managed to give her made her smile. "You're right. I can't give up. There must be another way to find the answers. I won't give up on Silas. He's too important to me."

"I don't know about 'important,'" Morton said. "It's a fun adventure, but not the end of the world if we don't figure it out."

"It's complicated." Abby had no idea how to explain her growing attraction to … what? A vision she'd had a few times? A ghost? A hallucination? She shrugged. "I promise you I'll solve this, no matter what it takes." At the look of "she's crazy" in Morton's eyes, she didn't add what really coursed through her heart. Silas.

"You promised me ice cream."

Abby straddled her bike. "Come on, milkshake man. We'll hit the Dairy Delicious on the way home. I always keep my promises."

"Especially to you," she whispered into the wind, wondering if her words would reach Silas, wherever he might be.

FIFTEEN

Abby opened her eyes to bright morning sunshine. She stretched, yawned, and rolled over to check the time. Her thoughts, the same as every day for the past week, centered on how close she'd been to the Munroe Bible, only to see it taken away.

She stretched again, kicked off the sheet, and picked up her phone. The date screamed at her. Turning over she rolled into a ball, pulled the sheet over her head, and let the gloom sink into her bones. Her dad's birthday. No more celebrations. Ever.

The hurt became a physical jolt, deep in her gut. Memories flooded her mind, shutting out the sunshine, the blue-sprigged cotton sheets, and the raucous cries of a crow outside the window. The first text she'd ever sent had been to him: HB 2 U.

Visions of birthday cakes, dripping candles, and her dad's beaming smile played through her mind like an old DVD.

"Happy birthday to you, happy birthday, dear Daddy," she sang in a quiet, tear-clogged voice. He always sang along, even on his own birthday, "Happy birthday to me."

"Abigail …"

The deep, soft voice surrounded Abby with comfort, a hug from an invisible source. She looked up, expectant, longing for more. Beside her bed stood the same young man she'd been imagining, only this time his outline was sharper, more distinct. He reached out one hand to touch her hair.

"Silas …?"

His right cheek dimpled, and he saluted. "Silas Munroe, at your service, ma'am."

"How is it possible?" Abby searched his gold-flecked eyes. "You died a long time ago."

"Life don't really change with death. But it sure is a mystery, Miss Abigail."

Abby reached for his hand. Hers went through his semi-transparent flesh as if pushing aside a cloud of cool steam. "You aren't really here. I'm losing my mind." But she had the sense that, as crazy as it seemed, he really did exist. And had come to rescue her. "I want to help you."

"Abby." Lisa's voice—grating, annoying—chased Silas away.

Abby crashed back into the real world, with a profound sense of loneliness and longing for Silas. Shaking her head, she refocused. Dad. Lisa. Reality.

Maybe, even after everything that had happened, Lisa might be having a hard time, too. Surely she remembered what the date signified and had some good memories. It might be one time when they would be better off together. Abby tossed the covers aside, dressed, and bathed her eyes in cold water.

Entering the kitchen, Abby expected the stench of burnt coffee, the murk of shut blinds, and a mother with red, swollen eyes to match her own. Instead, bright sunlight greeted her, accompanied by the crackle of sizzling bacon and the aroma of warm cinnamon rolls.

"There you are." Lisa leaned over to squeeze Abby's shoulders. "I made breakfast. It's been a while since I had time to take care of you, not that you need much caring for anymore."

Abby watched in amazement as her mother sat breakfast on the table and continued to prattle about nothing of any importance whatsoever. She sat down and sipped a glass of fresh-squeezed orange juice. Her stomach rebelled as the cold citrus burned its way down her throat. The bacon congealed in a greasy pool on the plate as it cooled. The dark cinnamon swirled into the center of the rolls. It reminded her of a circular labyrinth leading to hell.

"I'm not hungry." Abby put down her juice glass. "And I don't eat pork."

"Not hungry? You love cinnamon rolls." Lisa paused. "Don't you?"

"Not today." Abby shoved the basket of rolls across the table.

"Why do I even try?" Lisa cleared the table with jerky movements. "You expect too much, Abby. In fact, I'm not even sure what you want most of the time." Her shrill voice went up an octave. "I left the life I had made for myself and moved back here to take care of you when your father died—I *want* to be with you. I've tried to give you space, but still pay attention. I wish you would talk to me, really talk to me, even if I don't like what you have to say. But you walk around in a rage and nothing I do works; you act like we're strangers. It's lose/lose for me, no matter what."

"Well, this time you've outdone yourself." Tears filled Abby's eyes. "You were so busy playing mommy that you forgot today is Dad's birthday. You're two for two— absent from his death, forgot his birth. Way to go. I realize you didn't love either one of us enough to make things work twelve years ago. But somehow I gave you credit for remembering the good as well as the bad. Go figure." She stood up and pushed the kitchen chair so hard it fell with a clatter onto the tile floor.

"Abby, wait," Lisa said. "I want to explain …"

Abby interrupted. "Don't bother. I'll be in my room;

your explanations can keep you company." She ran from the kitchen, the slap of her flip-flops echoing on the tile floor in the sudden absence of voices.

Abby paced for several minutes after returning to her room and slamming the door shut, her thoughts centered on hating Lisa. When the anger morphed back into sadness, her momentum wound down like an old clock. She collapsed in a heap on the bed, unable to move at all. Questions wound through her brain. *Did Lisa come back out of duty or love? What happened to make her leave? Does she feel guilty? Am I a candidate for Bitch of the Year? And what's with Silas? Am I not only a bitch, but crazy, too?*

Abby made her bed, folded some clothes, and ran out of things to do. The need to keep busy sent her to her phone. Since she'd forgotten to charge it as usual, she went back to her laptop. She had to discover something concrete about Silas Munroe and his relationship to Abraham Lincoln. After forty-five minutes Abby rolled her neck and shoulders. Millions of hits on Abe, but nothing about him with anyone named Silas.

She took a shopping break and clicked on eBay. Browsing through purses, shoes, and bike accessories yielded nothing of interest. Then she thought about Morton. He would love some ghost supplies if she could find them cheap enough. She entered "spirits" and sat back. To her amazement, the screen lit up with a multitude of items for ghost hunting, nothing she could afford. Suggestions for further searches included Holy Spirit and Bible.

She entered "antique Bible" in the search block and sat back. Several appeared on-screen and she scrolled through, noticing as she did that most old Bibles looked similar. Some were listed with the auction starting as low as five dollars, others up to two thousand dollars. Kel had been smart to check out the price of her find.

"No. Way." She stopped scrolling. The Bible on the screen looked exactly like the Munroe Bible. Her hands started to sweat as she clicked on the picture and the description came up.

Antique Bible, circa 1840. This lovely old book boasts a quilted leather cover, brass hasps, and full-color illustrations. It is in fair condition. Wear evident on cover, some pages torn/missing. Newly listed, this historic gem won't last long. Seller: Confluence of Events Antiques & Oddities. Confluence, Pennsylvania, United States. Contact seller at:
www.confluenceofevents.com
Buy It Now price: $65 shipping $3.99

Abby took a deep breath. Morton had talked about the little town of Confluence as being nearby, down the Allegheny River. It's also where Kel and her friends had come from. But what if she spent that much money and it turned out to be the wrong Bible?

She sat back and searched for a fingernail that hadn't already been bitten back to the quick. They all looked bad, but she found a place to gnaw. When that didn't dispel her indecision, she went to twisting a strand of hair around her finger. She stared at the Bible on the computer so intently it seemed to float off the screen.

"Abigail ... trust yourself."

Abby's head whipped around; no one. She jumped out of the chair and went to the kitchen. She could see her mother and Jack through the window, standing beside the barn. There were no guests in the house. And no Silas anywhere.

She returned to the computer and sucked in a breath. The cursor had moved and was poised over the words BUY IT NOW.

Abby struggled to put a word to what Silas made her feel. She thought about the psychologist Lisa made her talk to once, who repeated over and over for an hour, "How does that make you feel?"

Rather than being freaked to the max, the voice and

vision of Silas made her truly *feel love* again. Somehow, he always knew when she needed comfort, hope, protection. Something about him, his chiseled chin, curly hair, and broad shoulders made her long to be held in his arms, to feel his heart beating against hers, to press her lips against his.

Abby's indecision vanished, replaced with a sense of certainty. She rummaged through her desk drawer until she found the credit card Dad had given her to use for emergencies after he got sick. It had never been canceled, and the money she had saved would pay the bill when it came. Back at the computer she entered all the necessary information and hit Complete Transaction. Several minutes later she had an email confirmation and expected delivery in three days.

Leaning back in the antique chair her dad had restored, she rubbed her hands on the smooth wooden arms.

"HB 2 U, Dad."

SIXTEEN

"Come down here." Lisa's voice, although faint between the first and third floors, nonetheless grated on Abby's nerves as usual.

Abby put aside the Civil War book she'd been flipping through. "Of course I'm coming, like I have a choice. I'm sure some very important project waits for me, like dishes, vacuuming, something to improve mankind. What a pain in the ass. No, I have to stop acting like this, it isn't the me I want to be."

She stopped muttering as she rounded the bend in the first-floor stairs. On the marble-topped entry table sat a huge package addressed to Abigail Whitney. "*Yes.*"

"What exactly is in there?" Lisa stood with one hand on the package. "The UPS man left this on the porch; did you order something? The return is from an antique store. I didn't know you were into antiques—or that you had money to blow on frivolous things." Lisa's jutting jaw, and frown said more than her words did.

Abby reached for the package. "It's nothing."

Lisa's hand clamped down on it. "It's big, it's heavy, and I want to know what it is."

"Yes, well, it seems to be addressed to me, not you,"

Abby said. "So if you don't mind …"

To Abby's surprise, tears formed in Lisa's eyes and spilled in silence down her cheeks. "I suppose you have a right to your privacy. I forget you aren't three years old anymore. I wish—oh, never mind."

An unexpected ache filled Abby's heart. "Hey, it's not a big deal, just an old book I found on eBay. I have enough money saved up, so don't worry about another bill."

Lisa managed a small smile and went back toward the kitchen.

Abby lugged the package upstairs to her room, mind churning. The heavy parcel shook Abby's old dresser as she plunked it down. Ripping off the tape, she lifted out the Munroe Bible. She ran her hand over the quilted leather cover, embossed dove, and gilded lettering, then bent down to sniff the musky parchment. "What secrets are you going to tell me?"

"Hey, Abs. You in there?" Morton knocked on the door and then barged in, uninvited. "What's up? Your Mom's crying in the kitchen, and I heard you up here. You guys have a fight again? You should be nicer to her, you know. At least your mom can cook and walk around and stuff. You gotta let the past go."

He held up a glass. "I got some orange juice on the way through; it goes great with M&M's—chocolate and citrus, yum. Want some?" He wandered around the room, then noticed the old Bible on the dresser. "Hey—you got it."

Abby grabbed the book from Morton. She rubbed at a smear of chocolate on the cover. "Can't you at least wipe the candy off your hands?"

"You do know how miserable you can be sometimes, right?" Morton said. "Besides, M&M's are supposed to melt in your mouth, so I didn't know there would be chocolate on my hands."

Abby rolled her eyes. "I'm going through this book again. There must be something in here to help us figure out the big mystery about Silas. If there *is* a mystery. I'll start in the front and work through one page at a time."

"Are you for real?" Morton said. "This thing must be a foot wide and a bazillion pages long. We'll never get done."

Abby put one hand on her hip. "'*Never*' used to be my favorite word. I'd 'never' do anything too hard; I thought my life would 'never' change, my dad would 'never' leave, my mother would 'never' come back. Well, look at what's happened. Every day's a struggle, my Dad is dead, and my mother is worming her way back into my life. I *will* solve this mystery; don't tell me I won't."

"Yeah, sure, whatever." Morton studied Abby. "Did you know you look like your mom when you stand like that?" He ducked when she swatted at his shoulder.

"Let's get started." Abby opened the Bible. "It's divided into books, with chapters and verses. The first book is Genesis."

She pulled Leticia's letter from the drawer and studied the text. "Look at this, near the end. I thought it must be about a guy named Gene III, but that doesn't make any sense. What if it's a clue, you know, to check out Genesis, chapter three? Looks like they used Roman numerals instead of numbers back then."

Abby opened the Bible and turned to Genesis. In chapter three, five verses down, she found a phrase underlined: <u>knowing good and evil</u>. In the margin, sideways, she saw a hand-lettered notation: PS XXXVII. "Morton, look at this. She's sending us to another place. PS, PS ..." Abby flipped through the pages. "It must mean the book of Psalms, number thirty-seven."

Morton crossed the room balancing orange juice in one hand while he shoved the last of the candy in his mouth with the other. He tripped, lost his balance, and fell. The candies spit out of his mouth and bounced across the floor. Juice rained through the air onto the hardwood, splashing stray droplets on the Bible.

"Look what you've done. Where's your brain? In your

stomach as usual?"

Morton got to his feet. His face blanched, and he pulled his hands back as if burned, tucking them behind his back. "I'm s-s-sorry," he said. "Here, I'll take care of it." He reached forward, grabbed the heavy Bible, and dropped it with a resounding thud. It landed in the puddle of orange juice, splashing Abby's legs.

Abby gritted her teeth. "Do. Not. Help. Me." She raced to the bathroom, returning with two bath towels. She groaned when she saw Morton mopping the floor with her pillowcase. She threw the towels at him.

Morton cleaned the floor while Abby lugged the Bible to the nightstand by her side window. Sunlight streaming through the lace curtains made fancy designs on the quilted book cover, softening it into a work of abstract art. The smell of old paper and orange juice, incongruent together, filled the room.

Glancing out the window she saw Jack on the barn roof hammering new shingles. His back gleamed with sweat, and the muscles in his right arm bulged with the effort. She watched him, wondering about his secrets.

Jack sat back on his heels, wiping his face with a red bandana. Shielding his eyes from the sun, he gazed over the treetops down the bike trail. A small smile played around his thin lips, and he nodded. As he turned back to the roof, he caught Abby staring at him and scowled. She waved, but he ignored her and went back to work, wielding the hammer with vicious energy.

"Jerk," she said. "What's your problem?"

"Look, I said I'm sorry. You don't have to call me names."

"Not you. It's Jack."

"Told you so from the very first time I met him." Morton smirked.

Abby shrugged and picked up the sticky Bible. After examining the front cover, she leafed through the pages. "The leather protected the inside. I'll clean off the rest of the juice. Just be careful from now on."

"You're the one who insisted we stay up here. I do better in the kitchen with food." Morton cringed when Abby frowned. "Don't forget I'm still a kid."

"Yeah, okay; truce." Abby handed him a pad of paper. "You can be the secretary."

Morton giggled. "And do what, get you coffee?"

Abby ignored him. She opened the Bible to the first section, the Old Testament, and found the marked verse in Genesis again. "Write this down: knowing good and evil."

While Morton wrote, Abby muttered to herself. "Good and evil. Dad good, cancer evil. If Silas did something good, how could it be evil? What about Jack, which one is he? The good, understanding, hot guy who rode in on a bike or the evil, moody, mystery guy who appeared out of nowhere? How do I know? How do I find out?"

She sighed and stared at the Bible, a little prayer playing through her mind, hoping someone out there heard her.

LAUREL HOUCK

SEVENTEEN

Morton threw down the plastic pen labeled Ambien: sleeplikeababy.com. "I'm tired and don't want to be the secretary anymore. I have writer's cramp, I have to pee, and I never got lunch. Silas has been dead for over a hundred years; he can rest in peace later."

Abby stretched. "Almost done. We're in the second half of the Bible, the New Testament. This is the book of Hebrews." She flipped through the remainder. "Nine more to go. Just be glad Leticia left margin notes at each clue, leading us to the next one."

"Come on, Abs," Morton whined. "I'm out of M&M's; I'm desperate. Just scan the rest, you already got plenty of words."

"This isn't a book report. It's not about the number of words. We're searching for clues, remember? I don't want to miss anything."

Silence stretched in the room. Morton folded his arms.

"How about this?" Abby said. "Use the bathroom, we'll finish up, then get pizza."

"With pepperoni, mushrooms, and green pepper?"

"Whatever; I'll pick off the meat," Abby said.

Morton left; Abby heard the toilet flush, then the

splash of water in the sink. He returned and collapsed on the bed. "As long as you get the crust with cheese inside."

They went back to work. Abby's eyes strained to read the small print and search through columns of words. Finally she reached the last page of the Bible in the book of Revelation.

"Here's hoping we get a revelation from Leticia. Let's see if it makes any sense." She plopped down beside Morton, box springs squeaking in protest.

Morton bounced up and down on the bed, grinning when the noise became louder.

"You are such a child."

"What's going on here?" Jack stood in the doorway. "Sounds like you two kids are having lots of fun." He raised one eyebrow.

Abby jumped up. "We're reading a Bible, that's all."

"Uh-huh, sure." Jack peered around Abby. "It *is* a Bible."

"Yeah, we're reading about ..." Morton began.

"God," Abby said. "Maybe you've heard of Him. What's up? Did you miss me?" She smiled, wishing she had put on some make-up.

"I need the key for the big cupboard in the barn. Your mother thought you might know where it is." He waited, tapping one booted foot on the floor.

Abby shrugged. "No clue. What's the big hurry?"

"The 'big hurry' is there's a job to finish before I leave for the bike rally in D.C. and my little get-together with President Keller. I haven't got all day." Jack's voice cracked. "Do you have the damn key or not? A key is the *only* thing I'm missing."

"What exactly is your problem?" Abby said.

"I'm not here to flirt with little girls. I have a job to do, and no one and nothing is going to interfere. The key?"

"Find the stupid key yourself, genius. Now get out of my room."

Jack's eyes narrowed, and he started to speak, then

seemed to reconsider. He turned and slammed the door shut on his way out.

Abby didn't know whether to be angry or hurt. Why couldn't he just be decent and uncomplicated?

"How come you didn't tell him about Silas and the Bible?" Morton said. "Maybe nasty is his regular personality, and he can't help it. Genetics, you know. His parents must be jerks, too."

"The more I get to know Jacques Charpentier, the more I don't trust him." Abby's eyes narrowed. "His mood swings creep me out. It's none of his business what I do in my own house. And why are you defending him? I thought you didn't like him."

"But if Jack ..." Morton said.

"Forget Jack. We have to figure out what Leticia's trying to tell us."

Morton put his arms behind his head. "Hurry up. I'm hungry."

Abby picked up the yellow legal pad and read through each entry copied from the Bible, trying to absorb the meaning from the archaic language. "Some of these are redundant."

Morton frowned. "Huh?"

"You know, Leticia underlined lots of sentences with 'wicked' this and 'wicked' that. They all sound the same. I'll pick out phrases that aren't repetitive and see if they make any sense. Listen:

... Knowing good and evil ...
The wicked watcheth the righteous, and seeketh to slay him.
This is my beloved Son, in whom I am well pleased.
Ask, and it shall be given you; seek, and ye shall find ...
And for this cause he is the mediator.
... The same yesterday and to-day, yea, and for ever.
He which testifieth these things saith, Yea:... Amen ..."

Abby looked up at Morton; he shrugged. "I wrote them

the way the Bible had it. I never understood those old words, even in church. It's just a bunch of junk, Abs. Maybe Leticia underlined stuff she liked. It seemed like a good idea, but ..." He shrugged again. "So, pizza, right?"

Abby conceded defeat and ordered pizza. She went downstairs to wait for the delivery and found her mother on the porch swing staring into space as the chains clinked in rhythm. She perched on the step, facing the drive.

"I wish you hadn't ignored me for the past few days. I'd rather have you yelling at me than saying nothing at all." The chains on the porch swing went silent.

"I got mad." Abby turned halfway around.

"Do you really think I forgot your dad's birthday?"

"Well, yeah, you did."

Lisa's voice caught. "I think about him every day. Each time I look at you I see him—brilliant smile, blue eyes, blond hair. I tried to make things nice the other morning because I knew it would be a tough day for you. It backfired, I guess, but I resent you thinking he meant that little to me. Your dad and I loved each other once, Abby. You are the visible miracle of that. We both loved you. I still do."

Abby faced her mother. "But you chose to leave. And you didn't come back."

Lisa shook her head. "I never planned to stay away forever. Time passed and everything got blurry for me. People make choices, some good, some not so great. And those decisions can bite you in the butt—and hurt others, too. But you don't have the exclusive rights to grief around here."

A white car with the Vocelli's Pizza logo pulled up. Abby paid for the pizza, opened the screen door, and paused. "I miss him so much."

Her mother walked over, reached around the pizza box, and gave her a brief hug. "I know, honey. I know." She went back to the swing.

At the risk of letting the pizza get cold, Abby stood

inside the front door and leaned against the wall. She couldn't recall Lisa ever being transparent about her life. Her rejection had always seemed thoughtless and spiteful. But there had been real pain in her voice. What had really happened twelve years ago? Yet another unsolved mystery.

"Hey, where's my pizza?" Morton's voice drifted down from above.

"Yeah, okay." Abby returned to her room and gave Morton the pizza. She picked pepperoni off one slice and choked it down. After he left she couldn't sit still, aching for her Dad, understanding that nothing would bring him back. Afraid to hope for a real relationship with her mother. Wishing Silas would appear, knowing it to be a crazy thought filled with unfathomable emotions. Jack appealed to her—who wouldn't find him gorgeous—but not in the same way as Silas. But a flesh-and-blood guy had to be better than a … ghost … or whatever.

She paced around the room, picking things up, putting them down, adjusting the lampshade, biting her nails, glancing at Leticia's notations from the Bible. Studying the pages in her hand, she organized the Bible phrases into a paragraph, adding punctuation and updating the language:

Knowing right and wrong, the evil watched the honest and tried to kill him. I am proud of my son. Look for it and you will find it. For the true cause he became the go-between. The message is always the same. The one who wrote this swears it is true.

Abby picked up the paper and began to pace again, reading it aloud, trying out different meanings. "So, *someone knows the difference between right and wrong.* That could be anyone. *A bad person tried to kill an honest man.* Who are these guys? *Leticia is proud of Silas,* that's easy."

She folded the page in half. "*If I look for it I'll find it.* Whatever "it" is. *Someone became the middleman for the true cause.* She probably means Silas; the Civil War must have been the cause. *The meaning is always the same.* Okay, time hasn't changed anything. *Leticia swears it's all true.* Which means exactly what?"

Abby threw the tablet on her bed and spent the remainder of the day doing chores around the house. By evening exhaustion caught up with her. She took a shower, shaving her legs and washing her hair. The aroma of body wash, pleasant and flowery, combined with the warm water, relaxed her. She towel-dried her hair and braided it wet, hoping the waves she would have in the morning would impress Silas if he appeared.

In her room she pulled on striped pajamas from Pink via Goodwill. Although ready for bed, she had gotten no closer to solving any real secrets, to figuring out how to let go of her dad, how to love her mother, or how to deal with her feelings for a man who didn't exist in the real world. Because in spite of her lack of experience with romantic relationships, her soul knew it had found its true mate.

Hands under her head, Abby lay on her bed until night wrapped itself around the old house. She stared at the ceiling for a long time, barely noticing a lightning-bolt shaped crack in the plaster. The Bible phrases began to take shape in her mind, swirling like mist through the framework of Leticia's old letter and what she had read about the Civil War.

She grabbed the pink stuffed pig she'd slept with since her toddler days and looked into her eyes. "Okay, listen up, Piggy, you gotta help me out here. The 'true cause' is the Civil War; I'm sure about that. Silas was a soldier for the Union Army. Who would be famous enough that an ordinary soldier and his mother would think of him as 'honest' ... someone well known, important? What about Abraham Lincoln, old Honest Abe? But it couldn't be him ... could it? In the letter Leticia said Silas did something for Mr. Lincoln. What if Silas saved the life of the president?

She sat up in the dark. "Someone tried to kill President Lincoln. Silas died saving the president's life, making his mother proud. It's a secret, but the answer can be discovered and is always going to be the same. Leticia knew the truth, but made sure the secret would be protected. It's a pretty big leap, but at least it's a place to start."

Abby got up and looked out her front window at the yard below, glistening in a shaft of moonlight. Her gaze traveled to the moonlit sky. "Good-night, moon," she whispered, remembering the book her dad read to her each night at bedtime before she could read.

She jumped when a car backfired, then climbed under the covers and drifted into a dreamless sleep.

EIGHTEEN

Abby stirred awake. She checked her phone: four o'clock in the morning. She didn't have to pee, so what woke her? She squirmed deeper under the cotton sheet and adjusted the lightweight blanket under her chin, faint river sounds lulling her back into sleep. The pillow, indented where her head rested, enveloped her in comfort.

Just as sleep began to gnaw at the edge of consciousness, Abby came wide-awake. She heard scratching, random but distinct, and sat up in bed. The noise continued, accompanied by a low, feral growl. She got up, shivering, sleep impossible.

Pulling aside the lace curtain at her window, Abby peered into the yard. Night shadows remained deep and dark, back-lit by moonlight, turning the landscape into the black and white from one of her father's old film negatives. The only noise coming from outside, the distant rush of river against stone, sounded nothing like scratching. She eased into the hall, arms wrapped around her chest as if they could protect her from—what? Mice? Rats? Raccoons?

A low, almost human hum followed the next flurry of scratching.

Not a mouse, something bigger; definitely not good. Why didn't Lisa hear this? She must have taken a sleeping pill again.

Abby crept closer to the wall, realizing the sounds came from behind it. When she tapped on the partition it sounded hollow. The noises stopped. She leaned her ear against the plaster—silence.

"Good. Whatever you are, just go out the way you came in." Abby waited, heard nothing more, and returned to bed. Jack could check it out in the morning. She burrowed back under the covers and closed her eyes.

After a light, restless sleep, Abby awoke early and tried to make sense of the night noises from the hall, wondering if it had been the lingering fragment of a dream. The sounds from guests downstairs meant Lisa would be busy preparing breakfast in the kitchen. Abby stretched, yawned, and got up to the bathroom. She stopped in front of the wall on the way back to her room, staring at it as if contemplating a work of art at a Shadyside gallery.

She ran her hands around a faintly-raised, rectangular outline a little higher than the top of her head. With her palms splayed on the surface, she felt the bumps and furrows from layers of painted-over wallpaper. With a poke at the plaster, a ragged one-foot section crumbled under her hand; she inhaled a puff of stale air. A smallish, dark shape hurled itself through the opening. Abby fell backward, heart pounding; the figure disappeared into her room.

She tiptoed to her door to shut it but couldn't resist peeking inside. On top of her dresser, hissing, teeth bared, back arched with stand-up fur, stood a black cat. Its pupils were wide, ears flat to the head, and tail bristling. Abby froze, barely breathing.

"So you're the one who disrupted my rest," she said in a monotone. "Just calm down; I'm not going to hurt you, pretty kitty-kitty-kitty. How did you get inside the wall? How long have you been there? You must be hungry."

Abby walked toward her nightstand; the cat spit a warning. "Take it easy. I'm your new best friend." She plucked a packet of goldfish crackers out of the drawer. "Do kitties eat cheese crackers? Want some? It's the best I can do for now. Come on, yummy, yummy fishies for the sweet kitty."

Speaking in a soft, even tone, Abby eased her way across the room until she stood in front of the cat. She held out her hand, one yellow fish-shaped cracker in the palm, and lifted it. The cat sniffed all around her hand and between her fingers, took a delicate swipe of pink tongue across the cracker, and ate it. After a few more treats it jumped off the dresser and onto the bed, pawed at Abby's quilt, and began to wash itself.

"You're so scrawny. No collar either, guess no one owns you. Hope you aren't bringing fleas into my bed. I don't know much about cats, but you look like you need someone to love you. And I could use someone to love."

The cat cocked its head, as if understanding every word Abby said.

"Maybe we could put you to work as a barn cat. The perks are great, all the mice you could ever want." She reached out to pet the cat. It hissed again and swiped at her with a paw, claws extended. "I get it; calm down. I'll let you alone. I don't like people messing with me, either. At least we know you have the equipment to catch those mice if you stay."

Abby left as the cat resumed its bath. In her mother's room she located an antique ceramic dish with the word KITTY stenciled in brown on yellow-glazed pottery. She removed the potted plant sitting in it, rinsed the dish in the bathroom sink, and filled it with cool water. Back in her room she set it on the floor beside her rocking chair.

"Here you go. Goldfish make me thirsty, how about you? And who knows how long you've been hiding in that wall without water? Check it out; you get to drink from Lisa's old dish. She'll love that, not."

The cat waited until Abby moved away from the water dish before jumping down to examine the bowl. The small pink tongue darting out of a whisker-embellished mouth made a stark contrast to dull black fur. After drinking, it returned to the nest in Abby's quilt, sitting alert and still.

Abby joined the animal on the bed, careful to keep some distance at first, but mesmerized by the brilliant copper-colored eyes that stared at her. She reached out a tentative finger and stroked the cat's back; it didn't move.

Bolder, Abby opened her hand and ran it down the length of the spine. In spite of the odd sensation of bone close to the surface, the soft fur tickled her hand. She lay down on her side, continuing the light, smooth caress. "Pretty little kitty …"

The cat straightened white-tipped paws, stretched, yawned, and moved over to nestle in the crook of Abby's arm. It purred, deep and throaty, as she continued to stroke its back. They both fell asleep as a puddle of early morning sun moved across the bed.

Abby woke to a hissing sound, followed by her mother's strident voice.

"Abby? Are you sick?" Lisa gasped. "What in the world? Is that a cat?"

Abby laughed. The sight of Lisa's shocked face, the strange cat hissing, and the clock that read "11:45 a.m." were all too surreal.

She spoke to the cat in a soothing voice. "Chill kitty. She's okay, she won't hurt you. She's happy you came to live here, right Lisa? She knows you're just what we need."

Abby looked at her mother, pleading. "It's a long story, but can we keep her? I know it's the obvious kid cliché, but I *will* take care of her. You even said a cat would be helpful with mice in the barn. And cats practically take care of themselves."

As if on cue, the cat stretched, jumped off the bed, sauntered over to Abby's mother, and sniffed. After receiving a brief pat on the head, the cat rubbed against her leg before returning to Abby.

Lisa started to shake her head and speak, paused for what seemed like an eternity, then smiled at Abby. "We'll try it, for now. Make sure she doesn't belong to anyone else. We'll get her checked out at the vet in town and buy some supplies. I guess this means we can advertise a resident cat at Bikers' Rest."

Abby jumped out of bed. She reached to hug her mother but dropped her arms to her sides before they made contact. "Thank you so much. I mean it. And no, I'm not sick. I'm sorry I overslept and didn't help downstairs." Abby realized it had been a while since she talked *to* Lisa instead of *at* her.

"Does it have a name?" Lisa said. She raised her eyebrows when she saw the water dish, embellished with the kitty logo. "Hmm ... my antique Roseville crock ... I'll get you a plastic container for water. Your dad bought this for me a long time ago as a joke since he wanted a cat, and I didn't. Anyway, what are you going to call it?"

"I'm thinking she's a girl." Abby looked at the cat. "Shadow?" The cat ignored her. "Midnight?" The cat yawned and licked a paw. "Kitty?"

The cat meowed, walked to the water dish, and took a delicate drink. "I guess her name's Kitty. Not too imaginative, but she seems to claim it."

Lisa reached for the ceramic dish, and the cat hissed at her. "Well now, Kitty, looks like you not only claim the name, but my china, as well." She hesitated and sighed. "Adam would have loved a cat in the house; it's all yours, Kitty." She looked at her watch. "I have to get some groceries and run a few errands. I'll be back in a couple hours." She started out of the room, then turned, frowning. "I almost forgot when I saw the cat. What happened to the wall? Did you do that?"

"Yeah, I guess I did." Abby recounted the story of finding Kitty.

"We'll need to remember to shut the screen door all

the time so no other critters wander inside. I'm not worried about the esthetics up here, but it does need repair. See if Jack can fix it. It shouldn't take long to just close the hole." Lisa started to leave again, then turned back. "Throw the sheets in the dryer for me, too, okay? Thanks." Without waiting for an answer, she hurried downstairs.

"No problem." Abby watched as Kitty sauntered across the room and hopped up on the table by the window, then onto the old Bible sitting there. Both were illuminated in a shaft of sunlight. She stared at the Bible, distracted by thoughts of Silas—both the mystery, and also his presence in her life. When her mother's voice floated up the stairs, she jumped.

"Abby? Get busy with those sheets. I'm leaving."

Abby sighed. She dressed and paused on the way through the hall to examine the wall. A chunk of plaster on the floor and the jagged hole made it look like a derelict tenement. Abby thrust her hand into the opening, feeling a slight draft of cool air, which meant an opening at least big enough for a cat. Or maybe something more.

Abby took one last look at the wall and glanced into her room. "I guess all mysteries will have to wait for another day, Kitty."

The cat meowed and turned her back on Abby. Settling into the pool of sunlight streaming through the window, she fell asleep on the Bible.

NINETEEN

"You and my mother are both making me crazy."

Kitty jumped up on the kitchen table and began to nibble some scrambled eggs spilled there earlier by a guest.

Abby shooed the cat off the table and then searched through the labels in the pantry for people-food a cat might like. "Mushroom soup, green beans, chamomile tea, spaghetti, tuna—tuna, yuck. Better you than me." After emptying the canned fish into a plastic dish, she threw the sheets in the dryer, grabbed a piece of fruit from the bowl on the counter, and opened the back door. Kitty slipped out and disappeared around the corner. Abby went in search of Jack. The buzz of a saw behind the barn made it easy.

Munching on a Fuji apple, Abby paused to watch Jack work. With his back to her, the muscles across his bare shoulders rippled as he fed planks of pine across two sawhorses and through a circular saw. One rivulet of sweat trickled from his hairline to a mid-point on his back, a fascinating slow-motion descent. His fair skin glowed with a hint of sunburn-red. Bits of sawdust floated in the air like confetti around his white-blond hair—the same color as hers. Destiny? Khaki shorts topped muscular, blond-furred calves. She *wanted* to want him. A real guy, not an apparition. Maybe if she tried harder a connection would spark, and she could forget about her feelings for Silas.

Abby scrunched the waves in her hair and ran her little finger across the lip-gloss on her lower lip. She took a crunchy bite of apple just as the saw bisected the final board and it thudded to the ground.

Jack jerked upright and whipped around. "What the hell are you doing, sneaking up on me like that?" He shielded his eyes from the sun with one hand. The other hand held the power saw. "Sorry. Guess I'm a little jumpy, eh?" He walked to her—the saw still humming in his right hand.

Abby took a step back as the trailer for a chainsaw horror movie played in her mind. She stared at the blade of the saw, gleaming and sharp in the sun. "What're you doing?"

Jack turned it off and sat it on the ground. A sudden, easy smile crinkled the corners of his eyes. "You startled me, that's all. I got focused on the job. Sorry about the language. My vocabulary got worse in college, not better. My dad freaks when I swear, says 'that's not the education I pay for.'" He wiped a red bandana across his sweaty forehead. "It's getting hot. Want to keep me company on a break?"

Abby kept her distance, attracted and repelled by Jack, all at the same time. "My mother has a job for you in the house."

"Sure. What's she need?" Jack picked up a pale blue T-shirt the color of his eyes from the stack of wood against the barn and pulled it over his head. "I might be a little stinky for an inside job, but I'm ready to serve." A tight smile appeared on his lips as he saluted. "Do I need the tool box or just my magic hands?" He held up both hands, palms out, and wiggled his fingers.

Abby smiled. Bad guys didn't wander around on bicycles searching for roofing jobs so they could terrorize people. She smiled again at the thought of a bad guy on a bike. And at how little there would be to steal, even if that's what he had in mind.

"I'm forgiven for my foul mouth?" Jack said. "I'll remember my manners in the house, *Mademoiselle*."

Abby laughed. "I can't say it in French, but no worries."

"*Merci*," Jack said. "That's how you say thank you in French. Either way, I promise to behave myself. What do you need? I'll bring the duct tape; it's good for any job."

"There's a hole in the wall that needs fixed—it's a long story. But I don't think any kind of tape will work."

Jack laughed and gathered tools and a can of patching plaster from the barn. He followed her inside to the third floor, sneezing at the top of the steps. "Must be the plaster dust. I should have brought a mask." He pulled the bandana from his back pocket and tied it around his nose and mouth, making him look like a bandit. The cotton muffled his voice. "What happened? I missed the earthquake."

"I heard sounds behind the wall last night. When I pushed on the plaster it crumbled." Abby held her hand to the hole. "Feel this; there's a draft. Let's take out another section and see what's behind here before we seal it up."

Jack knocked against the wall, and then around the edges. "It's hollow, but I think the lumber is for support, not a doorframe. Walls *are* empty spaces, with wires, studs, and pipes behind them. And sometimes rats." He pulled down the bandana, wrinkled his nose, made a silly rat face, then shrugged. "It's not some archeological site. Don't make this more than it has to be. We'll only have to remove a little more plaster for a neat repair; no big deal." He got the tools out of the gray plastic toolbox. "Great; no putty knife. I'll be right back."

After he left, Abby considered the space in front of her. *He said to remove some plaster; why not get a peek at what's back there? What does he know? He's a roofer. It'll have architectural interest for him. I hope.*

Abby picked up the work gloves Jack had dropped and put them on, even though they were two sizes too large. She inserted her hand into the space, careful to avoid the rough edges. Grasping a handful of plaster, she pulled; a section of wall crumbled away, leaving a now-gaping opening. Nothing but black could be seen inside, but she got the sense of open space, not a jumble of wires and wood.

She retrieved a small flashlight from her bedroom, pink with her name painted on the side in purple nail polish. Her mind's eye saw something else. Holding her dad's hand in the hardware store ... countertop at eye level ... begging for a flashlight so she could be his helper ... Abby sighed.

Returning to the wall, she shined the light into the inky-dark hole and gasped. As the thin beam moved across the void, it illuminated brick walls and wooden steps. Cobwebs swaying from bare wood strips decorated the low ceiling.

Jack returned and leaned in next to her. "*Mon Dieu*, what did you do? I said take out a little more plaster, not destroy the whole thing. You should've waited for me."

"Check it out." Abby handed him the light. "We have to take down the entire wall."

Jack rolled his eyes but peered in the opening. He whistled. "Very cool. Must have been a servants' entrance of some kind. Wonder where it ends up?"

"Once we open the wall, we'll find out."

"Whoa, wait a minute. Your mother said to fix it, not to make it worse. And she's the boss. When you two decide what to do, let me know. I'll come back for the tools if she decides on demolition instead of repair. For now I have a barn roof to finish, *Cherie*. You know, real work." Jack blew her a kiss and left.

Abby put both hands on her hips. She had Jack's tools and two strong arms. And she didn't mind taking the heat from Lisa. She smiled when she heard footsteps. "I knew you couldn't stay away, Jack. Let's get this wall down."

"Uh, sorry to disappoint you. It's just me." Morton crossed the hallway. "What're you doing?"

"You're just in time." Abby lifted her hand in the air.

Morton gazed at her, eyebrows raised. "You're glad to see me?"

"You're not gonna believe it. There's a set of steps hidden behind the wall, and we're going to excavate it."

"Like an archeological dig?"

"Exactly. Feel around here, the raised area; it's a big rectangle. Help me rip out the plaster in the center. I want to get it done to surprise Lisa."

Morton gulped. "Is this gonna be a good surprise or one of those that get us in trouble? Cause I don't want any problems with your mom."

Abby shrugged. "I'm doing this. You can help or not. I'll take full responsibility with my mother." She picked up a hammer and heaved it at the wall. Chunks of plaster, dust, and old wallpaper flew through the air. She laughed and took another big swing.

Morton blinked several times, then reached into the toolbox and grabbed a rubber mallet, attacking the wall with gusto. "All right. This is great. Extreme Old House Makeover meets Indiana Jones."

In the aftermath of demolition, silence hung as heavy in the air as the thick dust. Morton wheezed and Abby coughed as the grime settled on them.

"Hilarious." Abby laughed. Morton's face, hair, and clothes were covered with a matte white layer of powdery plaster. When he took off his glasses the area around his eyes appeared smooth and clean. "Now you're a raccoon."

"Yeah, well, you look like one, too," Morton whispered. "Now what?"

"We check it out," Abby whispered back. "Why are we whispering? No one else is here, and even if they were, it doesn't matter. Go into the bathroom and get the flashlight under the sink." She pulled the pink penlight from her pocket.

Abby shined the light around the edge of the opening. A wooden frame surrounded it. Bits of plaster, hunks of old wallpaper in faded floral prints, and a few bent nails adorned the lumber. It looked old, the wood grayish-white and splintered in places.

"You were right, it *is* a doorway," Morton said, returning with an old metal flashlight. "Does this thing still work?" He turned the glass end toward his face and flicked the switch. A wide, bright beam of light illuminated his eyeglass lenses.

"Now you look like an alien. This is serious business; I can't work with an alien."

"Yeah, funny." Morton turned the light off and on. "You might need my special powers in that dark hole."

"Yeah, I'm sure." Abby swapped flashlights with Morton and shined the wide beam into the aperture. A set of wood steps descended into darkness. Rough red bricks, joined together with daubs of coarse mortar, created a passageway. The low ceiling had exposed beams. It smelled musty, even though a slight air current ruffled Abby's hair and propelled lazy bits of debris. A layer of fine dust covered the steps.

"Check it out. Some animal must have been in here." Morton pointed to one set of paw prints in the dust.

"I'll explain later."

Abby put one foot on the first step, testing it. Although the wood creaked, it held firm. "I'm going down. Follow me, but wait until I get to the next step." She looked at the strain of T-shirt against Morton's abdomen. "We don't want to put too much weight on any step at once. And be careful."

"Yeah, okay." Morton reached into his right pocket and pulled out a handful of M&M's. "Want some?" When she shook her head he tossed them all in his mouth, jaws opening and closing like a bulldozer.

Abby carefully put all her weight on the first step, then the second. She braced herself against the brick wall; the rough stones chilled her hand. The flashlight illuminated the near area, but the light got swallowed up into blackness below. One step at a time she moved downward, farther into the gloom.

After several stairs, she whispered back to Morton. "I see some light, but only in spots. I'm not sure where it's coming from." After a few more steps, she shined her flashlight straight ahead. "There's a wall at the bottom. I'll bet it's that blocked-up alcove in the kitchen—the one I thought could be an old fireplace. We might have to go back up."

"There isn't much space in here to turn around."

"Quit whining. It's just an ancient set of steps. Probably a servants' entrance or something, that's what Jack said."

"This is an old farmhouse, not a Victorian mansion," Morton said. "I don't think farmers had servants, no matter what Jack thinks."

"We can worry about that later. I just want to get to the bottom."

As she got closer to the base, each stair groaned louder, with soft spots in the center. "The wood might be rotted," she called over her shoulder. "If it feels weak, stop right away or stand on the edge."

Abby got to the next-to-the-last step and reached out for the partition at the bottom. Rough wood strips and the sharp metal of nail points met her fingertips. At the foundation of the wall, several chinks revealed light seeping through.

"Light's coming from behind the wall. It has to be the kitchen on the other side."

Focused on the panel instead of the tread, she put all her weight on the bottom step.

With a snap, the rotted wood splintered. Abby tumbled through the jagged hole where the step used to be, into free space below. She gasped as a large sliver ripped her arm on the way. The flashlight flew from her hand, followed by a dull thump and the tinkle of breaking glass. She landed with a *thud*, face down on packed earth in total darkness.

A scream lodged in her throat before she sank into unconsciousness.

TWENTY

"I love playing in the dirt." Abby smiled way, way up at her tall daddy. "It smells like worms and mud pies. Do worms eat the mud? Do they like getting dirty? I like getting dirty, but I know better than to eat mud."

"I know you do." Her dad brushed the dirt away from Abby's nose. "You don't look much like my princess with mud on your face. But no matter; you still get a princess kiss from me."

Abby turned her cheek for the kiss. Her head hurt. She groaned and rolled onto her back. Her eyes opened to semi-darkness.

"Abby, Abby, are you alive? Oh, jeez, this is awful."

Morton's voice echoed in the space around Abby. She reached up to touch her forehead; her fingers felt sticky when they dropped back. Her stomach protested at the odor of blood; vomit rose in her throat. She swallowed, hard.

"I'm okay." She lay there for a moment longer, trying to savor the warmth of being with her dad again. Had the happiness in her life become only the stuff of dreams and visions?

"Talk to me." Morton's voice went up an octave.

"What should I do? Are you hurt? Should I call 9-1-1? Oh man, this is terrible." The rapid crunching of M&M's followed his statement.

Abby sat up, and after the room spun around several times, only a headache remained. "I'm okay. Shine your flashlight down here; mine broke."

With Morton waving the beam around, the pinpoint of light did little to alleviate the darkness. It intensified the headache instead. "Focus it on me. I'm going to get up and walk, and you follow me with the light. I want to see if there's a way out of here." She stood and explored the perimeter of the area in the meager glow.

"It's just a small room. I can't find a door. There's some kind of shelf, but no exit. Go back up to the third floor. We have a ladder stored in the attic. And be careful."

"Sure thing." Morton raced up the steps, his wheezing audible.

Once the noise of his departure faded, it seemed very quiet and even darker. No outside noise penetrated the stillness. Under the smell of soil an unpleasant odor lurked, non-specific but foul, a dank stench. Abby wrinkled her nose. A soft sound above her head broke the silence.

Like a silhouette on a Halloween painting, Kitty perched on the edge of the broken step, looking down.

"Kitty, stay."

At the sound of Abby's voice, the cat sniffed the opening and leaped, landing on her feet. Abby scooped her up. "You goofy cat, you could have been hurt." Abby inhaled her furry warmth and reveled in her solid, real presence. "You did better than I did getting in here. Now how do we both get out?"

"Are you talking to yourself?" Morton's voice came from far above. "Don't lose it; I'm coming. Oh man, she's losing it all right. I found the ladder. Hang in there."

With much banging and muttering, Morton got the aluminum ladder down the narrow staircase. "Abs, I got a lantern from the attic, too, and some matches. I'm coming to get you."

Morton lowered the six-foot ladder into the room below, eased his bulk onto the top platform, then climbed down to Abby. He lit the lantern, jumping when he saw the cat.

"Morton, meet Kitty. I found her last night behind the wall. That's how all of this started." Abby took the lantern and held the light aloft. "Let's see what's here."

Morton peered at Abby's forehead. "You're bleeding. We need to get you some help."

"I appreciate the Boy Scout thing, but this won't take long." Abby gazed around. "It's a really small space."

"Yeah," Morton paced the area. "It can't be more than about eight square feet."

Abby walked to the wall. "Look at the narrow shelf. It's a wooden plank of some kind. This must have been a root cellar. There's another shelf on the other side." She shined the light at Morton. "What does that expression mean?"

Morton examined the platforms. "Who makes a root cellar that's hidden? Or a storage room with only single shelves? They couldn't have stored much here."

"It's old and boarded up, not hidden. And it's close to the kitchen so they could get the jars or whatever out of here when they needed them. When they got a refrigerator, it wasn't useful so it got closed up. There's nothing else it could be." She hesitated. "But you're right; why not more shelves? And why so inaccessible? There's no evidence of a door."

Morton licked his lips. "What if it's a secret room they used to hide runaway slaves? I saw a picture in a book one time with a room like this, from a safe house in Indiana. The boards were where people slept. I'll bet your house used to be a stop on the Underground Railroad."

Abby laughed. "Get real. You told me people 'think' there 'might' be places like this in Boston, but no one ever found one. That's called an urban legend."

"Still ..." Morton surveyed the enclosure. "Nothing

else makes any sense."

Abby frowned. "I don't know. It seems weak to me—root cellar to slave hideout. So for right now, let's not tell anyone, okay? At least not until it's noticed."

"Why not? This could be huge."

"I don't know. It's a feeling. Didn't you ever do something just because of a feeling?"

Morton thought. "Nope. But girls do that stuff, I guess, and I can keep a secret as good as a girl. C'mon—let's get out of here. This place is creeping me out."

Abby turned in a circle. "Just a minute. Help me look for a blocked-off doorway. There has to be some other way to get in and out of here." She ran her hands along the two walls without shelves, searching for evidence of an exit. "There are some indentations, but I can't find a frame like the one at the top of the stairs."

"If it hid slaves, it would have been crude," Morton said. "Not much finishing work went into hiding places. Maybe there's a tunnel to somewhere else, but after all these years it'd be hard to find."

"Aren't you even curious?" Abby said.

"Yeah, well, curiosity killed the cat." Morton cringed when he looked at Kitty. "Sorry. Okay, but can we make it fast?"

He pried Abby's pink flashlight out of his pocket and pointed it at random spots.

"Under the shelves it's stone, but the top walls look like packed dirt." Abby ran a ragged fingernail over the surface, shearing off a curl of brown earth. "It's more like a pit dug in the ground than a room."

The tiny flashlight flickered. "Abs, we have to go," Morton said. "I don't want to be down here without a light. I know you have the lantern, but I want light of my own to get back up the ladder and the steps."

"Shake it; that helps."

Morton shook the flashlight. It got brighter. He shook it again, lost his grip, and it went flying into a dark corner of the room.

Abby stood still and mentally counted to ten. "My dad bought me that." She handed the lantern to Morton. "Hold the light over here. I have to find it."

Getting down on her hands and knees, Abby reached under the waist-high shelf and felt in the shadowed corner. Her fingers curled around her flashlight. She shuddered when a delicate tickle ran across her forearm. As she jerked, her hand brushed against something cold and hard, protruding from under the packed earth floor. "I found something else. It's partially buried."

Abby grasped at the metal and pulled. It didn't budge. "I'll have to come back and dig it up. Whatever it is must have been here for a long time, so a little longer won't matter. I'd rather find the entryway."

"Wait, use this." Morton handed Abby a penknife. "Dig around with the blade."

"Always the Boy Scout." Abby jabbed the point of the knife into the dirt around the object's edge. A little at a time, she could feel it being exposed. After digging for several minutes, she handed the knife to Morton and pulled at the article with both hands. The clank of metal echoed in the confined space as she held it up.

Morton gasped.

Abby dropped the cold metal as if it burned her fingers.

They stared in silence as the sputtering oil lantern illuminated the horrific sight.

TWENTY-ONE

"What is this?" Abby drew in a breath, suspecting the answer even as she asked the question.

"No way." Morton shook his head. "I can't believe it. I'm right about this place."

A shudder went up Abby's spine. She couldn't take her eyes off the object. "It's a handcuff."

"Yeah, but lots worse."

"Bring the lantern closer."

Abby turned on her flashlight, picked the artifact back up, and held it in front of the two light sources. The semi-circular piece of metal hung open at one end, with a length of short chain attached. A metal peg dangled from a hole on the side. When she put the peg through the hole, it closed tight. She winced at the metallic click.

"There's some kind of writing on this tag, but it's still too dark to read. Let's go up to my room." Abby passed the handcuff to Morton then rubbed her hands against her thighs. "You take this ... thing. I'll carry Kitty. We can come back later for the ladder."

Morton shoved the metal into the waistband of his shorts and scrambled up the rungs with the lantern, groaning as he stretched for the stairs. He peered into the room below at Abby. "Can you see okay to climb with the cat? 'Cause I'm out of here, Abs."

Scooping Kitty up in one arm, she ascended. "I'm right behind you."

Abby set Kitty down on a step and watched her streak past Morton. She balanced on the very top of the ladder and hoisted herself up, careful to avoid the broken step. The murmur of familiar voices drifted into the stairwell from the other side of the partition. Morton and the handcuff could wait a few more minutes. She put her ear against the plywood, careful to avoid protruding nails and splinters.

"Let me get you a drink, sweetie," Lisa said. "You must be hot."

Jack laughed. "You know it. You're making sure I get a good work-out."

Abby located a small hole in the divider and peered through. At first she blinked in the bright light; when her eyes focused she saw the corner of the kitchen, by the back door. Jack stood there, lounging against the frame, face red and sweaty.

Lisa walked over and handed him a can of pop. "Here you go, honey. Nice and cold." She reached up and smoothed the hair off his forehead.

Abby's stomach roiled. Sweetie, honey, touching? Since when did they become such good pals? Something wrong, very wrong, went with this picture.

Jack set the can on the counter. "Thanks—for everything."

Lisa smiled. "You're welcome—for everything." She reached up and put her arms around his neck, hugged him, and kissed his cheek.

Jack hugged her back, and then pulled away. "What about Abby? You haven't told her yet, have you?"

"No, I'm not sure she's ready." Lisa sighed. "Soon, I hope. It would make everything so much easier." She rubbed a smudge of dirt off his cheek. "I love you and want her to know."

"Yeah, well, you'll know when the timing is right. I have to get back to work." Jack sauntered out the door, and Abby heard Lisa's footsteps fade out of the kitchen.

Lisa and Jack? Together? Abby stopped her thoughts before she had to puke. She climbed over the broken step and raced up the remaining stairs toward the light at the top. She emerged into the third-floor hallway and paused to gaze around, blinking as if she had awakened from a nightmare. The image of Jack's bed in the barn, the sheets always rumpled, the blanket on the floor, swam into her mind. And the time she found Lisa's shoes, discarded right inside the barn door.

The sun streamed through the windows, the scent of lilac lingered, and from outside a birdsong pierced the air. Abby went into the bathroom, sponged her face with a washcloth, and took two Tylenol. Back at the door of her room, she stopped. The handcuff on her unmade bed looked out of place next to the crisp sheets. Everything about the day had become disjointed and out of place.

Kitty jumped onto the bed and sniffed the object lying there. With a soft growl she hopped to the floor and left. Abby watched her go, entered the room as if in a trance, then sat abruptly on the mattress. It bounced and the springs squeaked.

"Abs, you okay? You look kinda pale or something." Morton peered into her eyes. "Maybe we should get the doctor to check you out. There's blood and everything."

"No, I'm fine." Abby reached up and probed the wound, wincing. "Just a little cut. It's this—thing—that's freaking me."

She held back the "thing" about Lisa and Jack. No need to share that with Morton. Now it made sense that Jack saw her as a kid; he just happened to be involved with her mother. Instead of a boyfriend, would she get a stepfather? Disgusting.

She focused on the handcuff. "I saw a picture of

something like this in my dad's Civil War book." She shuddered. "Is it a … slave shackle?"

"Yep." Morton showed her a picture on his phone labeled Authentic Antique Iron Slave Shackle, 1800's.

Abby carried it to the window and held it up in the light. She examined a round metal tag, attached with a twisted, figure-eight-shaped length of rusted wire. "I see a date, 1822, and the initials H.C." She looked closer. "There's something engraved on the metal button where it's attached: T. H. PORTER." She pulled a sock off the floor and rubbed at markings above and below the name, gasping as the dirt fell away. "Morton, check this out. Above the name is the word DEALER, and below it says IN SLAVES.

She thrust the shackle at Morton. "Someone kept slaves here. This is awful. I didn't even know people in Pennsylvania had slaves. I thought they all lived in the South and worked on plantations. We were supposed to be the good guys." Goose bumps traveled up her arms.

"Don't you get it?" Morton's eyes gleamed. "Slaves weren't *kept* here. They were *hidden* here. Your house *must* have been a stop on the Underground Railroad. How cool is that? We'll get someone in from the Historical Society. Maybe even National Geographic will come and take pictures. We'll be famous, Abs. You and me on the cover of Archeology Magazine. They'll excavate the whole place. We'll get a plaque on the wall with our names on it."

Abby shook her head. "No way. Not right now. There's too much other stuff going on. Besides, we don't know if it's such a big deal. Maybe someone collected Civil War memorabilia and this piece got lost. It might not mean anything."

"But …"

"You can't tell anyone yet. We'll look around ourselves, and if we find anything else, I'll talk to my mother. Promise to keep it a secret? The room and the shackle?"

"Abs …" Spit flew out the corner of Morton's mouth.

"It's my house. We'll do it my way. Okay?"

"You just want Jack to be part of this instead of me." Morton's cheeks flushed "I'm the fat kid with a sick mom and no friends, and he's the handsome, mysterious foreign guy. I get it. That's stupid, but you're right, it's your house. Next time call him to get you out of whatever hole you fall in." He threw the shackle back on the bed, where it landed with a clang, then stomped down the stairs.

Abby hung her head and winced at the faint slam of the front door. Kitty sauntered back into the room; she picked the cat up and held her close.

"I can't worry about Morton right now," Abby murmured into Kitty's fur. "I'll straighten it out with him later. I know you can keep a secret, right?"

Kitty purred, then struggled out of Abby's arms and jumped onto the rocking chair for a nap. Abby wrapped the shackle in an old Hilton Head Island sweatshirt, shaking her head at the irony of a slave shackle in a sweatshirt from South Carolina. But there were more pressing problems.

Lisa clearly couldn't be trusted. She had to be confronted about her affair with Jack. Head on, no bullshit. How embarrassing to have been attracted to a guy even in a minimal way, only to find out his taste ran to older women. Much older.

"I can't deal with it, not alone. But there's no one else to help me." Abby's stomach heaved, bringing a foul, burning sensation into her throat. Her head and heart battled for which could pound the hardest.

"Abigail … you ain't alone."

Silas materialized by the window, translucent but very real. He nodded and sent her a smile of warmth and compassion, while floating over the bed to her. His arms opened wide and closed over her shoulders.

Abby experienced the embrace of a cool, steadying presence wrapped around her. She stood for several minutes in the oasis, eyes closed, leaning into the comfort.

"This isn't the way the world works. How can you be here with me?"

"I swear on my ma's Bible, I don't know." Silas stroked her hair.

"Maybe time doesn't matter when two souls are meant to be together?" Abby experienced his substance, from the rough wool under her cheek, to the gentle touch on her hair, to the joy coursing through her veins.

Silas hugged her tighter. "This time I'll protect you. "

Abby opened her eyes and gazed into his face, seeing strength, determination, and love. She closed her eyes once again as she raised her lips to him.

Silas brushed a kiss across her mouth, murmuring, "Sweet Abigail."

Heat flowed through Abby until suddenly, a sense of loss displaced desire. She stood alone in the room; Silas had left. But she knew he would be back. And that whether she understood it or not, everything she'd thought or imagined had now changed forever.

She touched her lips that had been pressed against his, squared her shoulders, and marched downstairs to confront her mother.

Because of Silas, her life once again had meaning. Her love had a home.

TWENTY-TWO

Abby found Lisa in the kitchen sitting at the table, drinking a condensation-covered can of root beer. "Hot?"

Lisa smiled. "As a matter of fact, I am. I decided to stop for a minute to catch my breath." She lifted the can in her hand. "Want one?"

"No, I didn't have much exercise today, at least not the kind you seem to have had. In fact, I've never *worked out* the way you do."

"That sounded cryptic. You didn't even ask me what I did."

Abby grimaced. "I don't have to ask. And I don't want details, please."

"What is that supposed to mean?" Lisa's smile faded and her eyes narrowed.

"Let me tell you a story," Abby said. "Once upon a time, while minding my own business, I happened to find my mother and the hired help clenched together in the kitchen on a sunny afternoon. Whatever they had been doing together made them hot, so they shared a drink. Then they whispered sweet nothings to each other, had a little kiss, declared their love, and parted. The End."

Lisa jumped up, shaking her head. She reached for

Abby. The can toppled over; dark, foamy liquid ran across the table and dripped to the floor in a brown puddle. She ignored it. "Oh, Abby, *no*. You can't possibly think Jack and I, are, well, together that way. You don't understand."

"Right …" Abby tapped her temple. "I don't understand because you don't think I'm ready to hear it. Isn't that how you put it? Well, news flash, I will never be ready to hear about you screwing Jack. You're old enough to be his freaking mother, not that you have the least idea what a mother is supposed to be." Abby choked back tears.

"This is an awful misunderstanding." Lisa ran her hands up and down her arms as if a sudden chill had entered the warm room. "Sit down, let me explain everything. I'm very fond of Jack … I love him and …"

"You disgust me." Abby ran out the back door and toward the barn.

The screen door slammed. Lisa strode across the yard. She glanced at Abby but didn't stop.

Abby grabbed her bike and sped into town, skidding into Dairy Delicious on reflex. Usually a chocolate milkshake could freeze out the pain of most problems, but not this time. She had no idea what to do. And she knew she couldn't stay at a dairy bar forever.

As Abby sat at the outdoor table, milkshake untouched in front of her, Lisa sped past in the truck. She drove across the bridge and headed out of town. Abby pedaled home. Bikers' Rest appeared deserted until she headed for the third floor. The sound of hammering got louder as she ascended.

Abby reached the top of the stairs and glared at Jack.

He tossed the hammer into the toolbox. It landed with a loud clang. "That about does it."

Abby winced, the pounding in her head intensified at the sight of him. She surveyed the wall repair hiding the staircase once again. A big piece of plasterboard covered the opening, with a gaping perimeter.

"I'll plaster the edges later," Jack said. "I told your mother she might want to consider opening the false wall at the bottom someday and make a back entrance into the kitchen between here and there, but it's her call. She's the boss; except for you, of course." He winked at Abby. "I have to get back to the barn roof. I'll be leaving soon for D.C. and the bike rally. And I want to get the job done before I go."

"I think you've done plenty while you were here. More destruction than repair."

Jack shrugged. "Whatever that means."

"You don't know what I'm talking about?"

"No clue." Jack picked up the toolbox.

Abby wondered if Lisa hadn't had a chance to tell him that their secret had been shattered. Which meant she could avoid confronting him, he would leave, and Lisa, well, that wound would never heal. She just had to stay calm and act normal.

"So you're leaving for the bike rally. Do you really expect to meet the president?"

Jack shrugged again. "I'll make sure I get up close and personal with the commander-in-chief. My dad is being honored at the rally, as the father of a fallen marine. He's sitting on the viewing platform and will make sure I'm part of the action. I'm certain that Keller will be using the occasion as a photo op to boost his popularity; he needs it. He should spend more time getting soldiers out of a war zone and less time worrying about his image. If he had done his job in the first place my brother would still be alive. And so would other peoples' brothers and sons and daughters." Venom laced through Jack's words, cobra-like and deadly.

Abby shivered, not sure what to do, not sure what he expected, not sure about anything. She defaulted to a non-threatening subject. "It's so amazing you and your dad will meet him, even if you don't agree with everything he's done. Politics are complicated, and I'm not that into it. But

I know how much you must miss your brother. My dad—"

Jack interrupted, "Your dad was old. Older people die; it's called natural causes. That's the way it works. You need to get over it. My brother was young and didn't deserve to be killed. It's Keller's fault; he's the president. You're incredibly naïve, even for an American."

The shock of Jack's words made Abby reel back in surprise. "First of all, my dad was not old. And I don't need to 'get over it' until I'm good and ready. I loved him, maybe even more than you loved your brother, who knows? What *is* your problem? Your brother chose to join the Marines. I'm sorry he died, but as you said, 'that's the way it is, and you need to get over it.' Blaming the president is stupid; you're brainless to think it's anyone's fault. War is war; no one wins. Maybe you should worry more about your own behavior, since it's something you *can* control."

"What's next?" Jack sneered and put his hand over his heart. "Are you going to wave a little American flag and sing the "Star Spangled Banner"? Grow up, Abby. It's people like you with their heads buried in the sand that insure people like me will suffer grief. I thought you understood. But you're so self-centered that all you can think about is the death of one old man."

"Don't you dare say another word about my father." Abby's hand shot out and the resounding crack of it against Jack's cheek echoed in the hallway. She snatched her hand back and pointed to the steps. "Get out."

Jack rubbed the reddened handprint on his face. He turned and marched away.

Abby went into her room and looked out the side window, arms wrapped around her waist, trying to subdue the shaking. She watched Jack stride from the house to the barn and climb onto the roof. The sound of frantic hammering soon filled the air.

She pondered the dilemma. As much as she had

wanted Jack to like her, at the end of the day it had just been a stupid fantasy. Things had been getting better with Lisa. Shared meals, laughing at the same jokes, even working together to make Bikers' Rest a success had jump-started the bonding process. Probably all mothers and daughters fought sometimes, but lately the bitterness of Lisa's absence had faded. Now that relationship had been tainted forever.

Sudden longing filled her heart. Not for Jack, Lisa, or even her father. She yearned for Silas to be with her all the time. Strange that only with him did she feel whole. What did that mean? It meant that in some indescribable way, she had fallen in love with a ghost. What she felt for him was more real than any emotion she'd ever experienced.

"Abigail."

Abby caught a whiff of campfire and coffee. She turned, expectation making her heart pound. "Silas!"

He stood at the end of her bed. The translucence had faded, his appearance as a living man fully restored. "Here I am."

"How did you know … that I wanted you?" Abby discarded all thoughts of this being anything other than what it was to her: someone she loved, here when needed.

Silas smiled. "Me and you, we share one heart. Time don't mean nothing in eternity. I just been waiting to love you."

Talk of love, soul mates, and shared hearts had never been part of Abby's dating life. It had always been pizza, movies, and quick kisses. A few boys had come and gone; she didn't miss them. Jack had grabbed her attention; she wouldn't miss him, either.

"This can't be real." Abby reached her hand toward Silas. "You aren't real."

"Bodies surely do die." Silas took two steps toward her, closing the distance between them. "But love, real love, never dies. Do you know Walt Whitman? He was a poet in my time, put some good thoughts on paper. He said, 'I tramp a perpetual journey.' That's what we all do. The Good Book is a help." He clasped her hand, his thumb stroking the soft skin between her thumb and finger.

She closed her fingers around his, this time reveling in his flesh, substance, warmth. He leaned in closer, and Abby closed her eyes, anticipating a kiss.

Instead, a gentle breath passed from Silas to Abby. It tasted of vanilla and cinnamon.

A feeling of total peace filled her, leeching through her mouth and filling her entire body. She opened her eyes. Silas had gone. She noticed the old Bible sitting on the table. Abby ran her hand over the puffy leather cover. Her grandmother had called a Bible 'the Good Book.' Is this what Silas meant? Why hadn't he stayed to tell her his story? How could she get him back again?

"Silas? Are you here?" Abby waited a full five minutes. When he didn't return, she sighed and turned her attention to the Munroe Bible.

Upon opening the book she saw a crack along the bottom edge. It had survived since Leticia received it in 1843. Until it met Morton. Maybe it could be glued or something. She inserted her pinkie into the split and inside the cover; a quick, sharp pain on her fingertip made her draw it out again. She sucked on the cut. "How come a freaking paper cut hurts so much? And what's a piece of paper doing in there?"

Abby turned the Bible so the opening faced the light from the window and got down on her knees to be at eye level with it. She grabbed a pencil from her desk, inserted the eraser end into the opening, and pried the broken edge wider. It seemed to be stuffed with something.

From the bathroom Abby retrieved an antique straight razor Lisa displayed as a decoration. Carefully she slit the long side of the Bible cover and across the top. She peeled back the quilted leather. Inside she found an oilskin packet, tied with twine. One separate sheet of paper sat on top of the protective layer, held close by the cord. She slid the entire package from within the Bible cover and untied it.

"Hey—Abs. You up there?" Morton called from the second floor.

"Yeah. And hurry."

"How's the head?" Morton entered the room, puffing from running up the stairs. "Why did I have to hurry? What's that?"

Abby realized her head no longer ached. "First, I'm sorry I acted like a jerk. But look what I found."

"Apology accepted. I'm used to you." Morton examined the oilskin. "It's old waterproof stuff, you know, before they invented plastic. Someone wanted to protect it. All but that paper on top." He crowded in beside Abby and ran a finger across the surface.

"That 'someone' must have been Leticia. It's her Bible."

Morton reached around Abby and untied the twine. The loose paper fluttered through the air. He grabbed for it, tripped, and landed on the floor. Raising his fist in triumph he opened his hand. The ancient sheet of parchment fluttered to the floor in pieces.

TWENTY-THREE

"*Crap.*" Stepping over Morton, Abby gathered together the remnants of paper and gently deposited them on the dresser. "Now look at what you've done. This had to be important, and now it's trash."

Morton stood, his face flushed and his eyes wide. "Abs, oh man, I'm like the worst friend ever. Total klutz, loser …"

"Enough." Abby blew out a breath. "It's too late now."

Morton shook his head. "Nope. Never too late. I know about this stuff 'cause I watch reruns of CSI, crime scene investigation to you. We got this. Get glue and a piece of cardboard. It's all good." Under his breath he muttered, "I hope."

It took patience Abby lacked and perseverance Morton had to spend the next hour gluing together the fragile shreds in order.

"Phew." Morton stood back when they finished putting the puzzle together. "Ta-da!"

Abby surveyed their work. "I'm glad it's still readable. I recognize the writing. It's Leticia's."

Thoughts about Lisa and Jack became inconsequential. Abby took a deep breath and scanned the fine cursive across the bits and pieces:

Judge ye not harshly. There is a truth that lies beyond the Good Book, in slumber forever. My Silas, I love him. Leticia Munroe.

Abby put the paper down. "What does that mean? And what kind of truth would be more than the Bible? Everyone read the Bible back then. What does she mean by 'truth that slumbers forever?'"

"It's weird." Morton shrugged.

Abby picked up the oilskin. "Some of the answers must be in here."

With trembling fingers she unwrapped the protective layers, revealing a small, blue booklet. The cover gave no indication of its title or author. She opened it and almost dropped the packet.

On the front page in bold, slanted cursive it stated: *Diary of Pvt. Silas J. Munroe, 103 PA Volunteers. This is the truth, I swear.*

"It's Silas's diary." Abby sat back on her heels and ran her hand over the notebook, her finger tracing the signature. "Now we'll know why he should be a hero, but died in shame. I can clear his name. You know what that means?"

"It means we won't have any more questions to answer. And you'll come swimming with me instead of spending the summer doing research."

Abby's eyes filled with tears. "No. It means we solve the mystery, and I do something for my Silas. This isn't just an adventure to me. It's a—quest."

She hesitated, journal in hand.

"What do you mean, '*my* Silas?'" Morton chuckled. "Are you looking for a boyfriend in a cemetery?"

"You wouldn't understand. I don't understand either. But I wonder, do I even have the right to pry into Silas's and Leticia's lives?"

Abby moved the diary to her left hand and chewed on

her right thumbnail. She noticed the quiet—no wind, no birdcalls, Morton sitting on the bed without making a sound, like the world held its breath. What about Silas? He, too, was silent. Maybe it would be better to walk away, leave it alone. What if Silas turned out to be a bad guy? She touched Silas's name and closed the diary.

"You can't be for real," Morton sputtered, spitting a half-chewed M&M out of his mouth. It skittered across the floor. "You have to read the diary. You have to. If you don't, I will. And I might get chocolate all over it."

Abby whirled around. "Keep your sticky hands off of it. I just need a minute to think. This is a big deal. We might be discovering a secret the whole world will want to know. Or we might find out something that's better off hidden. What if Silas isn't a hero after all? I couldn't take it. I'm not as tough as you think I am."

"Abs, history is history. You can't change it anyway. It's not like they're your relatives, so why worry?"

"I guess. But Silas is, well, important to me. I don't want to read it, not now." Abby went to the window, hoping the sight of the big oak tree, the river in the distance, and the flower garden would somehow calm her, help her to make sense of her feelings.

Instead she felt a trail of soothing cool on her burning neck. In place of the scene she expected to see, Silas's face appeared in the old glass, his shock of dark hair dipped over his wide, hazel eyes. His mouth opened, and a plume of white mist drifted between his lips. "*Abigail ... have faith in me.*"

Any uncertainty about opening the diary vanished, as Silas's precious face also faded.

"Abs? Where'd you go?" Morton shook her shoulder.

Abby blinked and looked at the window. Outside, the leaves on the oak tree rustled in a breeze, the ribbon of river gleamed in the sun, and a riot of colors surrounded the white fence around the yard. She wished Silas would return and read his journal to her. But he'd made it clear she had his permission to go through his private words.

"I'm ready now." She sat in the rocking chair. After closing her eyes briefly, she picked up the diary, turned the page, and began to read out loud.

"*December 10, 1861*

I been thinking on this war. William argues with me all the time. He sez the South shud be left alone. Folks here are startin' to get angered at him. I showed him a book Miss Elizabeth lent me. It was writ by Mrs. Harriet Beecher Stowe, along about 1852. I agree with her: 'slavery is the most cursed thing in the world.' I will fight for this, no matter what William thinks. I know right from wrong. He took leave of his senses, I reckon.

December 15, 1861

I leave today to fight for my country. Ma is angered that I go with Christmas near. But Dewey Long says if we bring a man with us, we git 10 days furlough. Jeb Chambers is joining us so I plan to come home for the holidays. Ma's afraid to tell William I fight for the North. Guess we call him Johnny Reb now. Priscilla wished me God speed and writ me some poem. Abigail is sad but understands I do this for her."

December 18, 1861

The trip to Armstrong County made a long one. I thought to git a warm meal and blanket when we reached Kittanning, but Camp Orr mor like prison. We passed thru a high board fence from snow outside to hell inside. There is much sickness and suffering. All are cold. But if our Lord cud suffer for me, I kin suffer for a just cause.

December 19, 1861

Ma knit me woolen gloves or my fingers would be too freezing to write. I ain't getting no furlough after all. Jeb done changed his mind once he saw this place, and he took off for home."

Abby paused. "He and Leticia had to spend Christmas apart; that sucks. I'm dreading the holidays this year without Dad." She flashed back to tromping through the snowy woods each December with him, finding the perfect Christmas tree and chopping it down. Crisp air, snowflake tongue warmed with hot chocolate—all gone.

Morton shrugged. "I haven't had Christmas with my father, like, forever. He took off when my mom got sick, and I was just a little kid. At least you had your dad for a while and now your mom is with you—and healthy."

With effort, Abby pushed her mother out of her mind. She yearned for Silas's calming influence, but it seemed obvious he came and went on an agenda she didn't understand. Taking a deep breath, she continued to read from the diary.

"December 25, 1861

Christmas. I miss home, but we are busy even on this day. I learn to be a soldier and even got a uniform. No one knows where we are going or what we will be doing after training, but I hope to git some of them Rebs real good. Priscilla sent me a poem, hardly fit for a soldier, but she bein' a decent sister I forgive her. One part sounded good, but I won't tell the fellers: 'Pretty little robin, With your scarlet breast, O may tormentors never find, The way into thy nest.' I pray those Reb tormentors do not come to our nest.

January 1, 1862

Dewey got so sick, with the shakes and vomiting up even weak beef tea. He don't want to go to the camp hospital. One feller from Westmoreland County says if you git sent there you may as well say good-bye. Some other soldier heard they call a hospital in Alexandria Camp Misery. Hope Dewey gits better for the New Year.

January 12, 1862

Thank the Lord, Dewey is well again. I know war and death dance together, but we don't want to die before seeing battle. I don't want to die at all. Got a box from home with socks, sausages, bread. Christmas came late for me, but I am grateful.

February 4, 1862

Got our orders, we leave on February 24 for Washington. I hope I git to see President Lincoln there, but maybe not. He is a busy man. Some folks in the newspaper say he is weak and 'spilling precious blood.' Some say he should resign and let Vice President Hamlin take over. Me, I know nothing. But I think the president is a great man and kin git the job done.

February 24, 1862

We left Camp Orr at sunup to travel to Pittsburgh. From there we go to Harrisburg. I feel like a real soldier. People wave to us when we pass by. Charlie got a letter, said Jonathan Whitlach is in prison in Dixie. Guess no one waves to him now.

February 26, 1862

Today we got our flag from the governor. We leave Harrisburg for Baltimore, in Maryland. Then on to Washington, the Capitol of the Union.

March 3, 1862

Arrived in Washington today. We set up camp on Meridan Hill, between 14th and 16th Streets. We have time here to rest and git ready. We leave on March 28 and join the Peninsula Campaign in Virginia. I'm a tad worried of battle, but tired of marching for nothing and don't much like this city. It smells bad, people are everywhere, and even at this time of year flies are everywhere, too.

March 6, 1862

President Lincoln reviewed our Regiment today. He is a tall man, but stooped over. Maybe he seems weak to some, because of his thin shape and worried look, but to me he is brave. I would rather fight a war than be in politics.

March 10, 1862

I got called in to headquarters and figured on some trouble or other. But no! Ma's prayers worked. God must be smiling on me. President Lincoln wants to meet a common soldier. A group of us drew straws and I git to be the One to stand for the Federal troops. Ma will be so proud of me. Even if I die in Virginia it will be worth it, since I git to meet the president first.

March 12, 1862
I came to the White House to meet President Lincoln. They brought me to the outside under a tree. Senator Zachariah Chandler is waiting here with me. I am so excited my hands are wet with sweat. This is the best day of my life. Me, Private Silas Munroe, nineteen years of age, from the County of Allegheny in the great State of Pennsylvania, git to put my sweaty palm in the president's hand on this day. Praise be!"

Abby stopped reading. "He skipped some pages; that's weird."

"Who cares?" Morton said. "Besides, if you keep reading maybe you'll find out. This is getting good."

"I hope we find out why he's a hero. I still think it's bizarre what Leticia wrote in her letter. Is he a hero just because he got to meet the president?"

"What about the 'shame' part?"

Abby closed her eyes and could see Leticia's letter in her mind. "It said something like, he lies in shame when he should be a hero." She opened her eyes. "It's gotta be in here somewhere." She flipped past blank pages and found one more section. She read the final entry in Silas's diary.

"March 13, 1862
This is the truth, and I bear no false witness. On March 12, in the year of our Lord 1862, I did try to kill President Lincoln with my own hand. I failed. Senator Chandler is eyewitness to this event. May the Lord have mercy on my soul.
Pvt. Silas Munroe."

TWENTY-FOUR

Abby blinked. Silas tried to kill President Lincoln? He wrote the confession himself. She re-read the page, twice. Nothing changed.

Morton's mouth hung open. A speck of orange candy clung to his lip.

"It makes no sense, none whatsoever." Abby shook her head back and forth. "I'm no history geek, but my dad told me all about the Civil War. The only assassination attempt on Lincoln's life came a lot later, by John Wilkes Booth at some theater."

"It happened on April 14, 1865," Morton said. "At the Ford Theater."

"How can you remember that?"

"I don't know. It happened on Good Friday, right before Easter. I'm better at history than sports." Morton patted his stomach.

"But what about Silas? You read what he wrote right before this. On the same day he's supposed to have tried to kill him, he called President Lincoln 'a great man.' He admired him, so why would he try to assassinate him?" She leafed through several more blank pages at the end of the notebook, then went back and scanned each page again.

"Look at this. Right along the binding, close to the center, some pages have been removed."

Morton examined it. "Someone took a razor blade and did surgery on it."

Abby nodded. "Exactly. Leticia must have removed important information. But if she protected this and hid it, and it tells about her son's shame, why remove the part that must tell the reason he's a hero?"

"I don't know." Morton scratched his head. "Like I said when you showed me her letter the first time, he's her kid; no matter what he did he must have been a hero to her. Maybe she wrote that to make a bad situation look better, you know, to spare the family from what Silas really did. Isn't it time to eat? I'm starving."

Abby ignored him. "Must I always state the obvious? Leticia loved Silas, she loved him a lot. Why would she remove a section of his diary that tells the world good things about him and leave in his confession? That doesn't make any sense. What about those Bible passages she underlined? It seemed to say someone else tried to kill the president and Silas was the one who saved him." Abby thought for a minute, concentrating on all the facts swirling through her mind.

"Remember the tombstone at Dravo Cemetery? Silas died on March 27, 1862. That's only two weeks after he wrote about trying to kill President Lincoln. It's too convenient. There's more to this, I know it. Remember, Leticia also wrote about keeping a secret and not telling William, whoever that is. And she said Silas rests in peace; who would rest in peace after trying to kill the president?"

"Abs, chill," Morton said. "The Bible stuff is your opinion. Who knows? Maybe Leticia underlined things she liked that don't mean anything. Your imagination can be scary. And you sound like a conspiracy theory freak. Didn't you ever hear about KISS?"

"If you think I'm going to kiss you, you're crazy." Abby put her finger down her throat and produced a fake gag.

Morton puckered up his lips and smacked them together. "No, it means Keep It Simple Stupid. Anyway, Silas probably wrote about his trial, and then maybe they put him in jail or hung him, and he couldn't write anymore. His mother might have destroyed it to protect his memory. That's the big secret she didn't want anyone to know. Since he didn't succeed with the assassination, it's one of those footnotes to history. Stay up late some night, and you'll hear about it on The History Channel."

"But still, why save his confession? Why not destroy that, too?" Abby thought her head might explode. "Maybe she saved that part because it has his signature, the last time he ever wrote his name. And she hid it because of the awful thing he tried to do. Maybe you're right; he was a hero to her because she loved him. It still doesn't make sense to me, but I guess not everything in life makes sense."

"Great. I'm going home to help my mom make dinner. Later." Morton clattered down the steps. The faint slam of the screen door moments later left the house silent.

Abby closed the diary, put it back inside the Bible cover, and shoved the book under her bed. She yawned and plopped on the quilt, arms and legs limp and splayed out. Instead of making things right, she found more problems. And Silas hadn't shown up to explain anything.

Sighing, she dragged her weary body off the bed and down the steps. Wandering onto the front porch, she sunk into the soft cotton cushions of the big wicker rocking chair. The peaceful view usually relaxed her. Spring flowers had given way to summer blooms, and the heady scent of roses wafted through the air. She inhaled the aroma, like comfort food for the nose.

A couple rode past on the bike trail, laughing; they waved, and Abby waved back.

"Sure, why not have fun? Just because my life sucks doesn't mean everyone's does. Great, now I'm talking to myself."

She couldn't shake the sluggishness that had captured her since reading Silas's confession. Clearing his name had given her a goal. The burgeoning love growing within her now seemed to be for a murderer. It couldn't possibly be true. How could someone, who had been as gentle and tender with her as Silas had been, commit such a violent act? Would she have to give him up, like everyone else she had loved? Could she? Surely he'd explain everything the next time he came to her …

Abby jumped as something brushed against her leg. She relaxed at the touch of soft fur against her bare skin. "Hey, Kitty, how's my girl?" Kitty wound around and around Abby's ankle, whiskers tickling. Abby picked her up, stroking her back until she settled, purring, draped over the arm of the rocker and Abby's lap.

"Where have you been? Chasing those nasty little mice? You might be small, but you're mighty. I'll bet every rodent between here and McKeesport is afraid of you."

The combination of rocking, a gentle breeze off the river, and Kitty's warm presence lulled Abby from pensive to sleepy. Her head settled against the back of the chair, and her soft snores soon ruffled the fur on Kitty's back.

As her sleep deepened, she watched Silas float through the gate, up the path, and onto the porch, as if carried along on the wind. He still wore the tattered, dark blue uniform, and this time he carried an old rifle. His dark hair almost covered one eye, and his dimple pierced his cheek.

"*Abigail.*" His muffled voice echoed.

"Am I dreaming? Or are you really here with me?"

"*You sure are dreaming,*" Silas answered. "*But I am real.*"

For some reason this made perfect sense to Abby. "Did you do it? Did you try to kill President Lincoln?"

Silas saluted. "*I ain't allowed to speak about it. Trust me. Trust my love.*"

Abby peered at him. "I don't believe you did anything wrong. But I need your help to prove it."

Silas smiled a sad, lop-sided grin. "*But I need you.*"

162

Now that he came to her often, Abby studied him closer than before as he hovered in front of her several inches off the plank floor. He had pale cheeks, sideburns, and sad eyes, smoky-green like a forest plant growing in the shade. A sparse growth of whiskers and wisp of a mustache barely covered his handsome face. Dark brown curls extended below his cap. He wore no boots; his toes peeked through the layer of old rags wrapped around his feet.

"Where are your shoes?"

"*They wore out. I don't need 'em now.*"

"It's all so confusing. Your grave is at Dravo cemetery. I read your diary. But I also touched your hand. I kissed you. And ...*"* Abby stopped, embarrassed to continue.

"*You kin tell me.*"

Her voice came out in whispered confession. "And I love you, Silas. Even though it makes no sense. But I know it's true, more than anything I've ever known in my life."

Silas nodded and removed his cap; his hair floated around his face like a cloud. "*Kin I tell you the truth, Abigail? Will you keep my secret?*"

"Yes. I promise, and I always keep my promises. At least I always kept them to my dad. But he's dead, too." An ache seeped through her body, starting in her toes and traveling through her bloodstream up her legs, into her heart. The grief lodged there, pulsating with a life of its own. The unpleasant tingle of it hurt.

"*Don't be sad.*" Silas knelt in front of her chair. "*Your pa, he will always love you, and he's at peace. Give your sorrow to me.*" He reached forward and passed his hand in front of her eyes, ragged fingernails turned so close to her face she saw each particle of dirt embedded around the cuticles.

Abby shook her head, a slow-motion effort. "No. Sadness is the only thing I have left of my dad. You can't take it away. I need it. I need him."

Silas smiled. "*You only think you need to be unhappy. I kin take your burden for a little while, then I'll give it back if you want it."*

Abby exhaled. A black mist came from her mouth.

Silas caught it in his hand and flung it into the current of air, blowing it away with his white-tinged breath. Then he rested his head on her lap.

The blackness drifted into the trees and disappeared in the orange glow of sunset.

"I feel so light." Abby stroked his hair. "What can I do for you, to show you how much you mean to me?"

"I want you to know my secret—and share my burden."

"I'll help you." Abby smoothed the hair back from his face, leaned down, and kissed his temple. "Did you do it, did you try to kill President Lincoln? Please tell me you're innocent."

"Words are but lines writ on parchment, here today, gone tomorrow. Believe in me, Abigail. Believe in yourself. Believe in us. That's the secret."

"But that doesn't tell me anything. Help me. What should I do?"

"Abigail … my love." Silas drifted off the porch, following the smoke of Abby's despair into the sky.

TWENTY-FIVE

A sharp hiss filled the air, followed by a loud sneeze.

Abby woke up and stared at the shape blocking the sun. "Silas?"

"Silas? Who is Silas, *Cherie*?"

"Oh. Jack. What do *you* want?" Abby shook her head, trying to dispel the fog lodged inside. Her mouth tasted stale, eyes gritty, neck cramped. She sat up from her slumped position in the rocking chair.

Kitty jumped off her lap, slunk across the porch, and disappeared under the railing into the side yard.

Abby struggled to integrate the present into the past, yearning for more of Silas ... less of Jack. Flesh and blood had let her down. Love had found her in the person of a spirit. She didn't need to understand it, only to embrace it.

Jack reached down and brushed her cheek with the back of his hand. "You looked sweet and peaceful. Do I need to protect you from some local farm boy?"

With what she knew about Jack and Lisa, Abby bridled. "Did you want something?"

Jack dropped into a chair beside Abby and picked up the newspaper on the table. "Just taking a break, that's all. I have some work to finish before dark." He glanced at the front page. "Hmm, 'Cycle Trip Celebrates Underground Railroad. A new bike route opens from Alabama to Canada, providing the means to … blah blah blah. You people get so excited about this Underground Railroad trivia. You should be reading about the injustice going on right now, not hundreds of years ago."

"History is important. We're supposed to learn from the mistakes of the past, so we don't repeat them in the future. That goes for people as well as governments."

"You think that happens?" Jack rifled through the rest of the newspaper. "Like this, for example, buried in the back of the paper. 'Car Bomb Kills Local Soldier.' The U.S. government learned nothing from its past mistakes. The Underground Railroad only existed because one group of people had the power to hurt another group of people. And how did the politicians solve that one? They sent boys into the Civil War to do their job for them. Along the way those boys died, in droves. Just like they do now all over this blasted world. So who learned anything from the past?"

Abby thought about Silas. "Don't you think people go to war because they believe in something? That's what soldiers do. I'm sorry a car bomb in a foreign country killed a local soldier, but he went there to fight for his principles. It's not always about politics; sometimes it's about ideals. You're a big talker about values until you have to do something about it."

Jack threw the paper on the floor. "You are so naïve. Do you really think my brother signed on to eat a bullet in a sweltering desert? He went there because the politicians were too lazy to fix things themselves and convinced everyone they had 'a duty to protect America.' Bullshit. President Keller is the one who should have died, not my brother."

Almost against her will, Abby noticed how ugly Jack's features had become during his tirade. How had she ever thought him to be handsome? Instead of pale gold, his skin looked pasty and unhealthy. The light blue of his eyes had become slim outlines to his huge, dark pupils. Clear drops of spit collected in the corners of his sneering lips.

She stood up to face him. "People get arrested for making threats against the president."

"What, you plan to call the Secret Service on me?" Jack slumped into the chair. "My brother died, Abby. What if it had been your father in a war?" He put his head in his hands, a shuddering whisper escaping as he exhaled on one name: "Etienne …"

Abby paused, remembering her simmering rage at her dad's doctors, the hospital, hospice nurses, her mother, and everyone else during and after her father's battle with cancer. Her anger at Lisa and Jack, although more recent, gave way. "Jack, I'm sorry about your brother. I know it hurts." She dropped to her knees and put her arms around him.

He buried his face in her shoulder and let out a shuddering sob.

"You'll feel better when you finish your work here and get on with the bike trip. You've had too much time on your hands to think about Steve. Once you start riding again, get to the bike rally in D.C., then get back home, you'll have had time to work through everything. I feel better when I'm busy and have a goal."

Jack pulled away and stood, wiping his eyes. "You try so hard, I'll remember that. It's a gift you've given me. But at the end of the day, someone has to take responsibility for my brother. I have a goal, too. And loyalty. And ideals I plan to put into action." He stomped across the porch and back to the barn. Frenzied hammering soon filled the air, drowning out bird chirps and the tinkle of wind chimes.

Abby sank back into the rocker and watched Kitty leap onto the railing and then return to her lap. She stroked the downy fur behind her ears. She knew friendship with Jack—her mother's lover—would be impossible. She wanted to hate him, and Lisa, too. But hatred took too much energy. She longed for the newfound love she had for Silas to spill over onto Lisa.

The crunch of tires on gravel and the low hum of the truck engine interrupted her thoughts. Jack stopped hammering and stood to peer over the edge of the roof. Abby sank even further into the cushions as the vehicle skidded to a stop, scattering stones. Lisa climbed out of the driver's side, leaving the door open, and hurried into the barn.

Jack climbed down and followed her. The barn door swung shut.

Abby sat Kitty on the porch floor as instant rage boiled up inside her chest. "How bold can they get? Jack knows I'm here, but apparently that's meaningless. Doesn't he care about anything? I'll give them a few minutes and pop in to say hello. Can't wait to see what they're doing." Her mind reeled from the image of naked, sweaty bodies joined together—with faces belonging to Jack and Lisa.

In spite of the churning in her stomach, Abby made her way to the barn, taking her time. She tried to formulate a speech to blast them with righteous anger, but the words wouldn't come. Her feet moved as if they had a will of their own.

The barn door remained ajar, enough for Abby to slip inside unnoticed. She paused to let her eyes adjust to the gloomy light. Dust motes drifted in the air; the scene appeared gauzy, a Lifetime television movie come to life, resurrected as an X-rated film. In the rear stall, to the left, Jack and Lisa faced each other.

Lisa waved an envelope in the air. "I went into town to get the certificate from my safe deposit box at the bank. I want Abby to see it, and then she'll understand."

"Why be so worried?" Jack said. "Abby will get it eventually. She's a good kid."

Lisa wiped tears off her cheeks. "She misses her father so much. I'm not sure there's room in her heart for you and me. You can't take his place, even if you want to, and she already hates me for leaving all those years ago. I've made a mess of everything."

Jack opened his arms, and Lisa stepped into the circle. "Hey, you've taken care of me, now I'll return the favor. Let me talk to her first, and then you can explain everything."

"You think that'll work? I love her so much; I want things to be right for all three of us. We need to be a family."

The hope in Lisa's voice made Abby cringe. As nice as it was to know that Lisa loved her, did she really expect her to accept Jack as her father?

"Let me make this easy for you." Abby stepped out of the shadows and approached the back of the barn. "Here I am. Want to explain now? I'm a little tired of my life playing like a cheesy reality program. It's bad enough my mother abandoned me. I had no friends, but Dad didn't understand about mean girls. So he became my only real friend. Then he died." She stopped to clear her throat, the threat of tears pulsating at the back of her eyes.

"Abby, wait ..." Lisa reached out.

"No, you wait." Abby held her hands up to stop her mother. "You came back to make up, to be my mother, and instead you hook up with a teenage roofer? Maybe you've always been a slut. Is that why you and Dad ended up in divorce court, and you disappeared? I guess history does repeat itself, right Jack?"

"Let me explain." Lisa's hands dropped to her sides. She took a deep breath and looked straight into Abby's eyes.

"You have no excuse, so save it." Abby turned to go.

"Abby. Wait." Lisa took another deep breath. "Jack is your brother."

TWENTY-SIX

Brother. *Brother?*

Abby braced herself against the rough wooden stall, wondering if some hideous alternate universe had descended onto Bikers' Rest. A wave of dizziness and nausea rolled through her.

"*Cherie,* you're going to pass out." Jack's words reverberated in Abby's skull.

"Sit down, honey." Lisa's voice echoed from a distance away, through a wind tunnel on the other side of the world.

Abby shook her head and collapsed abruptly on the barn floor, raising a puff of dry chaff. She pulled up her knees and lowered her head between them, taking deep breaths. A shock of cold on the back of her neck brought reality tumbling back. Jack stood behind her, ice pack in hand. Abby pushed him away and stood, putting distance between them. She noticed her hands shaking and shoved them in her pockets.

She focused on Lisa, willing her to make sense of the senseless. "I thought you said Jack is my *brother.* You mean, like we're all brothers and sisters in the human race?"

"No." Lisa held Abby's gaze. "As in, I'm your mother

and his." She held the envelope aloft. "This is his birth certificate."

Abby swayed again. "I'm going to sit down on the porch."

The single-file march back to the house could have been a funeral procession. No one spoke. Lisa snuffled and wiped her eyes. The crunch of gravel underfoot, the subtle echo of a car horn, and the drone of a bee were amplified in the strained silence. After climbing the steps Abby sat in the wicker rocker, Lisa pulled a chair to face her, and Jack perched on the railing. He avoided eye contact and appeared ready to run.

Lisa slapped both hands on her knees. "I'm usually a direct person—like you Abby. So I'll just put it all out there. Then ask me anything, and I'll try to answer."

Abby nodded, mute for once.

"I got pregnant in high school. Never thought it could happen to me, same as every other kid. But it did. My boyfriend moved away with his family; he wanted nothing to do with the baby or me. The October after graduation I gave birth to a healthy baby boy, which didn't fit in with my college plans. I gave him up for adoption; it seemed like the best thing to do, not just for me, but for him, too. Then I tried to forget and move on."

"You tried to forget your own child?" Abby knew she sounded judgmental and held up both hands. "Sorry."

Lisa nodded. "I got a waitress job, started drinking, barely remember much else. Then I ran my car off the road into a construction site one boozy afternoon. One of the workmen helped me out and ended up asking me for a date—your dad."

"Was it love at first sight?"

"Hardly. But he treated me very well. I knew he loved me, and when he asked me to marry him it seemed like the perfect solution. I'd be respectable, he never had to know about the baby, he'd help me to forget." Lisa sighed.

"So you never loved my dad?"

"I did in my own way. I'm not sure I even knew what love meant back then." Lisa raked her shaking hands through her hair. "But you have to understand what an emotional wreck I'd become. It never works to bury problems. They only surface in some other, more destructive way. But that's hindsight. Anyway, we got married, and when you were born I thought my past would never bother me again."

"But it did." Abby's flat voice belied her agitation.

"I'm afraid so. Blame me, not your dad." Lisa's words came out as a halting whisper. "You were the sweetest baby, but any baby reminded me of the little person I gave away. By this time he would have been ready for kindergarten, but in my mind he remained a tiny, helpless infant, being carried out the door of my hospital room, handed over to a stranger. So I got reacquainted with my old friend bourbon, made very bad choices, and tried to blame everyone else. By the time you turned three I gave up. On myself and everyone else."

"That's when you got the divorce and left us." Abby remembered a photo taken with her dad. They were wearing pointy paper hats and blowing out three candles on a cake. He held a remote camera timer in his hand. No mother in the picture.

"You don't need the boring details, but eventually I got sober and enrolled at Gannon College in Erie. I earned a degree, found a job, focused on making it one day at a time, and tried to forget yesterday. It even worked, for a while."

"You tried to forget another child. Me."

Lisa's face, devoid of color, drooped like a wilted carnation. "I'm so, so sorry."

"I'll pick it up from there." Jack nodded to Lisa and looked at Abby. "I told you my mom died. I didn't know until years later that she and my father had adopted me. I'll never forget the day Dad showed me the paperwork. I missed having a mother, couldn't stop thinking that somewhere my birth mother existed and might want to know me. So I found her."

Abby snorted. "That's a crock. You were just a kid."

Jack shrugged. "My father provided the information he already had and Etienne—my *half*-brother, helped me to do the rest. He took care of everything. That's the kind of guy he is—was."

Minutes of silence went by. "How did you find Lisa?"

Jack glanced at Lisa. "Once I had her name, I tracked her to Gannon and found out her current address, only about thirty miles from us. I called, she agreed to meet us, and Dad took us over to her place one Sunday afternoon."

"Surprise …" Abby said.

Lisa patted Jack's knee. "Truly. At the time I thought the shock would kill me. But when I looked at this sweet child, with his blond hair and blue eyes—so like you, Abby—my heart melted. Jack's adoptive father let me get involved in Jack's life, and I found I could be a decent mother after all."

"And you didn't want to include *me* in your new life because …" Abby said.

"My life with your father had been a mess because I messed it up. He preferred I stay away, and my guilt tricked me into thinking it would be best for you." Lisa frowned. "Yet another in a long line of my mistakes."

"Dad kept you from seeing me?" Abby had to concentrate on Lisa's words, even as anger blossomed at her father. And at yet another betrayal.

"Call it a mutual decision. I know you think he could do no wrong, but no one's perfect."

"You have to give Lisa some credit," Jack said. "When she heard about your dad's death, she couldn't wait to get back to you."

"You were part of Jack's life for ten years," Abby said to Lisa. "Steve's, too."

"They both became the best part of *my* life," Lisa said. She grabbed at Jack's hand. "We missed Steve when he left for the service, and now, well, I can't believe he's dead."

"Why didn't you tell me this when you got here?" Abby said. "Or at least once Jack arrived. Why the secrecy and lies?"

"Not lies, exactly," Lisa said. "I didn't think you were ready for the whole truth. I hoped we could have a relationship before I told you my past sins and produced a brother you never knew about."

"Did Dad find out you had a baby and gave it up?"

"I told him before we separated," Lisa said. "By then I had nothing left to lose."

"And he didn't tell me I had a half-brother." Abby wrapped both arms around her stomach. "You both deceived me."

"He didn't know about Jack as anything more than a nameless baby," Lisa said. "I had no idea where he lived or anything else about him. I never imagined I would."

Abby turned to Jack. "You came here on purpose because of Lisa. Is the rest of it true, the bike rally, meeting President Keller, all that?"

"It's all true," Jack said. "Except for one thing. I didn't just come to see Lisa; I came to meet my sister."

Abby looked from Jack to Lisa. Now she noticed that they had the same smile, quick temper, and athletic build. And that Jack's hair and eyes matched her own. It must be true.

Without a word Abby stood and went in the house. Lisa and Jack let her go. She had a brother. She was a sister. Nothing was what it seemed to be. Again.

TWENTY-SEVEN

Abby went into the kitchen, followed by Kitty. She filled a clean glass from the drainer with tap water, took a few sips, and rolled her head to relax the tight muscles of her neck. Her heart raced at the foreign concept of having a sibling—a brother—family of her own to love again. The reality of it didn't compute. "Come on, Kitty. I have to lie down and get some sleep, or I'll go crazy thinking about everything."

After emptying cat food into a dish, Abby made a crunchy peanut butter and jelly sandwich on wheat bread and ate it on the way to her room. She lay on her bed and stared at the lightning bolt crack on her ceiling for a while, hands under her head.

Jack: Bizarre and strange on one hand, understanding and sweet on the other. Lisa: Messed up several lives, but trying to make amends. Abby wondered if she'd ever given either one of them a real chance to get close.

Abby got up and went to the bathroom. She brushed her teeth, flossed, and brushed again. She pushed aside her bangs to study a small pimple high on her forehead, applying a dab of acne cream to it. After gazing at her eyebrows in the mirror, she rummaged through the box of junk in the medicine cabinet for the tweezers. She plucked several hairs between her brows. Replacing the tweezers she pulled out the nail clippers and cut off a broken toenail. Using an emery board she tried to shape the remainder of her fingernails, then rubbed lavender-scented lotion on her hands and forearms.

She stared at herself in the mirror. "I'm out of things to do, and I'm still not tired." After a brief inspection, she trimmed her bangs, using the manicure scissors.

With her impulsive makeover complete, she went into the hall and stopped at the newly boarded-up wall covering the hidden stairs. She ran her hands over the perimeter and laid her cheek against the plasterboard, trying to absorb inspiration from the room below. She had trouble imagining slaves hiding in the basement. Who first opened the house to runaways? Leticia and Silas? How did people know this was a safe house? Questions flew through her brain, but no answers, her mind like a game of Olympic Ping-Pong.

In her bedroom Abby threw her robe on the chair and climbed into bed. She picked up a magazine and flipped through the pages, unable to get involved with stories about singers, movie stars, and horoscopes. Instead, Silas and Jack played in the theater of her mind, on constant re-run.

She rolled over and turned out the lamp. After the initial shock of darkness, her eyes adjusted to the ambient light coming in the window from the full moon. She studied the shapes of her furniture, counted squares on the quilt at the foot of the bed, and wiggled her toes as she hummed "Yankee Doodle."

She tried to get comfortable, instead getting entangled in the covers. Lifting the sheet in the air, it billowed like a parachute before settling in soft creases over her legs. She repeated the lift, billow, settle sequence. Still awake. The old Baby Ben alarm clock on her dresser ticked away the nighttime minutes until it reached two o'clock.

A loud *yowl* came from outside. Maybe some stud cat on the prowl for a date with Kitty? The thought made her smile, and she closed her eyes, imagining a cat wedding in the front garden, complete with catnip cake, a bouquet of miniature red roses, and Kitty in a tiny white veil. She began to get drowsy, riding the fence somewhere between awake and asleep. The stupor wrapped her in comfort, like wearing her red moose-track robe on a winter night.

Crack.

Abby sat straight up, startled by the sound of—what? A broken tree branch? A car backfiring? The barn roof collapsing?

She threw the sheet off and ran to the front window. The yard, illuminated in the moonlight, showed the outlines of flowers, the fence, silhouettes of trees, but no branch on the ground or headlights nearby.

Crack.

The reverberation seemed to come from behind the house. Abby went to the side window. The barn loomed in the foreground, outlined against the sky, roof intact. The door stood ajar, a sliver of light glowing from within. A shape materialized from the tree line, slinking through the grass. As if conjured from Abby's dreams, Kitty crept across the yard.

Crack.

Kitty froze in place and remained that way for a heartbeat, then streaked into the barn, tail between her legs. Abby pulled on her robe as she ran out of the bedroom, not knowing what was happening, but sensing something very wrong.

"I'm coming, Kitty." She leapt down the stairs two at a time, sped across the second-floor landing, down the steps, through the living room and dining room and into the kitchen. The tile floor chilled her bare feet; she skidded on the throw rug by the mudroom door but avoided falling by grabbing onto the doorframe.

With her momentum stopped, Abby hesitated. What

had spooked Kitty? Something—or someone—had made the noises she'd heard. At night they were isolated between the empty bike trail and a section of woods. Should she get help? If Lisa hadn't already awakened, she must have taken a sleeping pill. Anxiety built on indecision; she chewed on a nub of fingernail. At least she could bring Kitty inside.

Abby opened the back door, wincing at the metallic grating of the old hinges. She tiptoed across the splintery porch floorboards, then eased down the steps. Avoiding the gravel walk she stepped into the damp grass. Soon the bottoms of her pajama pants slapped wet and heavy against her ankles. She shivered at the dampness creeping up her body.

"*Ouch.*" Abby stepped on a jagged rock as she approached the barn. She stopped, like a kid playing freeze tag.

The night remained deathly still—no breeze, no insect sounds, even the river on mute. The humid air signaled the possibility of a storm somewhere nearby. Moonlight illuminated the everyday things around Abby, making them indistinct, dark things lightened, light things darkened. When nothing responded to her outburst, she scurried across the open space, formulating a plan. Circle the barn. Avoid the trees. Check things out. Go in the barn. Grab Kitty. Back to the house. Breathe.

Abby reached the barn and snugged up against it, the back of her robe snagging on the rough wood. Her breath came in short puffs that matched the rapid thuds of her heart. She edged around the perimeter of the building, pausing often to listen. At the rear corner, she hesitated; once she rounded the bend she would be out of sight of the house and sandwiched between the empty barn and a line of trees.

She shivered. Jack should be inside. Her brother. Not an empty structure. Nothing to fear. Abby took a deep breath, the phrase "Take a cleansing breath" from an exercise class popped into her mind. She stopped, listened, and turned the corner. Rustling bushes and the *snap* of a stick came from the woods. She stood, rooted to the spot, straining to see through the dark. A shape appeared, then two, then three. Abby realized she had been holding her breath and exhaled as the two does and a fawn continued to feed.

She imaged what it would have been like to sit at the breakfast table tomorrow morning with her dad, laughing with him about her idiotic nighttime adventure. Then she realized her mental picture had them at the oak table in the kitchen at *this* house, not the old house. Startled, Abby understood she had a thought about her father that didn't involve death, pain, or sorrow, one that didn't hurt at all. Silas had done that for her. In giving her his love, he'd released her pain.

Moving away from the shelter of the barn wall, she sauntered into the level, grassy corridor between the barn and trees. The cool grass on her bare feet, her toes like white minnows in the moonlight, and the stillness were peaceful. Until she stepped on something unyielding, cold, and uncomfortable. She bent down and dragged her fingers through the grass. They closed on a small cylinder. She scooped it up and held it close to her eyes, straining to see in the dim light.

Short, hard, open at one end, closed at the other. Roofing hardware? Abby dropped it in her robe pocket and took two more steps, hurting her heel. She picked up an identical metal object and dropped it in with the first. When she stood, she noticed an odd, metallic odor in the air, where normally she smelled the scent of cow manure from a nearby farm.

Arriving at the barn door, she hesitated. But too bad if Jack woke up; she needed Kitty. "Here, Kitty, Kitty ..." Abby whispered into the barn.

Abby slid between the barn doors into the soft, lantern-lit interior. The dirt floor, firm and dusty with bits of old straw, made an odd contrast to the damp grass and rough stones outside. She tiptoed forward looking for Kitty, sighing when she felt the touch of downy fur against her ankle.

When she bent over to pick up the cat, the objects from her pocket fell out. They rolled across the floor through the dust and came to rest against the edge of the first stall. She shrugged and scooped Kitty up. The wink of light against metal in her peripheral vision stopped her.

With Kitty under one arm, she bent down and retrieved the identical cylinders, opening her palm to study them. With a sharp intake of breath, she released the cat. Bullets? She dropped one back in her robe pocket and held the other up in the air between her fingers. What type of a gun used a bullet this size? That had to be the sound she'd heard—but who would fire a gun in the middle of the night?

Abby's breathing accelerated. Her hands became slick with sweat, even though they were cold and numb. Her heartbeat reverberated inside her skull. The damp hem of her pajamas made her shiver. Her mind screamed: *Danger, get out.*

She turned to flee to the house for help, safety, Mom. Instead she ran into a solid wall of hot flesh. And experienced a sharp, pungent, metallic taste from the hand covering her mouth.

TWENTY-EIGHT

Abby tried to scream; it came out as a croak. She struggled against the strong arms that held her close, senses reeling from mingled aromas of sweat, fabric softener, and something that registered as fireworks. She pushed at the man's chest, unable to get even a millimeter of space between them. Finally she got her mouth opened wide enough to bite the offending hand.

"Abby, get a grip. Stop it."

Abby opened her eyes and looked up into Jack's pale blue ones. "Jack?" She blinked and stumbled as he released her.

Jack's hand shot out and steadied her, then he stepped back. "What's wrong? You ran into me and freaked out. Were you sleepwalking? What're you doing out here at this time of night, eh?"

Abby bent over, rested her hands on her knees, and took several deep breaths. The barn seemed to be spinning around; she had the sense of being a spectator watching the action from someplace else. She also wanted time to decide what to tell Jack before facing him. At last her breathing steadied and her heart slowed to somewhere near normal. Her brain continued in overdrive. What just happened?

She glanced up at Jack through her lashes before standing, her eyes half-closed. His unruly white-blond hair stuck up at the back, and as she watched, he yawned and scratched his crotch, as a guy who recently got out of bed. Except for his eyes. Instead of being unfocused and red-rimmed, they were hyper-alert and intent.

"Abby, are you sure you're okay? I'm worried about my little sister. Why are you outside at two o'clock in the morning?" He waited for a response, and getting none added, "I'll walk you back to the house."

"What a gentleman. I can walk back by myself, thank you." Abby started toward the barn door and stopped. "Were you asleep when I came in? What woke you?"

Jack glanced around the barn. "I heard you and wondered if Lisa had a problem at the house and sent you to get me."

"I didn't make much noise. And I'm barefoot, and I didn't call you. In fact, I didn't even see you. I came in to get my cat."

"That must have been it. The cat chased a mouse, and it woke me. Or maybe my cat allergy started up. Then you freaked and the rest, as they say, is history."

Kitty poked her head out of a corner stall and strolled to Abby.

Jack sneezed. "Get that filthy animal away from me." Before Abby could react, he kicked a boot-clad foot in her direction. Abby grabbed for the cat, but Jack's aim was perfect. He kicked Kitty, sending her spinning out the barn door.

Abby shoved him in the chest, hard, and ran outside.

Kitty lay in the gravel, trembling, then stood on shaky paws.

"Are you okay? My sweet little Kitty." Abby picked Kitty up and ran her hands over the cat's legs and body, unable to find any sign of serious injury.

Kitty scratched Abby's arm as she struggled to be

released, hissing and spitting.

Back-lit by the lantern light in the barn, Jack loomed. "Shut that stupid cat up—or I will."

Kitty scampered away into the night.

Abby turned to face Jack. Her words came out deliberate, low, a savage growl. "You–miserable–disgusting–piece–of–crap. Where do you get off hurting an innocent animal, *my* animal? I wish she had scratched your eyes out; you deserve it. Don't you ever go near her again, do you hear me?"

Jack raised one eyebrow. "Careful, *Cherie*, you're drooling; not your most attractive moment. You should see yourself, wild eyes, hair messed, spitting. I believe there's a bit of untamed cat in you. I suggest you take more time to care about humans and less about animals. What about people who go to war, what about them? No one cares if they live or die; why should a cat mean anything to me?"

"You aren't worth my time, brother or not. Does Lisa know about your tendencies toward animal cruelty?"

"By all means go tell on me. But may I remind you that you're the one who came to the place I sleep and woke me," Jack sneered. "*Our* mother might wonder what her little girl is doing out at this time of night—in her jammies. Ah, poor child, I'll tell her. So taken with her big brother, little lamb who lost her father. She's just looking for love, sleepwalking perhaps, not quite right in the mind. And she's been through so much, first a crush on me, then finding out I'm the brother she didn't know existed. Jealousy and loss, terrible things. Perhaps she needs some counseling, or time—away—to get better."

Abby blinked. He sounded so sincere that she almost believed what he said. If he only knew she'd fallen in love with the ghost of a Civil War soldier. Although she knew—absolutely without a doubt knew—Silas to be real, everyone else would call her crazy. And after ten years with Jack, Lisa might believe anything he had to say.

She hung her head, and in doing so noticed Jack's laced-up boots.

"So, Jack. Wear your work boots to bed all the time, or just when girls come to call?"

He shrugged.

"Lisa is my mother, too. She sees what kind of a person I am, even if we haven't spent much time together. I don't go out and party, my best friend is a nerd named Morton, and my idea of adventure is a two-mile bike ride to an old cemetery. Why would she believe I've got mental problems? She might be much more interested in why I really came outside tonight."

"Yes, that question has yet to be answered." Jack crossed his arms. "Do tell."

"It's so strange. There I was, lying in my own bed, when I heard a loud noise from the back of the barn."

Jack's eyes narrowed. "And did you discover what caused this phantom noise?"

Abby arranged her features into what her dad had called a poker face. He'd taught her to play cards, to bluff, to keep a straight face. She reached into her pocket. "I found a little souvenir out behind the barn. Maybe you want it, since it belongs to you." She pulled out the brass cylinder, showed it to Jack, tossed it in the air, and caught it, enclosing it in her palm. "Shooting guns at the house; my mother will love that."

"The shell casings. You found the bullet shell casings." Jack considered Abby for a minute. "*Touché, Cherie.* You got me." He grinned, a sudden metamorphosis Abby found disconcerting.

"Care to explain to me—or to Lisa?"

"It's nothing," Jack shrugged. "I did some target practice in the moonlight because I have insomnia. I knew I couldn't do it during the day, too many people around and all."

"So you went out to do target practice at night. Right. And you think *I'm* crazy? Why do you have a gun in the first place? Let me guess—you brought it on the bike. How stupid do you think I am?"

"This is Pennsylvania, remember?" Jack said. "Everyone hunts. Didn't your dad go deer hunting every November?"

"No. And this isn't about him, it's about you."

"I just assumed he hunted because I found a deer rifle stored in the back of the barn and decided to try it out. I'm sorry if you're upset. And I apologize about the cat. I just lost my temper; middle of the night, allergies, you surprised me, all that." Jack walked over and tousled her hair. "Friends?"

Abby noticed how his eyes crinkled at the corners when he smiled, as if he did it all the time. She shivered, not from cold, but due to the unfamiliar, brotherly touch—from a cruel liar.

"I'm not ready for all this," she told him. "And I'm not sure I trust you."

"Of course. I have a trip into town in the morning to get more shingles for the barn. Meet me for lunch at the Chinese restaurant on the corner, by the bridge, and I'll treat. We can start over."

Abby thought about it. "Okay, lunch. See you at noon." She turned to go.

"Just leave those shell casings with me." Jack held out his hand. "I'll get rid of them."

"That's okay." Abby closed her fist over them until her fingertips blanched. "I think I'll hold onto them, since they belonged to my dad. It makes them special to me."

Jack frowned. "Yes, of course, your father's things are precious to you; I'm sure you want to take care of them. You must take care of yourself, as well. I'm so happy to have a sister, *Cherie*. I wouldn't want anything to happen to you."

A sudden burst of icy-cold wrapped around Abby's heart. "Just what is that supposed to mean? Are you threatening me?"

Jack lifted both hands and shook his head. "No, no. What makes you say that? I'm not a violent person; I hate violence. I'm sorry if you think I'd hurt you. I have a lot to make up for at lunch tomorrow, eh?"

Abby watched a contrite expression creep over his face, but in the moment before he hung his head, his mouth twisted into a hard grimace. Gripped by indecision, her mind sped through the options open to her: tell Lisa, call the police, chalk it up to imagination.

She chewed on her lower lip. His word against hers; he had more experience lying.

Abby forced a smile. "You aren't forgiven yet."

Jack nodded. He reached out, grabbed her hand, and kissed it on the back. "Tomorrow, then. Sweet dreams, little sister."

"Tomorrow, big brother." She hoped he didn't turn into her worst nightmare.

TWENTY-NINE

Abby squirmed in bed and pushed away kisses from her morning visitor. "Kitty, I get it. Time for breakfast, right?"

Kitty's tongue slashed across Abby's cheek, a warm, rough feel but pleasant, in a cat-breath kind of way. She glanced at her phone. "You crazy cat, it's only eight o'clock in the morning, and I'm still wiped out. What a night, brutal. Looks like you survived your run-in with our resident maniac in the barn. I guess you deserve a good breakfast after what you went through, but let's make it brunch instead."

Abby pulled the quilt over her head. Kitty pawed at it. "Give me a break. My eyes feel like sandpaper, my throat is sore, and I think there's a cut on my foot. Just one more hour, then we'll eat."

Kitty burrowed under the covers and snuggled into Abby's arms.

"Abs, you in there?" Morton had never met a boundary he couldn't cross.

"Go away. I'm sleeping."

"If you were sleeping, we wouldn't be talking. Open up, I have some great news."

Abby sighed, hugged Kitty, and dragged herself out of bed and into her robe. She opened the door. "This better be good."

"I lost four pounds." Morton patted his belly. "Can you believe it? All that exercise on the bike paid off. Maybe by the end of summer I'll have a six-pack—abs, you know, buff stomach. Hey, I made a joke. I'm telling Abs I'll get abs. Funny, huh?"

Abby looked at the soft roll of flab around Morton's waist. "Uh-huh."

Morton's grin faltered. "I just mean I'll be built, you know, muscles."

"I'm happy for you. But it's early, and I'm tired. Can we admire your new body later?"

"We have to hit the bike trail. No time to waste." Morton pulled a packet of M&M's out of his pocket. "I need to stay in shape. I already got your bike from the barn, so I'll meet you out front. Maybe your mom will give me breakfast while you get dressed."

"Did you see Jack?" Abby glanced toward the window. Did Jack have her dad's rifle? What should she do about his middle of the night shooting spree?

"I'm so sick of you talking about Jack all the time. He's too old for you, and he's slimy. I'm only telling you this because we're friends. You think I'm jealous of him, but I'm not. It isn't like that for you and me, and I know it. You're not into younger men."

"Slow down," Abby said. "I have something to tell you, and something else to show you." She took a deep breath. "Jack's never going to be my boyfriend."

Morton grinned. "Hooray. I knew you were too smart to get involved with him."

"Um, it's more complicated than that." Abby glanced toward the barn and back. "Jack's my brother." When Morton didn't react she added, "Lisa is our mother."

"You're kidding, right? This stuff only happens on TV. Wow." Morton wagged his head, then got serious. "Hey,

I'm happy for you. At least I think I am. He *is* weird."

"Yeah, well, let me tell you the rest." Abby pulled the shell casing out of her pocket and told Morton what had happened during the night, leaving out the veiled threat. Shouldn't she want Morton to like her brother?

Morton examined the brass cylinder, adjusting his glasses to peer at writing on the closed end. He whistled. "He told you this came from your dad's hunting rifle?"

Abby nodded.

"He lied. This isn't rifle ammunition. First of all, the casing is too small. And see what's engraved here? On the top is says, WIN, and on the bottom, 9 mm LUGER. That means it came from a 9-millimeter handgun. No one hunts with a pistol, at least not in Pennsylvania. Unless they're hunting *people*."

Abby hated to acknowledge Jack's blatant lie, even though sharing some DNA didn't address his honesty issues. "How do you know? There are exceptions to everything."

"This is Pennsylvania," Morton said. "Everyone hunts around here. Bill from the junk store took me once, just to watch, and he lets me look at the guns he gets sometimes. You should talk to your mom about this."

"It's not a big deal. Jack's leaving soon anyway. The barn roof is almost done, and he's going to D.C. for a bike rally on the Fourth of July. It's a non-issue."

"But—"

"But we better get going on our bike ride. I can't wait to hang out with a muscle-bound hunk like you."

Morton blushed. "Great. See ya in ten. And hurry up, you don't need to do all that girl stuff for me."

Abby put one thumb up. When she got downstairs after dressing, she caught a glimpse of Lisa sweeping the front porch. She made an abrupt turn and headed for the back of the house.

After setting out cat food and grabbing an apple on the way through the kitchen, Abby steered her bike onto the trail behind Morton. The helmet he'd hung on her handlebars gave her head claustrophobia; she preferred the wind rushing through her hair.

The grass shimmered in the morning sun, highlighted by dew. It reminded Abby of the dew on her pajama pants, the shell casings, and Jack's strange outbursts. But somehow none of it seemed so bad in the light of day. She moved her head side to side, relaxing tight muscles, inhaling a hint of recently-mown grass in the air.

A robin flew in front of Abby, screeching as it landed in a nest high up in a birch tree. A stanza from the old poem in Silas's diary came to her: *Pretty little robin, With your scarlet breast, O may tormenters never find, Their way into thy nest.*

She had to find the rest of Silas's diary. His tormenters may have found a way into his nest, but she vowed to chase them out. Could Jack be a 'tormenter' in her nest? Did he have to be chased out? Yet she didn't want to alienate her brother, couldn't lose the family she had just found.

Morton turned his bike left and glided to a stop.

"I can't believe we got to the cemetery already." Abby pulled in behind Morton. "Maybe you aren't the only one getting in shape. By the end of the summer, I'll be looking good, too."

"Nah, I like you better like this."

Abby's eyebrows went up.

"I mean, you look great already. And it's not 'like you' like you, just, you know, friends." Morton hung his bike helmet on the handlebars. "Let's go down to the river and skip stones."

"I'm going to look around up here for a while. Go ahead." She felt drawn to Silas's grave. The finer points of ghosting were a mystery. Did he rest here, in the cemetery, float about at Bikers' Rest, or exist in some sort of limbo? And what did the answer mean to any hope of them having a life together?

Morton stared. "Are you being nice to me? Are you

sick? Is this a trick?"

"Not sick, no trick—just giving up bitchiness for the rest of the summer."

Morton grinned and disappeared down the path to the river.

Abby went directly to Silas's grave. She bent down and cleared away rotting leaves, dead weeds, and an old bottle cap from the grassy mound.

"Did Leticia come and talk to you? I'm sure she did. I'm talking to you, and it's been almost 150 years since you were buried here." She placed her palm against the headstone, yearning for Silas to appear to her so she could tell him about Jack. And feel his calming presence.

"Thaaaank youuu fooor coooming." The syllables were drawn-out and whispery thin.

Abby snorted. "Very funny, Morton. You are such an infant."

"You should have seen your face." Morton laughed, and then plopped on an adjacent tree stump.

"Whatever." Abby went back to clearing debris off the grave. "Doesn't anyone ever take care of these things?" She pulled out a few weeds and patted the loose dirt in place. "At least there aren't any bugs today. It's funny, this seemed so scary the first time I came here, now it seems like a new home for people who moved on to another life. I guess it's like that for my dad. I'd rather think of him moving on than just ceasing to exist."

Abby worked her way to the top of the grave. "Look at this mess; it's embedded around the tombstone, almost up to the engraving. Hand me a stick." She took a small piece of wood from Morton and dug around the base. "Hey, check this out. There's something attached at the bottom."

"Attached?" Morton got on his hands and knees and peered into the space Abby had cleared. "Cool."

The foundation of the granite protruded in an oblong semi-circle. "It got buried under the dirt and leaves over the years." Abby felt the top edge. "I think it's hollow.

Help me pull this gross junk out of there." She grimaced at the accumulated gunk; soggy leaves, a few dead insects, grime.

When they finished it looked like a vase growing out of the stone.

"It's an urn," Morton said. "You know, for flowers. They were carved into some of the old markers. I guess someone wanted to decorate his grave."

Abby examined it closer. "It isn't carved. There's cement or something around the edges, like it's an add-on. Maybe Leticia couldn't afford a fancy memorial and someone made this later. The stuff around the sides is crumbling."

She ran her fingernail around the urn. The concrete turned to dust and sprinkled onto the ground, like salt on a pretzel.

Morton jiggled the urn, leaving it off-center. "It's loose."

Abby reached around him to adjust it. The urn came off in her hand, leaving an obscene, gaping hole at the bottom of Silas' headstone. She sat back on her heels. "I can't believe it. All I did was touch the thing, and now I've ruined it." Her eyes filled with tears. "Leticia must have saved every penny to put this here for her son, and now I broke it. I'm such a moron." Softly she whispered, "I'm sorry, Silas."

"Hey, Abs, it's okay," Morton said. "It just barely stayed there all these years. I can bring some Quikrete, and we'll put it back in place." He squirmed. "I hate it when women cry. I like it better when you yell at me."

Abby gave him a watery smile. "Thanks."

"For what?" Morton said.

Abby pushed him. "For calling me a woman, what else?"

"I didn't mean it. What I *should* call you is a pain in the butt."

Abby knocked the remaining cement from the edges of

the urn and handed it to Morton. "Hold this. I'll clean off the tombstone so we can sit it back in."

She ran her hand around the gap in the granite. "It's hollow at the bottom."

"Well, duh." Morton rolled his eyes. "How do you think the urn fits in?"

Abby felt inside the opening. "There's something in here." She slid two fingers into the narrow space and extracted a flat parcel. Her heart pounded. "I'm pretty sure people didn't routinely hide packages in their loved one's tombstone. This has to be important. Especially since it's Silas's grave."

"Open it and see." Morton leaned in close. "This is too cool, like being an archeologist."

The bundle, wrapped in dust-dulled oilskin and tied with twine, lay in Abby's palm. "It weighs almost nothing." She noticed her hands shaking, making the package jiggle. "And it's wrapped like Silas's diary pages from the Bible." She blew off the dust and untied the string.

"Maybe we should wait until we get back to your place to open it," Morton said. "You know, to preserve it."

"Who do you think you are, Indiana Jones? When we found Silas's diary I wanted to take my time, and you were miserable. So this time I'm not waiting. If you want to go home, go."

With careful, deliberate movements Abby unwrapped the covering; it cracked at the creases but didn't fall apart. Inside she found another bundle, wrapped in faded, frayed blue-and-white gingham. She peeled it away, revealing a thin stack of old papers, covered with familiar writing.

Abby's words came out in bursts. "It's Silas's handwriting. The edges are torn. It's the missing diary pages. This is what Leticia meant when she wrote about 'a truth beyond the Good Book, in slumber forever.' She left us a clue. I was too dense to figure it out. But now we'll know the secret." She took a deep breath. "What if he really *did* try to kill Lincoln? I can't take it."

Morton patted her arm. "It is what it is. Whatever he did won't change now. Read it."

Abby nodded and cleared her throat. A small gust of wind ruffled the pages. The top sheet flew across the cemetery. She clamped down on the remaining pages. "Morton, get it. Hurry."

Morton sprinted across the uneven ground, planting his black high-top on the paper as it drifted onto another grave. "Got it." He returned it to Abby, breathing hard. "Whew."

"Be careful; it's old and fragile." Abby lifted it from his hand to return to the pile in her lap. "Let's take it back to Bikers' Rest. I don't want to lose it now." She looked up at Morton's smug expression. "Yeah, I know, you already said that."

Abby re-wrapped the diary in the cloth and stored it in Morton's backpack. She replaced the urn on the tombstone, wedging it in place with stones.

On the ride home, two small butterflies circled her bike. The rest of the scenery passed in a blur. She focused on Morton's pack with the diary pages nestled inside, bobbing on his back as he rode ahead of her.

One thought burned in Abby's mind: *Silas has to be innocent.*

THIRTY

"There you are." Lisa greeted Abby as she entered the kitchen, Morton close behind. "I'm not used to you being up and out this early." She glanced at Morton, and then turned back to Abby. "Are we okay?"

"He knows about Jack. I'm working on being okay."

Lisa nodded and cleared her throat. "I have some things for you to do."

"Sure. I'll be down in a little while. Come on, Morton." Abby turned to leave.

"Whoa. Hold on there," Lisa said. "Let's do this in reverse. You help me first, and then do your own thing. That's called a compromise."

"This is important." Abby took another step.

Lisa put her hands on her hips, not a good sign. "I'm sure whatever I have for you to do is much less important, right? Well, wrong. We have this little business, remember? To make it run properly we have to work together. And we want it to run properly for various mundane reasons, like we want to pay the bills, eat, things like that. "

"I get it. And I think compromise is a good thing." Abby nodded. "I'll just run upstairs and do one tiny thing, then I'm all yours. Until lunchtime."

"Discussion over," Lisa said. "Jack tells me you're having lunch together in town. He's taking the truck and leaving in a few minutes. You will go with him and get the groceries on this list, you may have lunch, then come back. I'm sure your 'tiny thing' will be waiting when you get here."

Abby mentally stomped her foot. She had to read Silas's diary. "I want to help. But my hair's a mess, and I have to change clothes. And it makes more sense for me to get the groceries after lunch, so they won't have to sit in the hot truck while we eat. Jack will help me."

"Perhaps I'm not making myself clear. Jack has a schedule to keep. He won't be here much longer. He's getting supplies this morning and has to work this afternoon. Go comb your hair and be outside in five minutes." The buzzer on the clothes dryer went off, and Lisa hurried out of the room.

"Tough break," Morton said.

"Did I ever mention how annoying she is?" Abby frowned. "I'll call you when I get back."

Abby stowed Morton's pack under her bed. The slave shackle clanked as they slid together. How much more complicated could life get? A secret room, slave shackle, Civil War diary, bullets in the middle of the night, Jack's behavior—Abby looked at herself in the mirror. "You are a mess."

She pulled clean jean shorts out of the dresser and rummaged through the drawer for the pale blue, V-necked Hollister T-shirt, her favorite. Jack might be for-real crazy, but she wanted him to like her. She had to learn how to be a sister.

The truck horn blew, echoed by Lisa's shrill voice. "*Abby.*"

Abby grabbed her purse, got the grocery list off the refrigerator on the way through the kitchen, and ran out to the idling truck.

Jack got out of the driver's seat and opened the

passenger door for her. He smiled, but looked wary. "Good morning, *Cherie*."

"Thanks."

"You look good." Jack got in and put the truck in gear. "Your shirt is the same color as our eyes, you know." He grinned. "I'll drop you at the market and pick you up after I finish at the hardware store. Won't take long, then I'll make good on my promise of Chinese for lunch."

The errands took an hour, but they were still the first customers at Chin's China Palace. Abby looked around the room, as if fascinated by the faux Chinese décor. She avoided making eye contact with Jack. When she thought about him as a gorgeous older guy, flirting had been no problem. But she had no clue how to act toward a brother.

Abby ordered sweet-and-sour chicken, and Jack told the waiter, "Same." After the server left, he poured a cup of hot tea and slid it across the table.

"Sweet and sour? Is that just your lunch, or does it describe you?" Abby took a sip of tea, grimacing at the bitter taste.

"I could ask you the same question, sis. I think we all have a little of both in us, don't you?" He poured tea for himself. "Of course, the sweetness is all yours."

Abby turned the lazy susan in the middle of the table, chose a white packet of sugar from a bowl, and added it to her tea. "How's your journal coming?"

"My journal?" Jack said. "Oh, yeah, the journal. Why so curious? It's a journal, which means it's private."

Abby studied the change in him, caused by one innocent question. One minute suave, the next, defensive, as if she'd hit a nerve. Something about the journal must be a big secret.

"It's just a question. You're writing a journal—isn't it about the bike trip?—and you said I'm in it. I'm not asking for your deepest, darkest secret."

The waiter arrived with their order and Jack changed the subject, telling Abby about Chinatown in Toronto and his life at the university. When they finished, the server returned with the check, orange slices, and fortune cookies.

Jack grabbed the check and pushed the dessert tray across the table. "Go ahead, open yours first."

Abby cracked open the cookie and laughed. "Who writes these things? It says: *Never wear your best pants when you go to fight for freedom.* I guess when I become a freedom fighter I'll wear my paint-splattered jeans. It's your turn."

Jack read his fortune in silence. "These are stupid. Let's get out of here. I have one more stop before we get back to Bikers' Rest." He crumpled the small piece of paper, threw it on the table, and walked to the front of the restaurant to pay the bill.

Abby picked up the wrinkled fortune and smoothed it: *You have a curious smile and a mysterious nature.* What about this made Jack so angry? She put the fortune in her pocket and followed him.

"It's going to be at least an hour before I get done in town," Jack said. "I have to get the rest of the supplies to finish the barn roof. Want to come with me?"

"No, hardware isn't at the top of my shopping list. I'll hang out and meet you here." She dropped her head and added, "Thanks for lunch."

"The pleasure is all mine." Jack winked and sauntered down the street.

Now what? Boston had next to nothing to do for an hour. She wandered down the sidewalk.

"Hi there, honey. You're sure a sight for sore eyes."

Abby whipped around. Sitting in front of the salvage shop on an old folding chair she saw a familiar pot-bellied man, sun shining on his scalp, gray fringe of hair framing his face.

She smiled. "Um, hi."

"Remember me? I'm Bill—I own this place. Did you ever find that old Bible?"

"Sorry, I'm really bad with names. And yes, thanks, I

did find the old Bible. So, have a nice day." She turned to cross the street.

"Now hold on there a bit," Bill said. "Do you live out by Morton? I don't know as I seen much of you before the other day."

"My mother bought the old house by the trail, Bikers' Rest, you know about it?"

"Then you must be *the* Abby." Bill smiled around the toothpick in his mouth. "I met your mama, nice lady, and she told me all about what a special daughter she has."

Abby's eyebrows went up. "She did?"

Bill nodded. "Yep. So how do you like living in a piece of local history?"

"You know the history of our house?" Abby sat down next to Bill on an identical folding chair. "I'd love to hear more about it."

"What I know's more gossip than hard fact, honey, but let me see." Bill paused, looked up at the overhang, and blew out a big breath. "Well now, it's been empty for a few years, ever since old Harry Corson passed. He must'a been near ninety before he died, and lived there by himself all that time after cancer got his wife; he was born in that house." Bill looked at her. "I knew him, of course, from around town. Knew the whole family. Small towns are like that."

"His children didn't want the house?" Abby said.

"He and his missus never had kids," Bill said. "Don't know why. Maybe they were too busy taking care of his mother. She lived to a ripe old age, too, right there in the same house."

"His family must have owned it for a long time."

"As near as I can figure, his family lived in that place for quite a spell, way back when. He took his bride housekeeping there, helped keep it up; finally took it over when his own folks both passed."

"So it belonged to the Corson family? Do you know when they bought it?"

Bill leaned his chair back and crossed his arms. "Let me think a spell. I do believe it came down to Harry through his mother's family, the Munroes. Yep, Edna Corson's maiden name would'a been Munroe. She and my mother were in the same sewing circle."

Abby squirmed on the hard chair, as a frisson of excitement ran up her spine. Did this confirm that Silas lived at Bikers' Rest? There couldn't be that many families named Munroe in one small town.

"Do you know exactly how old the house is? Or if there's anything special about it?"

Bill chuckled. "Honey, I know a little bit about a lot of things, but not a lot about much of anything. But let me think. Sometimes old Harry got to bragging after a couple beers, said he had a relative in the Civil War that lived in that very house. I don't rightly know. Far as I recollect, that house weren't no different than any old house around these parts."

"There's a Civil War grave at Dravo Cemetery with the name Silas Munroe. The birth date on the stone is 1843."

Bill nodded. "That would fit. Harry always said five or six generations of his kin lived there. Mebbe he had reason to brag after all."

"If Bikers' Rest is that old, could it have been a stop on the Underground Railroad?" Abby held her breath.

Bill laughed. "Well now, I guess anything's possible, but since Harry never bragged on it, seems unlikely. I'm just glad someone saw the potential in that old place and preserved it. You and your mama have vision."

"Potential, right." Abby experienced a flash of pride for her mother. She checked her watch. "Thanks for the history lesson. If you think of anything else about the house or the Munroe family, let me know."

"Sure thing, honey. Come on back any time, and bring Morton; he's a fine boy. Been takin' real good care of his mama, her being so sick and all."

Abby waved and hurried away. Time to finish Silas'

diary at last—maybe in the very house he left to go to war. Could this be a sign that they had always been meant to be together? Did love exist like a silent river, just waiting to be found? Would her love for Silas create some supernatural way for him to be resurrected? Or were they doomed to never know the fullness of an earthly relationship?

A premonition washed over Abby, making her shiver even in the midday heat. Did she have to die to be one with Silas?

THIRTY-ONE

Abby sat by her bedroom window, sheaf of papers in her lap, staring outside.

"What's the problem?" Morton pulled his chair closer. "We waited all day to read what Silas wrote, and now you're zoning out on me."

"It's a big deal. We know this belonged to him because the cut edges match the other part of the diary we found in the Bible. We're about to discover the mystery of Silas and President Lincoln. We're reading his diary in the house, maybe even the room, where he grew up."

"That's it?" Morton said.

Abby hesitated. "What if we read this and it turns out Silas *did* try to assassinate Lincoln? I don't know if I want to know. It's like a movie with a sad ending; I make up something happy and pretend that's the real story. I already made up an ending for Silas that makes him a hero. I don't want to find out he's a villain after all."

She stopped short of telling Morton that it had become more than solving a mystery. It had become vindication of the man she loved. Even if that love had no basis in reality or explanation. Could she love Silas if he was guilty of such a crime?

"Then I'll read it." Morton grabbed for the pages. "You can ask me what it's about if you ever want to know."

Abby held them out of reach. "Back off. I'll read it."

"I knew I could get you to do it." Morton grinned. "That's called reverse psychology."

Abby rolled her eyes and focused on the diary pages.

"March 12, 1862

Terrible, terrible day! My heart is heavy, that I am witness to these events. I felt so proud when President Lincoln came in the garden. He stands tall, but stooped; more so after this day, I fear. I saluted. He shook my hand, and thanked me—me!—for serving the cause of freedom.

The noon hour being nigh, he bade me farewell soon after. A man jumped out from some bushes. I watched him point a gun at the president, and then heard a bang, so loud my ears was set to ringing. President Lincoln, he fell back unharmed, but the feller with the gun made to shoot agin. I give that evil-doer a shove the likes of which I never done before. People came a-runnin' and all hell broke loose. Soldiers dragged me away before I cud see anything more. I pray President Lincoln lives.

Abby stopped reading. "I knew it. Silas *didn't* do anything wrong. He *is* a hero."

"Something's not right." Morton frowned. "There's more to the story, if Leticia wrote he died 'in shame.'"

"He-did-not-do-it." Abby emphasized each word. "Weren't you listening? You want him to be the bad guy?"

"Abs, come on. History is history. You can't change things that happened already, even if you want to. All you can do is figure them out."

Abby thought about Silas. She knew in the depth of her heart that he had to be innocent. If only she could prove it. She picked up the next page of the diary.

"March 12, 1862

I am asked to serve my country. What shud I do? Ma, if you read these words, I pray you forgive me. I fear I must do what he asks.

The president himself talked to me. He is unharmed. He sez the feller with the gun is a Confederate spy, sneaked in from Canada to do harm to our cause. The Union Generals are afraid if word of this gets out, the Rebs in the South will get all fired up 'cause they came so close to killing our president.

This is the plan. Mr. Lincoln asked me to make a sacrifice for my country. I am to say I tried to kill him, so no one ever knows how close the Rebs come to making good on their threat. I have to go to prison, quiet-like, and wait a spell, like I'm waitin' to get hanged. People will forgit what's happenin' and I kin go somewhere safe until the war is over. Then the newspapers will print the truth. I'll be a real hero, Ma. You will be proud of your son.

So it don't get out, you kin't tell no one, except mebbe Priscilla, who knows what it is to keep a secret. Abigail's constitution is not strong; shield her from this, even if you have to get Twones in on it. Be special careful to keep it from brother William. I wish Pa were still alive so you weren't alone with this, but God will take care of us both.

I love you, Ma. I will write when I kin. Your loving son, Silas Munroe."

Abby hugged the pages to her chest, drawing strength from the words written in Silas's own hand. "It's so not fair. And the date of his death on the tombstone is March 27, 1862. That's only two weeks after he wrote the so-called confession. What happened to him?" A horrible thought struck her. "You don't think they really did hang him, do you? I knew I shouldn't read this. The answers only gave me more questions."

Another thought popped into her mind. Silas couldn't trust his brother; could she trust hers? The Confederate spy came from Canada. Jack came from Canada. Could he be some kind of a spy? Ridiculous. Right?

"I don't know what happened," Morton said. "I never heard about any of this, not in school, not on TV, not in books … nowhere. Sounds like you're a lot tougher than the first Abigail, like we'll ever know her identity."

Abby experienced a twinge at thinking about an Abigail who had known Silas during his life. Friend? *Girlfriend?* She shook off what she refused to identify as jealousy for someone long dead. The mere thought of Silas hurting and in pain seemed like too much to consider. Would he tell her the rest of the story? Or would she never see him now that his innocence had been proven?

She shook her head. "Did they have conspiracies back then? Would the government really have silenced him once and for all? This sucks. And now we'll never know what really happened. Leticia must have been so sad, not to just lose her son in the war, but to have this huge secret to keep."

"I wonder what the deal is with his brother William," Morton said. "It's freaky that Silas fought for the North, and his brother sympathized with the South."

"One more thing Leticia had to worry about."

Crack.

Abby squealed. "That's what I heard last night. Jack must be shooting the gun again."

Morton laughed. "Abs, you need to chill. Someone's setting off firecrackers, it happens every year at this time."

"At this time?"

"Duh, Fourth of July's coming up, remember? Fireworks at Point State Park, hot dogs, flags lining the streets, everyone wearing red, white, and blue."

"That means Jack's leaving soon." Tears sprung to Abby's eyes.

"Then I'll be celebrating for sure. He's scary."

"Like you know anything." Abby turned away. "Later, okay?"

"Yeah, well, he's a moron, even if he is your brother. I'm glad I'm an only child." Morton left Abby alone.

She looked out her side window at the barn. New shingles covered the roof, a dull matte black on top of the faded red barn wood siding. Jack did exactly what he said he would. But what about all the times he acted like a psycho? Were they really that bad? It had to do with his brother's death. Just like she had been a bitch every time her dad's passing came up.

Softer images came into Abby's mind, superimposed over the hard-edged ones. Jack had been sensitive and caring, too, and Lisa trusted him. She wanted to love him, wanted to have no reservations about her own flesh and blood brother.

Abby envisioned his light blue eyes and strong, calloused hands. Moments, like images on the computer, flipped through her mind: Jack's golden hair, shining like her own; tears of grief in his eyes; his hand ruffling her hair; Jack's face buried on her shoulder; their shared sameness in Lisa.

As if emerging from her thoughts, she watched Jack walk to the barn, sweat glistening on his back; he reached up and wiped it off with his T-shirt. He seemed to sense her presence and turned to face the house. Squinting, he covered his eyes with one hand and looked directly at Abby with a smile and a small wave. She pressed one hand, palm-out, on the glass.

"Abigail." Hands settled on her shoulders, warm, real hands. "Now you know."

At that moment Abby experienced a connection with Silas so powerful she had to hold onto the window frame to keep from falling. The thought of ever saying good-bye to him sent tears down her cheeks. She turned to face him.

Aside from a slight wavering, Silas could be alive. He swept the hat from his head and pushed the hair out of his eyes. "Been a long time since I wooed a lady. I best clean up a bit, or you will be sending me to the woodshed."

"I'm not sending you anywhere. Unless I can come with you." Abby faltered. "*Can* you stay with me?"

"I don't rightly know. But I am with you now." He closed his eyes and leaned into Abby, pressing his soft mouth against hers.

She returned his kiss, as if she could hold onto him with her lips for a lifetime. His arms surrounded her, both solid and fluid at the same time, their movement enticing her to want even more.

Silas broke the contact. He looked full into her face. "Mr. Whitman said, 'What is that you express in your eyes? It seems to me more than all the print I have read in my life.'"

"If my eyes are saying 'I love you,' then they're telling you what I want you to know." Abby hated to break the moment. But the need to understand overcame her reluctance. "How did you die? Who was Abigail?"

Silas nodded, solemn and still. "The first Abigail sure did love me, and I loved her. But she died because of me. As for the end of my story … " He shrugged. "You'll mebbe git that for yourself—or mebbe not. Does it matter?"

"Nothing matters. Except for you. Me. Us. We matter because in your death you've given me new life."

Silas swept Abby into his arms. He floated across the room, carrying her to the bed and placing her very gently on it. His form settled next to hers, pressing in close. "You are my reward, Abigail. It ain't a soldier thing to say, but you make my soul glad."

"Tell me we can be together forever."

Silas sighed. "Mr. Whitman says, 'Happiness not in another place, but this place; not for another hour, but this hour.'"

A great sense of peace came over Abby, tempered with vibrations that seemed to move through every cell in her body. Silas became light and airy, melding with her as his essence surrounded her. Total well-being flowed through Abby's veins, pulsating as every beat of Silas's heart synced with hers. It left her sated and drowsy.

"Abigail. You are my one and only love. Forevermore."

Abby awoke in her bed and reached for Silas. Her hand

touched empty air. She expected to feel a sense of loss. Instead, hope infused her with purpose. "Silas? Come back to me when you can. *Please*. Come back to me."

The answer she received, silence, did not surprise her.

"Abby, dinner." Lisa called from downstairs.

With a deep sigh, Abby patted the rumpled quilt, got up, and looked in the mirror. Nothing had changed. Everything had changed. She and Silas had been happy together "this hour." It had to be enough. For now.

She ran a brush through her hair and made her way to the kitchen, sliding into the chair across from her mother. "I'm not very hungry. We had Chinese for lunch."

"Eat what you want," Lisa said. "It's just nice to have your company. We've both been so busy since we moved. I bought some used DVD's for the guests, and there's at least one you'd like. Let's watch a movie later, after I run over to Mrs. Blank's with some strawberries I picked up for her."

"Sure. I have a couple things to do after dinner anyway." She thought about Jack's story about her dad's hunting rifle. "Did Dad ever get a deer?"

"What do you mean, 'get a deer?' Your father didn't hunt," Lisa said. "At least not when I knew him."

"Then why'd he have a hunting rifle?"

"As far as I know, he didn't own any weapons. Even if he did have one, there's no way he'd have kept it with you in the house. He was a stickler for safety first."

"So you're telling me Dad never owned a gun, and we didn't bring one with us when we moved?"

"That's right." Lisa frowned. "Why?"

"Morton got into talking about hunting, and I thought Dad used to hunt, that's all. I assumed he owned a rifle." Abby felt the creeping fingers of distrust move up her spine.

"Well, no guns here. It's not like we need one for self-defense, and I have no idea how to use one even if we did. Want some pie?"

"No thanks. I'll clean up the kitchen while you're out."

Lisa raised her eyebrows, but merely said, "Thanks, honey. See you later."

Abby leaned both hands against the sink, inhaling the lemony aroma of the dish detergent, an everyday fragrance as common as dinner. She hung her head. The memory of the sharp, metallic odor from behind the barn, and the smell of a fired gun, took its place

Jack had lied. He outright lied, again. She thought about lies. Silas lied to save his country, even at the cost of hurting his family. Why did Jack lie? Not to save the nation, that's for sure; he didn't even seem to like the United States. But there must be a reason, a good reason. And if she could discover what Silas lied about 150 years earlier, she could find out what Jack lied about today.

THIRTY-TWO

"Jack." Abby made an effort to look silly and unconcerned; she rested one hand on her hip and flipped the hair away from her face with the other. "Hey, what's up? Where are you going?"

Pausing at the door of the barn, Jack held his bike steady. "What's it look like? I need to get some riding time in, or I won't be in shape for the trip to D.C." He smiled. "Will you miss me, *Cherie*? I will be desolate without you."

Abby smiled. "You're so full of it. I came to ask you a favor." She walked close and looked up at him through her lashes.

Jack leaned against the barn door. "A favor, eh? What kind of favor could my pretty sister want on this warm summer evening?"

"You know how much I miss my dad. And how important his things are to me." She paused, dredging up helplessness to make him feel important humoring his brainless little sister.

Jack sneaked a glance at his watch. "Right, sure; what can I do for you?" His fingers drummed against the handlebars.

"You told me about shooting my dad's hunting rifle

last night. I want you to teach me how to load it and shoot it. Lisa's not here, it's the perfect time. Please?" Abby opened her eyes wide and smiled.

Jack's eyes shifted left to right before focusing on Abby. "Not a good idea. Someone could get hurt, and I don't want it to be you. Take some lessons at a firing range, and then when you know what you're doing, try out the rifle. I have to go." He started to push the bike past her.

Abby grabbed the handlebar. "Not so fast. If you don't want me to shoot, at least show me how to hold the unloaded rifle, you know, let me get a feel for it. I'll grab it; it'll only take a minute." She paused, and couldn't keep the edge from her voice. "Unless there's a problem. Is there a problem, Jack?"

Jack leaned the bike against the barn and returned to take Abby's hand. "I didn't want to tell you, and I know you're going to be very mad at me, but there is no rifle."

"No? Then what were you shooting last night?"

"Last night there was a rifle, today there is not." Jack shrugged an apology. "In town today I sold it, for Lisa. That's one of the errands I had to do. She wanted to get rid of it, and didn't want you to be upset. I'm sorry, but don't be mad at her. She's only trying to protect you."

Abby's stomach cramped, and she experienced a sense of hollowness down to her toes. Her brother: a liar who shot guns at night, a liar who lived in her house, a liar who should be the closest person in the world to her. What else had he lied about?

She pulled her hand away from Jack, repulsed after this latest evidence of his betrayal. "Go ride your stupid bike. Take a good, long ride. I can't wait until you ride out of here for good." She turned on her heel and marched back to the house.

"Sorry, *Cherie*." Jack's bike tires crunched over the gravel.

Abby watched him ride away, waited five minutes, and

then ran to the barn. "Let's see what you've been up to *Jacques*. I'm guessing you've been a bad boy."

Once inside the barn, Abby didn't know where to start. Her dad would have said to start at the beginning. Jack had to have a gun hidden somewhere. She would find it. She surveyed the interior of the barn, wiping sweaty hands on her thighs. The places to investigate seemed endless, and she didn't know how long Jack would be gone.

For ten minutes Abby searched, stall by stall, storage bin by storage bin, cupboard by cupboard. She ran her hands behind things hanging on the walls and between boards, steeling herself to ignore thoughts of spiders, mice, or snakes. Behind a grain trough and the wall she felt something soft. It couldn't be a gun, but it didn't belong. Grasping it with two fingers, she pulled; a stained red cloth emerged. She sniffed it; metallic, oily.

She flashed back to the stormy night when Jack returned from Pittsburgh with a red bundle he protected with his hat. One mystery solved. He went downtown to buy a gun. But why? Why did a long-distance biker need a gun? Protection on the trail? Possible, not probable. And although Jack would never tell her, his journal might.

She looked at her watch and hurried to the rear stall. The smooth floor gave no evidence of which board hid the lockbox. Scuffing at the dirt and hay revealed seamed wood, nothing else. "It has to be here. I saw him hiding it." She glanced at her watch again. "This is taking too long. And I'm talking to myself."

After rolling her aching head in a circle to lessen the tension, she backed up and studied the area. Getting down on her hands and knees, she brushed a small space clean and noticed one board not nailed down. She pressed the end, and it came loose.

Abby slid her hand in the opening and pulled out a small, black metal box; it appeared new, even though covered with dirt. On one side a shiny latch connected to a round keyhole, no key. A search of the hiding space revealed nothing, and the box wouldn't open. The key had to be somewhere, unless he wore it around his neck.

Sitting back on her heels, she gazed around the barn. Nothing but stored junk, bikes, tools. Of course. A hammer and screwdriver would bust it open in a hot second. Damn the consequences *and* Jack. From the tool box by the barn door Abby grabbed the hammer, a large screwdriver,. and a pry bar. She checked her watch again, and in doing so spilled the remainder of the tools on the floor. She didn't waste time picking them up, but returned to the rear stall, inserted the screwdriver under the hasp, and reached for the hammer.

"What the—who's there?" Jack's voice, strident and angry, filled the barn.

Abby froze for a split second, heart racing, breath caught in her chest. She set aside the tools, inserted the lockbox in its hiding place, and reached to replace the floorboard. The pry bar clattered across the floor and came to rest under the small nightstand.

"Come out of there, or I'm coming in to get you." The strident sound of Jack's angry voice came closer, accompanied by the whisper of his bike tires.

"*Pop. Hiss …*"

"What the hell?" Jack moved closer, his footfalls a soft undercurrent.

Working fast, Abby replaced the floorboard. She kicked dirt and straw over the area, picked up the hammer and screwdriver, and dove for the floor beside a ragged hole in the wall of the stall.

"Abby? What are you doing? Why didn't you answer me?" The veins on Jack's neck stood out, pulsating against his red, angry face.

Abby sat back against the stall and took a deep breath. "Oh, Jack, it's you. I heard someone come in and got scared. With Lisa away and you out on the trail, it could have been anyone. Don't scare me like that."

Jack pursed his lips. "You didn't recognize my voice?

That's strange. And what are you doing back here with those tools?" He walked close to Abby and squatted next to her, so close his breath made the hair dance away from her forehead. "I want the truth."

"*You* want the truth?" Abby bit back the retort. The time would come to confront him, but not now. "It's lame, I guess, but I wanted to surprise you. I thought I'd fix this hole in the stall while you were out. It's one thing you wouldn't have to worry about before you leave. I know you have a lot on your mind getting ready for the trip to Washington and the bike rally. I didn't mean to cause any trouble."

"You made things worse. I popped a bike tire running over the nails you spilled with the tools. Now I have to replace a tire along with everything else. Don't help me." He stared at Abby.

Abby gave him a weak smile, got up, dusted off her shorts, and sidled past Jack, careful to leave space between them. She picked up the fallen supplies by the barn door, noticing how her shaking hands made the tools rattle, hoping he wouldn't think anything about it.

Jack wheeled his disabled bike past Abby and pointed a slender finger at her. "Do not make me mad. You wouldn't like it. And I really prefer you aren't involved in things that are best left alone. Believe it or not, I want to protect you." He set the bike against the wall and watched while Abby finished with the toolbox and returned to the house.

Once inside, Abby locked the door and ran to her room. She peeked out the window, careful to stay out of sight. Jack stood by the barn door, hands in pockets, staring at the house, at her window. Menace surrounded him like a noxious cloud.

"I don't like feeling afraid in my own home," Abby whispered, realizing that's just what this house had become, her home. "You better not make *me* mad, Jack. *You* wouldn't like it."

THIRTY-THREE

"You went to bed early last night," Lisa said over her shoulder as she deposited the breakfast dishes in the sink.

"Sorry. I know we had a movie date, but I got sleepy." Abby paused. "I really wish we had spent the time together."

"You just made me so happy." Lisa's smile beamed. "But you do remember I'll be out of town for two days, right? We'll catch up when I get back from the seminar."

Abby racked her brain for any clue to what her mother meant. "Um, a seminar ..."

"I'm leaving tomorrow morning for the Inn Keepers' Seminar in Philadelphia. Abby, I told you all about this." She shook her head. "I'll be gone overnight—Mrs. Blank will stay here with you—that's why there aren't any guests but the "No Vacancy" sign is posted. Any of this sound familiar? And even though Jack's around, I'll feel better with an adult here."

"The seminar, right." Abby knew she'd been distracted, but not that she'd totally tuned out Lisa.

"I'll be busy today getting ready because I want to be on the road early. But since we have the place to ourselves, it's a good time to get some work done. I want you to clean out the attic, and get it organized. Make a pile of things for the trash, one for the thrift shop, and another to keep. We'll go through it together when I get back. It will give you something constructive to do."

Abby glanced out the window into brilliant sunshine and saw Jack putting his bike in the back of the truck. "It's way too nice to spend the day in the attic. I'll do it the next time it rains." With Lisa busy and Jack away, she could grab Jack's journal and figure out what went on in his brain.

"No, you'll do it today." Lisa put both hands on her hips. "Just about the time I think we can have an adult conversation, you revert to this. I'm busy, you've done very little around here, and it won't take that long. Our stuff will be easy and the junk leftover from previous owners will most likely go in the trash. You should be done by lunchtime if you get moving."

"It goes both ways." Abby glared. "About the time *I* think we can have a real conversation, *you* decide to act like a mother."

"I am a mother, *your* mother, which also makes me the boss. Get busy. And by the way, I like being your mother, even when it isn't much fun."

Abby's annoyance melted. "I think I might like it, too."

The screen door opened and slammed shut. "Hey, how's it hangin'?" Morton clomped into the kitchen. "Am I too late for breakfast, Mrs. Whitney?"

"Your timing is perfect, as usual. There's fresh fruit on the table; help yourself." With a smile for Abby, she bustled out of the room.

"Whoa. You guys have a serious talk or what?" Morton looked at the fruit bowl and pulled some M&M's from his pocket. "Breakfast of champions. Come on, let's hit the bike trail before it gets too hot."

"I have to clean the attic. You go ahead."

"Okay. Later." Morton got a bottle of water from the refrigerator, put it back, and pulled out a soda.

"Or, you could help me clean the attic, and then we'll ride together. You know how much I like to ride with you, right?"

"I hate anything with the word "clean" in it."

"I'll pack a lunch." Abby showed him a pan of brownies. "Peanut butter and jelly, chips, brownies …"

"Yeah, you got me. I know how to take a bribe." Morton gulped the soda, tried to crush the can, threw it at the trash, missed, and sighed. "I gotta get in shape."

An hour later three piles had begun to take shape in the hall outside the attic. Abby dusted off her hands. "I can't believe we moved so much junk. It would have been easier to throw this stuff out before we moved it, instead of moving it twice." She thought back to packing up the old house, the feeling that leaving it meant leaving her dad behind. "I guess neither of us felt like going through everything then." She dragged out a box labeled *Adam Whitney*, running her hands over the name. Another lifetime. She missed him … but the pain didn't hurt quite as much.

"Abs, check it out." Morton turned with a flourish.

Abby laughed. "It's you, not. Where did that come from?"

Morton modeled a hat, tilted to one side. The rigid black felt turned up in a rolled brim on the edges, old-fashioned and out of place balanced on his shaggy hair.

"I moved that old lantern and found a hat box with this inside. Can I keep it?"

"Check with Lisa, she's into antiques. What else is back there? The hat isn't ours, and neither is this." Abby moved the lantern out of harm's way and stared at the glass globe, searching for a glimpse of Silas; no face looked back at her. Maybe now that they had been … together … he would always be with her in a real way. She hoped.

"Hey, wait a sec." Morton picked up the lantern, holding onto the large brass ring on the top. "The first time you forced me to be up here I didn't get it. But whoa, check this out."

"Yep. Old lantern. Same as before." Abby rolled her eyes.

Morton lifted the lantern. "No. Well, yes, but there's more. Abolitionists used these as a signal for slaves traveling the Underground Railroad."

"Very cool history lesson, professor. But we have work to do." Abby stooped to fit under the sloping area of the roof and peered into the shadowed space beneath the eaves. A slight glint caught her eye, and she stretched to reach it. The delicate, sticky touch of a cobweb stuck to her arm. "Yuck, this is spider central back here. I hate spiders." Her hand connected to a large, ridged object. "Morton, help me pull this out."

"I might not fit in there." Morton glanced at Abby. "All right, I'll make myself fit." He sucked in his stomach and crawled behind her.

Together they dragged a filthy wicker trunk from the recesses of the attic. Abby lifted the tarnished brass handle.

"This trunk is ancient."

Morton grabbed at the top layer and pulled out a dress, blue and white checked gingham, with a long skirt and attached apron.

"Be careful. That's beyond old." Chills crept up Abby's arms. "Maybe it belonged to Leticia. It matches the fabric that covered Silas's diary pages."

"You're dreamin'," Morton said. "I know Bill said the Munroes built this house, but that's a long time ago. Everyone dressed in this kind of stuff back in the day."

"And this trunk has been hidden back there for a long time." Abby went to her dad's box and pulled out a history book on the Civil War, flipping through until she found the page she wanted. "I saw this the last time I came up here. It's just an old scene, but look at the women's dresses; they're the same style as this one. It may not be Leticia's, but it's the right era."

With great care, Abby went through the remainder of

the trunk, finding various pieces of old clothing including baby bonnets, cotton gloves, and high-button shoes.

Morton took the shoes. "Hey, they wore high tops, just like me." He held his sneaker next to the cracked leather boot. "Well, sort of. Abs, you aren't looking."

Instead, Abby stared into the bottom of the trunk. She lifted out a rectangular wooden box with a slanted top. When she opened the hinged lid, an old pen and a small glass bottle rolled forward. The pen had a wooden handle and pointed, metal end. The bottle's interior appeared coated with a dry black substance.

"That's an old portable writing desk. Bill had one at his store."

Abby picked up the pen. "Just think; this might be the very place Leticia wrote the letter I found in the Bible. Sweet." She sat down on the floor and pulled a sheaf of paper from the narrow drawer on the bottom of the desk. "It's like the paper she used, but in better shape. There must be twenty sheets of it in here." She counted the papers and stopped near the bottom of the stack. A familiar sensation washed through her, and she shivered.

"You're cold?" Morton said. "It must be a million degrees in here." He swiped his sweaty forehead then hung his tongue out like a panting dog.

"Silas? Are you here?" Abby waited and was rewarded with a gentle caress across her shoulders. She smiled.

"Abs. Seriously? What in the freaking world is going on?"

Abby considered brushing Morton off, yet he *believed* in ghosts. "This isn't easy. You don't have to believe me, but promise you won't have me committed."

Morton crossed his heart.

"I'm in love with … Silas … and he's a ghost. And he's here with us now."

"That makes me so mad. It's just not possible, nope, can't be true." Morton peered into the corners of the attic.

"But you told me ghosts are real. And then when I

agree with you, you freak?"

"Abs, think about it. I've been hunting for a ghost my whole life and zip, nada, nothing. You arrive—without any equipment or even any belief, and you hang out with a spirit enough to fall in love?" Morton sighed. "Why you and not me?"

A shimmer lit the space next to Abby. Silas materialized and saluted Morton.

Morton's jaw sagged. He glanced at Abby and stood straighter. "Yo, General."

"Private First Class Silas Munroe, sir."

"What's your secret?" Morton's eyes lit up. "Now we can figure out what happened to you."

Silas's image wavered. "No, I ain't able to do that. I made a promise." He kissed Abby's cheek and vanished.

Morton ran his hands through the empty air beside Abby. "Did that just happen?"

Abby sighed. "I don't know when he's going to appear or when he's going to go. You're the expert. Can he ever stay in this world with me? Can we have a future together?"

"No clue." Morton took his glasses off and polished them on the hem of his shirt. "But jeez, Abs, this is the coolest thing that's ever happened, like, in the history of mankind. But I guess if you really love him, it kinda sucks."

"Yeah. Big time." Abby stopped the thoughts tumbling through her brain. There were no answers to eternity, not from Morton, not from her, and not even from Silas.

She refocused and went back to the writing desk. "There's a letter at the bottom, but it's hard to read in this light." She set the blank pages back in the box, and the box back in the trunk, then went to her room. Morton sat beside her as she read.

New Store June 1862
I am very sick. Doc Stevens don't think he kin do nothing. I get

weaker every day. The pain in my stomagh gets worse. Auntie Winifred come from back east to help me. I kin't even get her special beef tea in me.

I am too weak to lite the lantern and hang it on the hitching post, and fear the runaways who seek shelter here wil not find it in these parts. It hurts my heart, even mor than the sickness hurts my stomagh.

Slavery is wrong. How is it William kin fite for the Rebs? Priscilla bandages the slaves who come here hurtin.' Silas died fur freedom. This life I leave is a strange one. But they are my children all, and I have loved them.

I wish to set the record rite, before I go to be with my sweet Silas and my dear departed husband. The war goes on, will it ever end? I kin't die peaceful-like with folks thinking Silas did wrong, but I kin't tell no one, neither. I promised Silas to keep his secret, and I always keep my promises, 'specially to him.

"What?" Morton edged closer. "What happened?"

"I don't know. It ends there. We still don't know the secret." Her shoulders slumped forward.

"Just when I thought we had it nailed," Morton said. "It's even getting to me."

"We do know this was a stop on the Underground Railroad. That means the room downstairs did hide runaway slaves, and the shackle is real. Maybe we'll have to be content with that much." She held the paper with Letitia's handwriting close to her chest. "She must have died before she could finish this letter. And Silas won't divulge his secret, not even now."

"Yeah, sad stuff." Morton stood up. "I'll haul the junk downstairs, then I'm going home. I've had enough excitement for one day."

Abby organized the belongings in the attic, taking Leticia's letter to her room to store in the Bible. Her movements were slow and mechanical. She longed for Silas but had no way to reach out to him. And to prove his innocence meant discovering information that didn't seem to exist.

Passion morphed into despair as Abby pondered the possibilities.

THIRTY-FOUR

Abby woke with a headache to the snare-drum sound of rain on the roof and the stickiness of humidity-dampened sheets. She groaned. Lisa would drive to Philadelphia today for her seminar, leaving Mrs. Blank—and her need to be in control of everything—in charge.

It took a full minute, but Abby sat straight up in bed. Silas had haunted her dreams, but she didn't remember if he had been with her or if she'd conjured his presence out of desire and need. She dressed and went downstairs.

"Abby, honey, I'm going soon." Lisa fluttered around the kitchen and put yet another note up on the refrigerator door. "All the numbers where you can reach me are here, including the hotel. My cell phone will be off during the break-out sessions, but the front desk can reach me."

The phone rang. She began running her hands through her hair when she hung up. "Mrs. Blank called. Her six-year-old grandson got sick, and she has to watch him until her daughter gets off work. He's got a fever, so she doesn't want to bring him out in the rain. Will you be okay until dinnertime? I hate to leave you here, but ..."

"Lisa, chill." Abby rolled her eyes. "I used to babysit for other kids before, well, at the old house. And I stayed alone a lot when Dad worked. I can call Mrs. Blank if I need something. And Jack is close by."

"Yes, of course. I better leave before traffic gets too bad on the Turnpike." Lisa tucked a lock of hair behind Abby's ear. "Sometimes it's like I'm in a time warp; in my mind you're still a toddler. I so regret all those lost years. You have to know that." She hugged Abby then held her at arms' length. "Have I told you how much I love you?"

The right answer, "I love you, too," stuck in Abby's throat. She focused on getting the information she needed. "Could we talk, just for a minute?"

Lisa snuck a glance at the clock over the stove, but smiled and sat at the kitchen table.

Abby didn't know where to start. She also had no one else to ask. "Do you think there's one special person for everyone? Like, two people who have always been meant to be together since the beginning of time? Even beyond the grave?"

"I don't exactly understand your questions. But of course we continue to love people, even after they've passed."

"But what about ... ghosts? Do they, I mean, can they love someone who isn't dead? And can a live person have a relationship with someone who died a long time ago?" Even to Abby, this sounded bizarre.

"Ghosts?" Lisa stared. "I never thought you were someone who believed in the supernatural."

"It's an academic question. Something I read on a blog."

Lisa chuckled. "Oh, well, you know the internet. Sounds like a blogger who had a few too many drinks." She snuck a look at her watch. "I love talking to you, but can we pick this up when I get back? I should be on the road. And don't forget to keep your phone charged."

"Sure. And thanks for listening; I appreciate it." Abby didn't shrink when Lisa grasped her hand. When she returned the squeeze, the chill poison of bitterness drained from her heart. Maybe they would end up having a real mother-daughter relationship after all.

As Lisa drove away in the bleak morning light Abby waved, following the tail lights on the truck until it rounded the bend and disappeared in the gloom. She had no idea what to do next. Silas had become her entire world. He had to be vindicated of any wrongdoing. But how?

After searching through the Bible and the attic again, Abby had no idea where else to look for answers. The rain made it impossible to go out, so she resigned herself to taking the day off and letting her subconscious work on the problem. After a restless morning of TV talk shows, a boring book, and a homemade chocolate milkshake for lunch, Abby didn't know what to do. She called Morton and got no answer, then opened the refrigerator to forage for a snack.

The back door opened. "Abby? Can I come in?" Jack stood in the kitchen doorway.

"You seem to be in already."

"Don't be that way." Jack produced his killer smile. "You know I'm leaving soon, probably tomorrow or the day after. I don't want it to be like this between us. You've been an only child all your life, but I did have a brother. Siblings don't always get along, but they do get over it, and they always stick together. Even though I have to go, I hope we can see each other again, get to be closer. I know it's possible."

His sincerity sounded so believable. Abby suspected she had begun to love her brother, in spite of his lies. She didn't know if the shared DNA made any difference. But her unconditional acceptance of him, despite his moods and bad behavior, went beyond superficial ties. Maybe it qualified as family. And she longed for that kind of relationship.

"Apology, if that's what it is, accepted. Now if you don't mind, I have things to do."

"Of course, *Cherie*. I just brought a little going away gift, for Morton and for you."

Abby raised one eyebrow and peeked in the paper bag he handed her. "This is really nice. It's the biggest bag of M&M's I've ever seen. He'll like it."

Jack handed her a wrapped box. The colorful paper, covered with red roses and tied with red satin ribbons, looked beautiful. "I recall your dad liked roses, and you do, too."

Abby took it. "You remember me telling you that? I can't believe it."

"Open it. I had it made especially for you."

Abby undid the ribbons and removed the paper. "Ahh—it's my favorite picture of my dad and me."

"I had it enlarged and framed," Jack said. "You showed it to me one day, and it seemed so sweet in black-and-white, with the little *'Daddy loves Abby'* on the bottom. I thought you might hang it in your room, so he could be part of the household again."

"Oh, Jack." Abby reached out and, without even thinking about it, snuggled into Jack's arms, crying on his shoulder. The pain from her father, from moving, from Silas, even from Jack, came pouring out in wrenching sobs, followed by quiet gulps, and then hiccups. She moved away from him, wiping her drippy nose on the back of her hand. "I don't know how to thank you."

"You already did thank me." Jack handed her a tissue from his pocket. "No matter what, we're connected." He ran his thumb down her wet cheek, smoothing away the tears. "Your father can't come back, and neither can my brother, but at least we've found each other. And maybe this little gift will make up for my bad moods and even for selling your father's rifle."

Abby stiffened at hearing his continued lie, especially after sharing her deepest feelings with him. "Yes, well, thanks."

Jack's eyebrows went up, but he nodded. "I'm taking

the bike out to see how it goes in the rain. I'll see you later. Okay, sis?"

Abby nodded and hugged the photograph to her chest, as if it could shield her from getting hurt again … as if it was a talisman that could protect her dad, Silas, and maybe even her brother.

She watched Jack duck off the porch into the rain, and then she set the picture on the counter. Waiting until he rode down the path onto the bike trail, she pulled on a yellow slicker.

"Time to read that journal. I *will* figure you out, I promise. And I always keep my promises. I'm going to find out if you're the good guy you want me to think you are, or someone else entirely."

She ran through puddles to the background of geese honking as they flew over the river. The rain poured out of the sky, heavier than she expected. The slicker offered limited protection. She slid open the barn door, ducking inside. Kitty appeared from behind her dad's bike, mewed, and wrapped around Abby's ankles.

"Yes, you're a good kitty. But now is not the time."
The pungent odor of dirt permeated the gloomy barn, made muddy at the entrance from rain leeching in. She plucked a hammer and screwdriver from the toolbox. Going directly to the rear stall, she removed the floorboard and dragged the lockbox from its hiding place.

Kitty sniffed at the hole and curled up on Jack's blanket.

Inserting the screwdriver under the lock, Abby gave it one sharp hit with the hammer. It popped open. She removed Jack's journal, replaced the lockbox in the floor, re-sealed the board, scattered hay on the floor, and moved to the open end of the stall. She could hide the journal in her rain gear if he returned early. Or put it back, and he would never know she'd been there.

Abby remained standing in case she had to move fast. She squinted in the gloom but was afraid to use a light.

Opening Jack's black leather binder, she scanned pages about college life, the trip, supplies needed, and finally her. "So he thinks I'm a 'cute kid.' That's what I went through all this trouble to find out?"

Crammed into the back pocket of the notebook she found a stack of envelopes, all addressed to Jack in care of Bikers' Rest. The return address, from Erie, listed Basile Charpentier—likely his father—as the sender. It would be wrong to read his personal mail. But maybe it would offer some explanation for his erratic behavior.

Abby checked the postmarks on the letters; they were rubber-banded together in order, first to last. She chose the one on top, the first letter Jack had received. After reading a few initial remarks, she closed her eyes. Her hands shook, her body became cold and weak, and she let out a ragged breath. She re-read the page in front of her, then tore open each envelope and leafed through the sheets, picking out random paragraphs.

You are going to kill President Keller. He deserves to die, and you will most certainly give him what he deserves. I know how hard this is for you, Jacques, but we've been over and over it, and this is the only way.

Your brother did not deserve to die, like some rabid dog, in a miserable, God-forsaken desert. Keller sent Etienne there, now I'm sending you to avenge your brother's death. You must be a machine of revenge, not just for Steve, but for all the soldiers who have been slaughtered. I know you don't want to do this, but I also know you will not disappoint me.

The American Secret Service agents think they can protect the commander-in-chief. What a joke. They watch the airports. They patrol the subways and the cars and the trains. They surround him with guards and give him bulletproof vests to wear. Then they let him loose at a crowded bike rally, a photo-op to boost his popularity. Who will look for an assassin on a bicycle? Especially when it's the grieving brother of a fallen soldier.

I will be on the dais waiting for you to arrive. When you do, the honor guard will escort both of us to shake the president's filthy hand, in Etienne's honor. If you are able to pass me the gun, I will do the work myself. But since that is unlikely, I put all my hopes on you, my son. Be a man, look Keller in the eye, and tell him it is for your brother's honor. Then pull the trigger and run. I will do my best to protect you, but in the end we both must do what we must do. And Etienne will find peace at last.

Abby shuddered, nightmare and normal colliding with a roar inside her head. "No, no, no, this can't be true. What am I going to do?" She looked up as Kitty growled, her back arched and her fur on end.

"Do, *Cherie*? I'll tell you what you are going to do." Jack's voice, a sibilant whisper of menace and loathing, breathed in Abby's ear. "You should have left it alone. You should have stayed out of it. I thought you knew the pain of losing someone you love. I thought we understood each other. I wanted to protect you, but you had to interfere."

As Abby turned, Jack pressed the cold, hard barrel of a pistol against her temple.

"Please, don't shoot me or the president. You're *my* brother, I love you. *Please.*"

"I don't want to hurt you. But Steve and my father were my entire life until now. You're too late to fit into my heart like they do." Jack paused and tucked the hair behind Abby's ear, rough, not the gentle touch of Silas. "Believe me, I never wanted to hurt anyone. It's justice, pure and simple. You understand; I know you do. If someone sent your father to his death, you would do the same."

"No, Jack, you have to stop. Your father must be out of his mind with grief to ask you to do something like this. It's not justice, it's murder. You know better. We can burn the letters, and no one will ever see them. You can stay here with Lisa and me, we'll be a family; this will all be over. We'll get help for your father. Please, please, please …" Abby's throat constricted, capturing her breath even as Jack had captured her body. "Please" seemed to be the only word she had left that made sense.

Jack cocked his head and pursed his lips, as if considering her plea. He lowered the gun and stuck it in the waistband of his bike shorts.

Abby bowed her head and released a deep, shuddering sigh. He had listened to reason. Everything would be okay.

But instead of walking away, Jack grabbed her by the wrists and wound duct tape around them.

"What are you doing? That hurts. Jack, *no*."

Pulling a red bandana from his pocket, Jack gagged Abby. Her words changed to whimpers, and she shook her head back and forth repeatedly.

Kitty launched herself at Jack, claws extended, but he swatted her away with ease.

He picked up the pry bar Abby had dropped on the floor and brandished it. "This is over for you, *Cherie. Au revoir*—good-bye."

An intense, sharp pain exploded on the back of Abby's head. Bright stars danced behind her eyelids as she slid into unconsciousness.

THIRTY-FIVE

Dark. Very, very dark.

Abby blinked her eyes open, and then closed them again. Her body tried floating into even deeper blackness, and she welcomed it; sharp pounding pain in her head brought her back. Moving from side to side intensified the pain, and the bright stars returned, then faded, as she drifted into a restless stupor.

She dreamed of Jack, sitting across from her in a Chinese restaurant that looked like the porch at Bikers' Rest. He held out a bouquet of roses to her in his left hand, a gun in his right. He wore a T-shirt that read "Big Brother."

"Sorry, *Cherie*," he said, a tender smile on his face. "You are sweet and sour, don't you see? I only want what is right, for I have a curious smile and a mysterious nature. Are you wearing your best pants as you go to fight for freedom? The fortunes from our cookies told the tale."

Dream-Jack laughed, and his face morphed into a demon face, pale, frightful, and deathly. He shot the gun, and roses came from the barrel. He lifted the bouquet and a bullet traveled across the table in slow motion, aimed at Abby's heart.

"Abigail ..."

Abby moaned and struggled to awaken, to respond to Silas's call. Once she opened her eyes, she wished for sleep again, remembering the gun at her head and the pain in her heart.

She peered into the dark. Not a speck of light pierced the gloom, as if her eyes were closed. She brought her bound hands to her face and touched her eyelids. Open. *"Silas? I need you. Please."* He didn't materialize.

Trying to ignore the headache, she sat up, slow and easy. She felt the back of her head and winced. Her fingers were wet and sticky, smelling of blood. The pry bar had done some damage. Nausea hit her full-force, her fingertips began to tingle, and she experienced an odd sense of detachment. She thought she might faint and lay down again until the feeling went away.

After the sickness passed, she sat up for a second time, listening for any sound that might be a clue of her location. Not a whisper, no insects, no running water, nothing to tell her anything. And still Silas didn't come to her rescue. She lay back down again, exhausted, and drifted to sleep, hoping she hadn't died. Because if she had, she should be with the man she loved—and instead she was alone.

When she came fully awake, her body went into heart-pounding, breath-grabbing, sweaty-cold panic that wrapped its hands around her throat.

Where am I? What am I going to do? Silas, someone, help me.

She became aware of the futility of her fear and focused on her body instead of her surroundings. Consciously slowing her breathing, she tried the relaxation exercises the nurses had taught her father to use when the pain meds no longer worked.

Breathe. Slow. Arms and legs heavy, limp, floating on a cloud. Imagine sun on the ocean, birds in the sky, warm breeze. Feel good, relaxed, well, strong.

It didn't work, and she started to hyperventilate.

"Abigail, don't fuss. I am here."

Silas. Her words didn't make it through the gag, but the terror receded, and her head felt better. The sense of being closed in remained overwhelming. She reached out with her bound hands and found empty space. Not buried alive. A good place to start.

Taking a deep breath, she inhaled the musty essence of soil, damp and loamy. A sickly-sweet stench, like dead mouse, lurked under the surface.

Abby got on her knees, and then pushed to a standing position. Struggling with the tape on her wrists did no good. She reached up, unable to touch the ceiling, then extended her arms in front of her body and inched forward. When she hit a barrier, she turned left and walked as far as she could, arriving at a corner. Packed dirt met her fingertips. She bent down and found a small pebble. By twisting and turning it, she embedded it in the edge of the dirt wall at shoulder level.

Abby took five steps. Dirt wall. Turn. Five steps. Dirt wall. Turn. Five steps. Dirt wall. Turn. Five steps. Dirt wall. Turn. Back at the pebble. The room measured about five feet square. She surmised it must be underground; Jack had somehow transported her and put her in. Which meant she could find a way out.

She dropped back to her knees and began a circuit around the room again, clumsy with her wrists taped together. Her knee landed on something hard. Reaching down, Abby ran her hands over a piece of cold metal, long and bent at one end. The pry bar Jack had used, the evidence of his attack buried with her. But maybe now *she* would find it useful.

She worked the bar between her knees to brace it, and ran the duct tape along the edge in a sawing motion. Her hands and knees became sweaty, and the bar slipped. She repositioned it and worked until, with a rip, her hands were free. She tore the tape off her wrists, wincing as it stuck to her arm hair, then jerked the gag from her mouth.

"Help. Help me!" Her voice cracked like a very old

lady, as her words were sucked into the packed earth surrounding her. She stood and moved to the wall. At each stop on the perimeter, she systematically shoved the metal into the dirt, until her arms ached. She found no exit.

"*Try again*," Silas whispered into her ear.

"Silas, please, don't leave me."

"*Never, Abigail. Never.*"

On her second trip around the room, the metal rod moved with more ease and force, guided by Silas's hands. It hit the wall and sunk in, the dirt spongy and pliable. Using the bent end, they dug at the soft spot.

"This has to be the way out. I'm afraid I'm running out of fresh air. What if I suffocate in here?"

A gentle touch wiped away tears she hadn't realized were on her cheeks. A puff of breath entered her nostrils, sweet and refreshing. "*Love is stronger than fear.*"

"We can do this together. Right?" Abby waited, but Silas's presence had gone. And yet the worst of the fear seemed to be gone, too.

Abby went back to work. The humidity made her sweat, intensified by hard labor. She dug for what seemed like hours, until she sunk to the floor, unable to continue. Thirst and exhaustion overwhelmed her. Panic and doubt nibbled at her mind, taking sharp little bites of her confidence. She tried gouging at the dirt wall with arms as rubbery as cold spaghetti, even while her thoughts traveled down their own path. How long had she been entombed? If she died, would she be with Silas? Wouldn't that be her dream, to love and to be loved for eternity? Why didn't it feel that way?

The bar slipped in her sweat-slick hands and fell forward. She dropped to her knees and groped for it, reaching through an opening in the wall, clearing away as much rubble as possible. She breathed deeply. The air, although stale, seemed fresher than in the room. But still no light. What if she got wedged into the small space?

Abby bent over and crawled through the opening. She

was in a tunnel, unable to stand. The walls hugged her on both sides, suffocating instead of comforting. Would the dirt collapse? Did an opening or a dead end await? The absurdity of the phrase "dead end" in the current circumstances reverberated. She giggled, suspecting that she had almost reached her breaking point.

Silas whispered in her ear. *"This way."*

"I'm afraid." Abby choked back a sob.

"You ain't afreed of death, but of dying. The tether that joins us ain't gonna sever until your time comes." The essence of Silas let go.

Abby continued on her hands and knees. Spots floated in front of her eyes, and she had to stop to take deep breaths every few feet. She grasped the metal bar and dragged it along in case Jack showed up again. The added weight made it hard to crawl. The sweat from her palms combined with the dirt floor, making mud that caused sucking sounds in the narrow enclosure. Her knees scraped on small stones, her back ached, and the darkness continued, unabated.

With a sigh, she stopped, unable to go any further. She knew 'her time' must have come. Why fight the inevitable?

"Abigail, follow the path. Your purpose is mine."

Refreshing coolness wound around her shoulders. Her panic subsided. She lost all sense of time, concentrating on moving her hands and knees together, one at a time, as though a baby learning to crawl. She tried to think, to plan, but the whole of her reality became the slow progress through the tunnel. Then it stopped, at a solid wall.

Abby poked the metal bar against the end of the tunnel, making a small dent. The narrow space gave almost no leverage, and her arms were weak. She tried to turn but couldn't, and instead crawled backward, intending to return to her starting point.

"Keep going." Silas's voice beckoned to her.

"Silas, I'm sorry. I don't want to die. Not even to be with you." Tears ran down Abby's cheeks as she collapsed on her stomach in the dirt. At the touch of a cool caress against her cheek, her fear subsided again, even as a shower of dirt fell into her hair and onto her back like raindrops.

The pry bar appeared in her hand from where it had fallen, without her even reaching for it. She thrust the curved end into the packed soil with supernatural strength. With a sudden jolt another space opened. She cleared enough room to squeeze through. Collapsing on the floor, panting, she remained still until her heart stopped pounding and she could breathe again.

"*You are safe, dear one.*" Silas whispered, feather-soft, into her ear.

Abby sensed he had left her. She stood. This place seemed larger than the first room; she couldn't touch the ceiling and had no sense of the walls. Pacing the perimeter confirmed it to be bigger in diameter. It remained dark but not pitch-black. She sunk in exhaustion onto a waist-high rough plank shelf attached to the wall.

"A platform?" Abby took a fresh look at the dim surroundings. She remembered being in the barn with Jack, the sharp pain to her head, the pitch black, and then the tunnel. Which she opened with the metal bar she had abandoned on the floor.

"I'm home. Silas, I'm *home*." Although she received no answer, she kept talking, hoping to lure him from wherever he had gone. "This is the room Morton and I found at the bottom of the hidden staircase."

Above her head a glimmer of light came through the broken step in a jagged shaft. She turned her face to it, reveling in illumination from the real world. So she'd found home and light. But no ladder to get her out. She balanced on tiptoes at the edge of the wooden shelf and stretched toward the opening, but couldn't reach.

She hopped off the shelf and picked up the pry bar. Holding onto the flat part of the tool, Abby waved the curved end toward the steps above, jumping to reach it.

After several failed attempts, the curve caught on a solid piece of wood. Careful not to dislodge it, Abby grasped the bar with both hands. Her feet swung off the platform and she dangled in space, wishing she'd done better in gym class.

Using more strength than she knew she had, Abby pulled herself within reach of the steps. Just as her fingers slipped on the bar, cool arms scooped her up. She grabbed onto the wood. The pry bar fell to the floor below as she was lifted to an intact step.

In the dim light, Silas smiled. "Welcome home, Abigail."

Abby threw her arms around his neck and buried her face in the coarse weave of his jacket. Her voice came out muffled against the wool. "You saved my life."

"No, you dun good. And love finished the rest."

They stayed melded together for many moments while Abby's emotions settled into something resembling normal. "Where do you go when you leave me?"

"It's like drifting on the river, dozing in the sun." Silas stroked her hair. "When you stir my dreams, I wake up and come to you."

"Will you ever stay 'awake' with me? Or will I die and be with you?" Once she got this close to him, death held little menace or fear. "And why are you sometimes a spirit and at other times flesh and blood?"

"I waited these long years for you, Abigail. But in all that time, the answers still ain't mine to know."

"What do you mean, that you 'waited' for me? I'm not the Abigail you used to ... love."

Silas silenced her with a deep kiss, his lips chasing any questions. She clung to him, willing him to stay with her, demanding in her brain that whatever or whoever guarded the universe would understand and be merciful.

But with a final stroke to her hair, Silas slipped away.

Abby ascended the steps to where Jack had boarded up the opening. She pushed against the lumber and plaster, but it held firm. The metal pry bar, which might have worked, lay out of reach in the underground room far below.

Sinking down on the top step, Abby rested her head in both hands and sobbed.

THIRTY-SIX

Abby's sobs subsided into whimpers and hiccups, ending when the mucous clogging her nose shut off her air supply. She wiped her face with the back of her arm, blew her nose into the hem of her shirt, and stood to examine the wall in front of her.

Jack had done a good job boarding it up. She took stock of her options. Her mom would be sleeping in Philly tonight instead of on the other side of the wall. Mrs. Blank would never climb three flights of stairs to look for her, assuming she had gone to bed. And her phone had long since died.

Abby could only think of one thing to do. She pounded on the wall with both fists. She screamed until her throat ached and the sound came out in scratchy bursts. No one came, as expected.

Time crawled by as slowly as she had crept through the tunnel. Although it seemed light at first in contrast to being underground, she realized the stairwell remained dim. But at the bottom of the staircase, a faint glow seeped in through the partition.

"Meow." Kitty's soft purr whispered hope into the gloom.

Kitty must be in the kitchen, where she had first accessed the stairs.

"Maybe I can find enough space to pull apart the plaster and crawl through. I'm coming, Kitty."

Abby put one hand against the wall and edged forward, testing each step before placing her full weight on it. She headed for the irregular patches of light coming in along the base of the wall beyond the broken step. Kitty's plaintive mews called for her. When she got to the partition, she ran her hands along it. The wood seemed thin, hopefully breakable.

"Move, Kitty."

Bracing herself against a step, Abby lifted both legs and kicked as hard as she could against the wooden barrier— once, twice, then a third time. A hole appeared in the plywood as dust billowed into the stairwell. Abby waved it away, took a deep breath, and jumped over the broken step. She landed face down on tile. Dazed, she glanced up to where Kitty sat washing her paws. Looking back, she saw the brick-framed alcove in the kitchen, with the secret stairs behind.

Abby stood up and grabbed for Kitty. She buried her face in the soft fur behind her ears. "I am so glad to see you. Everything else is beyond weird, like I'm swimming underwater and the world is blurry."

She put the cat down and got a bottle of water from the refrigerator, grateful that the electricity had come on again. After chugging the water, she saw a note taped to the freezer door. On bright orange paper it said: *Dear Abby, came over but see that you went to Morton's house. I'll be back in the morning. Mrs. Blank*

Another note under it, in Jack's handwriting, said: *Mrs. Blank, going to Morton's for the night. Mom said it would be okay. Will call you tomorrow. Abby*

Jack had taken care of everything. Except for his sister.

Abby looked out the window into murky dusk, melting into darkness. Rain pelted the ground and now had been joined by lightning and thunder. Abby shivered.

"It's a good evening to stay inside, Kitty. I need a bath and my bed."

Then she remembered the reason Jack hit her, the letters, his father's plan to kill the president, Jack's vow to follow through with it. She felt the aching wound on her head. And recalled the pain of her brother's betrayal. Instead of a bath she needed the police, the Secret Service, someone. If Jack came into the house, she might not live through another encounter with him, even if Silas helped her.

Abby ran to the landline to hit 911. The light above the sink flickered and went out. She held the receiver to her ear; no dial tone. No electricity, no phone, no internet. Where was Jack? How could she get help?

Holding the curtain aside a tiny bit, Abby peeked out the window at sheets of gray rain. Flickering candlelight came from the barn and, as she watched, Jack rode through the open door on his bike. His saddlebags were attached to the back, leather wet-gleaming in the rain. Pedaling fast, he glided past the house, down the path, and turned onto the trail, out of sight in seconds.

Abby's mind raced. She had no way to get help. And if she did contact the authorities, they would arrest Jack, maybe hurt him ... or even kill him if he resisted. But she couldn't let him follow through with his plan. He had to be stopped. Not just to save the president, but to save her brother from his own demons.

She ducked into the downpour and ran toward the barn, immediately soaked to the skin. A bolt of lightning cut across the sky. Thunder boomed, trees bent in the increasing wind. Skidding into the barn, she grabbed her purple bike and then let it fall to the ground. Climbing on her dad's Cannondale, she rode into the storm and turned right onto the Youghiogheny River Trail, heading southeast.

Darkness swallowed her up as she rounded the first

bend. The rain pelted Abby's arms and legs, stinging as though tiny nails were being driven into her flesh. Her head throbbed, and she wondered if a bike helmet would have helped or made it hurt even more.

Abby concentrated on the trail, the path almost invisible in the dark. No street lights, nothing to illuminate the way except occasional streaks of lightning ripping across the fabric of the sky. She huddled closer to the handlebars as a dazzling, jagged bolt flashed horizontally above the trees. It showed nothing more than sheets of rain, water-soaked trees lolling over the trail, and a glimpse of reflection from the river on her left.

The wind shifted, blowing rain into Abby's face. She realized how hard it had become to pedal with the added resistance, the only consolation that it would be harder for Jack, too. Wet ribbons of her hair whipped against her face and neck. Sodden strands of something curled around her ankles, and she realized she'd ridden off the trail.

She muscled the bike back onto limestone. The wet surface grabbed at the tires with a soggy hiss that impeded her progress. Her legs ached from pumping, and she had no idea how long she'd been riding. It seemed much farther than she had ever gone, way past the cemetery, as if a surreal, slow-motion nightmare was being played out in the storm.

While one part of Abby's mind concentrated on navigating the bike trail, another part considered how to stop Jack. Limited access to the trail meant leaving it to find a phone or a person; no one would be out here at night, much less in a storm. If she failed to get help, too much time would pass; Jack would get away. If she got help, Jack would be in trouble. Big trouble. Jail-for-life trouble—or worse.

As an experienced biker, Jack had the advantage off-road and on. He could hide all day and ride at night. His hate-induced insanity would lead him to do whatever his father said to get revenge for his brother. The loaded gun he carried meant other people could get hurt. But surely he wouldn't shoot his sister.

Abby had a sudden epiphany. She had become enmeshed in a love triangle. With Silas, whom she loved with passionate intensity. And with Jack, who shared the blood coursing through her veins.

She had to save them both.

THIRTY-SEVEN

A clap of thunder rumbled overhead, reminding Abby of the Fourth of July bike rally, maybe President Keller's last one if Jack had his way. Another boom shattered the night, accompanied by a lightning bolt that sizzled and lit up the sky. In that brief moment Abby thought she saw movement off the trail, just the barest hint of someone skulking in the line of trees near the river. It had to be Jack. No one else would venture out in the storm.

Abby glided into the weeds before braking to mask the sound of wet stones skidding against rubber. She sensed how vulnerable she must be, exposed even in the dark as she continued to ride through an open field. The soggy meadow grass made it difficult to keep moving, but she feared walking would waste too much time if what she thought she saw turned out to be nothing more than a figment of her imagination.

She reached a tall pine tree, stopped, and leaned the bike against the rough, wet bark. Her ears ached from the deafening water noise of rain and river, but the sound drew her like a magnet. She caught a glimpse of reflection from swirling white river water at the bottom of the embankment on which she stood and swayed, dizzy from the height. A burst of lightning, quick and saw-toothed like a zipper, arced in the sky. The trees stood outlined, solitary black silhouettes back-lit by the flash.

Abby swiped a hand across her dripping face and peered into the dark. "Come out, come out wherever, you are," she whispered into the wind. What was she doing in a storm, chasing someone she could never catch? And if she did find him, what then?

She waited for one more look around during the next burst of light. She had a sense of Jack; her gut told her to stay, and she did, like a Golden Retriever on alert. Lulled by the darkness and steady beat of rain on the branches overhead, Abby jumped at the simultaneous roar of thunder and multiple flashes of lightning as it crackled, strobe-like and horizontal, across the sky. That brief moment seemed to extend forever, as she spotted a figure bent over a bike straight ahead.

Jack.

The next flash came directly toward Abby. She ducked behind a pine tree just in time, as lightning hit a huge oak to her left. A sizzle and loud crack as the trunk split in half and fell, drowned out all other sound. The acrid odor of burnt wood permeated the night. Her eyes couldn't focus in the aftermath and she stood still, breathing in shallow gulps, waiting for her pupils to accommodate to the dim light.

Without warning, a pale face appeared inches away from her. Eyes feverish and lips pulled back in an evil grin, it was the Jack of a bad dream. But all too real.

"And so, *Cherie*, you found me, thanks to that bad tire, also your fault." Jack's voice whispered, a sibilant hiss cutting through the wind. "When I hid my journal and found that pit under the barn, I never suspected it would prove useful. But not useful enough, it seems, for here you are."

Abby shouted to be heard above the water and wind. "Jack, this is crazy. You need help. Let me help you. I get it; I get you. I miss my dad enough to drive me crazy, but killing the president won't make it any better for you. You'll die, you know. There's no way you can walk away if this doesn't stop now. Your father isn't worth it, and neither is your brother. He's already dead. I'm your sister, live for me."

Jack put his lips to her ear. "So I die. I'll be with my brother, and the president can rot in hell. You'll be better off without a brother like me."

"I don't want you to die. I don't want anyone to die." The warm wash of tears on Abby's cheeks contrasted to the chilly rain, and she attempted to hug her brother.

"Very touching. I don't want you to die either, but you leave me little choice. I wish you had stayed underground. You are such a sentimental little fool." He shot out his hand like the tongue of a viper, clasped her arm, and yanked her toward the river. Her slippery-wet skin slid in his grasp. He held tight. "I can't protect you anymore, God help me."

Abby's loose arm flailed and connected with her dad's bike. In one movement she pulled her other arm loose, wrenched off the tire pump, and ejected a puff of air into Jack's eye.

Jack grabbed the pump, threw it into the weeds, and laughed. "Did you think that little breeze would stop me?" He lunged at Abby.

She released the canister of dog repellent from the handlebar and sprayed it in Jack's direction, aiming for his eyes.

He stumbled to the side, howling, then tipped his head back to the cleansing rain.

Abby dropped to the ground, feeling for a branch, a stone, anything to use as a weapon. White-hot pain shot up her left ankle as she twisted it on the way down.

Jack picked up the lightweight Cannondale as if it were a toy. He heaved it through the air, and it sailed over the cliff into the water. He grabbed Abby under her armpits from behind and hauled her to her feet, dragging her toward the river. "You can peddle that bike to hell."

She writhed in his grip, kicked, tried to lower her head enough to bite his protruding hands. Her screams disappeared into the storm.

Jack panted as he struggled to subdue Abby. He managed to get her through the trees and stopped, teetering near the edge of the cliff over the river. Turning, he faced her forward.

Lightning flashed. Abby saw the froth of white water far below, beating against the rocks. Between where she stood and the surface of the Youghiogheny, nothing but open space existed. She tried to subdue her growing panic, picturing Silas, praying he would come to her aid.

Jack held Abby suspended as he attempted to move her to the very edge of the precipice. When she felt his grip loosen, she slammed her uninjured foot down on his instep.

Jack brought his knee up behind Abby's, and she collapsed on the mossy edge of the cliff. She rolled over and punched him high, between his legs.

He moaned and bent over.

Almost transparent through the rain, Silas appeared. He grabbed Abby by the hand. "Go, git away, Abigail. Don't look back."

With Silas's momentum, Abby got to her feel and scrambled to the trees. She limped for the bike trail, Jack in pursuit. She knew she couldn't outrun him.

"What the *hell*?"

At the sound of Jack's voice, Abby darted behind a tree and stood very still, back pressed into the rough bark, waiting for an opportunity to escape. She chanced a glance behind her.

Silas hovered in the air, his hair blowing straight back from his face. Resignation and anger moved through his eyes as he raised both hands and dove for Jack.

Jack's eyes widened. He covered his head with both

hands, submission and protection in one gesture. When nothing happened, he slowly dropped his arms. "I don't know what you are. Maybe I've lost my mind. But nothing can hurt me any more than I've already been hurt. All the power of this world or any other can't stop me."

He took a swing; his fist going straight through Silas. "If I can't hurt you, I'm betting you can't hurt me either. I have a mission. And I *will not* fail."

Mournful, as if an orchestra of violins were playing in a minor key, Silas moaned. "Keep yer filthy hands off her. She don't belong to you."

Jack laughed. "Either I'm hallucinating, or you're a pathetic ghost. She can be all yours as soon as I send her your way."

Silas flew into Jack but made no physical contact with him. He returned to Abby and gazed into her eyes. "I'm guessin' I kin touch only you—because we got one heart. I failed you again, Abigail." With a caress to her cheek, he disappeared into the mist.

At the sound of a soft footstep, Abby realized the rain and the rumbles of thunder had moved off down the river. Dripping foliage, rushing water, and another footfall; the night had gone from deafening to silent in a heartbeat. Jack was coming for her.

The faint glow of moonlight behind the clouds filtered through the trees. Jack's white skin and blond hair should be a beacon. Shapes became clear—trees, rocks, Jack's bike. But no Jack.

"Boo!" He appeared from the other side of the tree and grabbed a handful of Abby's hair before she could react. "*Mon Dieu*, you are a pain, *Cherie*. You and that monstrosity from the grave. But not for much longer."

Abby shook her head, but Jack held firm; her scalp burned. "Let me *go*."

"Shut up. Just shut up." He dragged her to the rim of the cliff.

Abby fought back, lunging for eyes, throat, any

vulnerable spot on his body.

Jack dangled her writhing legs over the storm-frothed river.

Abby lifted both feet and kicked Jack in the stomach, hard. The air came out of his lungs with a whoosh. His arms flailed like propellers. She used the momentum to throw herself onto solid ground.

Jack lost his balance. He fell forward toward the river and disappeared over the rocky edge.

THIRTY-EIGHT

"*Jack.*"

Abby crawled on her belly toward the place where land ended and empty space began, her fear of heights overcome by a gnawing ache in the pit of her stomach. "Better you than me, right Jack?" Abby sobbed as she inched forward. "Please don't be dead, tell me I didn't kill you. Oh please, just a broken leg, something to keep me safe; not dead, you can't be dead."

"*Abigail—run.*" The reverberation of Silas's voice had gone from a whisper to an insistent hum. "*Runnnnnnnn ...*"

Abby ignored Silas and curled her fingers over the moss-covered stone that announced the cliff's border. She laid her head down on her arms. In spite of the storm-cooled night air, sweat ran down the back of her neck to meet the chills crawling up her spine. She didn't understand why she cared about Jack, given what he'd done to her. But the fresh bonds of family were difficult to erase.

Abby lifted her head and inched forward to peer over the sheer drop into the churning river below. On the glimmering water she saw Silas. He hovered above the rapids, reaching out to her, pointing toward Bikers' Rest and safety. His uniform appeared more tattered, and his mouth opened wide in an O, as if afraid for her. Then he disappeared, sucked away in a wind gust.

The situation itself seemed so bizarre, so out of context from her normal life, that Abby laughed, unable to control her emotions. Again. A weed protruding from the moss tickled her cheek, and her mind flashed back to the touch of Jack's finger against her face in a rare moment of affection. She shivered. There would always be a place in her heart that cherished him.

She reached forward and found a tree root protruding through the side of the hill. By wrapping her hand around the slippery wood, she braced herself at the rim of the abyss. She took a deep breath and craned her neck to search for Jack in the water or on the rocks below, careful to stay as far away from the rim as possible. If she saw him, she would do whatever she could to get help for him. And never tell them what he had planned.

Squinting, Abby focused on the water, the rocks, and the hillside. "Jack?"

Crack.

A hot shaft of wind tore past Abby's cheek as a bullet missed her by inches. It lodged in a nearby tree, wood splintering on impact. She froze in place.

A cold, callused hand grabbed Abby's wrist.

Jack's contorted face materialized in front of her. One hand clamped on her wrist, the other held tight to a fissure in the face of the cliff. He teetered on a tiny shelf of rock.

"I'm not even close to dead, *Cherie*," Jack said through clenched teeth. "But you are."

"Jack, listen to me. I'm your *sister*, remember? We can work it all out. Please, listen to me. It doesn't have to be like this. I'll never tell anyone."

Jack paused, features blank for a split second. He searched Abby's face, as if seeing it for the first time. He shook his head like a wet dog, his eyes glazed, and he tightened his grip. With a flip of his wrist Jack yanked

Abby over the moss-slippery stone.

She hung, suspended in the air, legs flailing. A roar echoed in her ears, her pounding heart competing with the crash of river water on stone far below. She felt Jack's fingers slipping off her wrist, taunting, one at a time; with each loosened finger she slipped further toward oblivion. She closed her eyes, then opened them, aware that Jack's pale face had become the face of death. And the last thing she would ever see until Silas greeted her in eternity.

Jack cackled, lips curled over his teeth in a horrible grimace. "*Au revoir*, my dear sister."

Abby closed her eyes for a final time and went limp. An old Bible verse she had seen in the Munroe Bible drifted through her mind: "Oh death, where is thy sting?" She thought about her father and then Silas. They died, but they didn't quit. At that moment she knew she couldn't give up, not yet.

Jack released her wrist. Abby grabbed at the air with her free hand and swung her legs toward the craggy surface of the cliff. She fell several feet in a roller-coaster plummet, before landing on a sapling growing out between the rocks. The slender trunk bowed and swayed, but held her weight.

Abby pushed her foot forward into a crevice in the stone; a sharp pain electrified her sore ankle. Black spots danced in the periphery of her vision, and she fought the urge to faint. She rested her forehead against the cool surface of the cliff. Holding onto the tree with one hand and an outcropping of rock with the other, she willed her heart to slow down.

"What?" Jack bellowed from above. "You have nine lives like your stupid cat. Say your prayers; you're out of luck."

He eased his body down the rock face, feet-first. When he got within striking distance, he aimed vicious kicks at her hand, the reflectors on his bike shoe winking in the moonlight. He struck out again and again.

Abby groaned at the assault on her hand. The pain told her to let go.

Silas whispered in her ear, "*Hold on.*"

Releasing her death-grip on the rock while holding tight to the tree trunk with her right hand, she grabbed for Jack's foot. Clumps of wet hair blowing into her face and mouth made it impossible to see. Her left hand opened and closed as she grabbed for his shoe. Slick with moisture and mud, the leather slid through her numb fingers. He continued to kick. Their extremities did a bizarre dance in mid-air.

His untied shoelaces whipped her hand, the sharp sting like the torture of a hundred angry bees. Abby reached as far as she could without falling down the cliff, wrapped her fingers in the loose laces, and pulled hard.

Jack lost his balance. He fell past Abby without making a sound; seconds later a *thud* and a small splash.

Then nothing but the moan of the wind and an empty bike shoe dangling from Abby's bruised hand.

THIRTY-NINE

Abby clung to the rocky façade. To move meant looking down, way down, or releasing her hold and climbing up, way up. An image of Jack's body plummeting past flashed through her mind; her heart contracted. She couldn't stay clinging to the cliff. Words moved through her mind in an endless loop.

Forget him ... forgive him ... forgive me ...

Abby slid her bruised hand around on the stone until she found a niche above her head; she did the same with one foot, then hoisted herself up, a little at a time. She repeated the process, left then right, a slow, excruciating vertical crawl. Her arms ached, her already skinned face scraped on jutting pebbles, and her ankle throbbed.

Forget him ... forgive him ... forgive me ...

She reached the moss at the top. Close up she saw the tiny, individual shoots clumped together; in the dark it looked gray instead of green. The moon over her shoulder cast enough illumination to highlight a silvery sheen on the damp fungus.

Abby's searching fingers found a gnarled root. Using it as a handle, she pulled until she slid across the moss and collapsed on top of the cliff, feet still dangling over the edge. She dragged her body across the moss then stood, swaying. She bent over at the waist and put her head down. The spinning stopped but her stomach rebelled. She gagged and vomited on the lichen. The stench made her vomit again.

She wiped her mouth on the back of her hand and waded through the sodden switchgrass. The longing to cry, the ache to grieve, would have to wait. Although she knew she should keep moving, she collapsed on a tree stump. Jack could no longer hurt her. He also would never make her laugh again, dry her tears, or surprise her with a rose-covered box.

In the absence of immediate danger, exhaustion set in. She hung her head and noticed Jack's bike shoe still clutched in her hand. Picking it up, she held it next to her cheek, flashing back to the barn the first time she saw it on him. And the last time, as he tried to force her off the cliff. She flung the shoe into the woods and limped through the mud. Jack's bike and his backpack were half-hidden in the weeds, bike tools strewn about.

Abby hesitated, then reached for the backpack, holding it against her chest and breathing in the essence of Jack. A trickle of tears blurred her vision, and she succumbed to the battle between grief and anger. Numbness crept in and the tears stopped.

"Abigail … time to git home." Silas stood amongst the trees, straight, tall, and very real. He opened his arms.

Abby dropped the pack. She ran to him, standing enveloped in his embrace, his scent heady and comforting. His soft breaths caressed her heart, making it pump with hope. "I don't know what to do now. My brother …"

Silas pulled back enough to look in her eyes. "He ain't worth your tears. Rest easy." He kissed her forehead.

"What about us?"

Silas shook his head. "I ain't privy to such things. I been mourning these many years for failing Abigail. But the good Lord gave me a second chance. Fighting for you brought me eternal love."

"Since the day I arrived at Bikers' Rest, you've been my friend—and my love." Abby stood on tiptoes and kissed him. All the danger, fear, and distress morphed into passion. She pressed into him.

A rumble of thunder echoed from the other side of the river. Then another sound, soft and stealthy, caught her attention.

"Did you hear that? What if it's Jack?" Abby stepped away from Silas. Mourning Jack and facing him again were two different things. When Silas didn't answer, she looked for him, but he had vanished with the mist.

Before she could decide whether to run, hide, or fight, a hand clamped over her mouth from behind. She bit down, tasting blood and chocolate. The hand released her.

"Abby, whoa. *Ouch*, let go. It's me."

Abby whipped around. "Morton?" She flung her arms around him. "I'm so glad to see you. Your fingers, I'm sorry, I thought you were … well, I didn't even think." She stopped, out of breath, then pulled back. "Why *are* you here?"

Morton glanced around. "Where's Jack?"

"Gone. Just—gone."

Morton nodded. Another rumble of thunder, louder this time, made him shiver. "I got scared at home when the storm hit. A friend had taken my mom to a doctor's appointment earlier; flash floods washed out the road, and they couldn't get back. I didn't want to be alone. I tried to call you, but the phones were dead, so I had to wait. When the rain stopped, I rode over to Bikers' Rest. Then I got worried about you."

"Why?" Abby said. "I could have been anywhere."

"Nah, I knew something must be wrong between the open door at the house and the busted-up wall on the kitchen floor. I checked the barn and saw your bike, but not your dad's or Jack's. That seemed too weird. Then I found Jack's letters and figured out you went after him.

Stupid move, Abs. He's a nut case—he could've killed you and thrown your body where we would never have found it."

"Yeah, maybe, but what choice did I have? He is ... was ... my brother. And you tried to strangle me because ..."

"Because I saw Jack's bike and thought you were him and he had done something bad to you."

Abby hung her head. "Yeah, well, I did something bad to him instead."

"I'm not a lawyer, but I watch lots of TV." Morton patted her shoulder. "It's gotta be self-defense. And whatever you did, he had it coming."

Abby couldn't talk, think, or feel.

"I just want to go home."

FORTY

After a night that never seemed to end, Abby sunk into her own bed in the early hours of the morning, while darkness still lingered. Her face burned, her muscles ached, and her ankle throbbed. Fatigue weighed her down as if she could literally sink into the mattress. A gentle rain resumed, but even the soothing patter on the tin roof failed to lull her to sleep. Her mind refused to cooperate and let go. Instead it re-played the past few hours over and over again, in an endless loop.

The far-off murmur of thunder dragged Abby's thoughts backward. A mosaic of images flitted through her brain, fragments burned there after Jack disappeared over the cliff into the river. Bike tires hissing on wet limestone. Hating Jack/loving Jack. Electric candles glowing in the windows at the end of the bike trail. Home at last. Electricity back on, unable to reach Lisa, message left at the hotel. Numbness filled her.

Abby twisted and turned, pulling the pillow over her head. She didn't want to live it all over again. But the montage wouldn't stop.

The simple act of finding the right phone number had seemed daunting; calling the F.B.I. even more so. The knock on the door came soon after. Then the telling that had to be repeated and repeated—Jack's letters, his dangling bike shoe, frothing waters. The hush of whispered conversations between men wearing dark suits and angry frowns made the murky hours of night last forever. Waiting, waiting, for something to happen as minutes ticked away, prolonging the nightmare. Chewing her fingernails until nothing was left to chew. Wishing Silas would appear to whisk her away.

When it seemed impossible to sit still the news arrived: Jack alive and in government custody, belongings confiscated. The police found his gun, pried a bullet from the pine tree, and discovered an inscription on it, "For Etienne." His father arrested.

Abby massaged her throbbing temples. She couldn't believe they expected to keep everything a secret, even for 'National Security,' whatever that meant. Maybe Jack would go to a hospital instead of prison, maybe they would be reunited someday after he got well. That's what they said; were they telling the truth? She had to believe it, or never, ever rest. He had to be okay. She would learn to be okay.

Names and faces from the long night were already blurry, except for Mrs. Blank wringing her hands, murmuring prayers over a rosary. And images of the men in dark suits leaving Bikers' Rest before daylight, as if nothing happened. Case solved, next terrorist please.

Tears spilled onto her pillow. Dad dead. Jack gone. Silas—somewhere.

"Rest now." Silas slipped under the sheet beside her. The buttons on his uniform pressed into Abby's back as he pulled her close.

"I want to stay awake. With you." Abby's eyelids, against her will, became heavy. The gentle tickle of Silas's fingers stroking her arm lulled her into dreamless sleep at last.

Sunlight streaming through the window roused Abby.

Silas had gone, but the impression left by his head remained on her pillow. She kissed the indentation, wondering if this would be her life from now on. Loving a ghost would not be easy. But love him she did. No matter what it might mean. She heard faint noises from below and crawled out of bed.

She limped across her room and found her phone on the dresser. Seven o'clock? And there were already people downstairs? She yawned but knew she had to check it out. When she reached the kitchen, she stopped and stared.

"Hey, Abs! Top o' the mornin' to you." Morton did a little jig and put a plate of pancakes on the table, next to a glass of chocolate milk.

Abby fought the urge to rub her eyes. "You made breakfast? Why aren't you with your mother?"

"Whoa. One thing at a time." Morton held out her chair. "My mom has to stay at her friend's house until the fire department gets the road open. I called, and she said it would be okay for me to hang here. So I slept on your couch. And yeah, I made the pancakes. Check them out; I put in some M&M's."

Abby sat down and took a cautious bite. "Not bad. I thought my mom must be home early when I heard the noise down here."

Morton raised one eyebrow. "Mom? Not Lisa anymore? What happened?"

"I figured some things out when I couldn't sleep last night, that's all."

"Gotcha. I'm gonna take out the trash. Right back." Morton grinned. "I'm the good guy today, right?"

"*Every* day." Abby put down her fork and carried the dirty dishes to the sink, quickly pushing the pancakes into the garbage disposal. Her reflection in the window glass stared back at her, like a younger version of Lisa. No perfect person existed. At least she had returned when Abby most needed her.

On the counter Abby caught sight of the photo Jack

had enlarged for her, *Daddy loves Abby*. She picked it up and whispered, "I always thought *you* were perfect, even when I grew up. Then I found out you kept my mother away. You must have had your reasons." She sighed. "I guess everyone makes mistakes."

She ran her hands over the picture frame Jack had chosen and closed her eyes.

In her mind she could imagine his blue eyes, crinkled at the corners, his white-blond hair, the feel of his calloused hand tousling her hair. And vowed to focus on what had been right between them, not wrong.

Morton interrupted her thoughts. "Have anything else to eat?"

"You're a food machine. Give it a rest. And since you're here and such a 'good guy,' will you help me clean up the mess from yesterday? When I kicked out the wall from the secret stairs into the kitchen it was about survival. But I want to start over with my mother, and the plaster and wood all over the floor won't help."

Morton surveyed the damaged wall in the kitchen alcove. "Let's open it the rest of the way and take out the old wood. If we do that and sweep, it'll look better."

They worked for an hour, pulling the old boards away from the bricked arch. When they finished, Abby ducked under the frame. "It's awesome. The stairs to the third floor are here and you can see the Underground Railroad room below. I hope we can keep it like this." She stopped. "Morton, check it out. There's a shelf inside the wall, with some old jars."

Morton reached in and pulled out a dusty glass jar with a metal lid. "You know what I think? I think in the old days there must have been shelves across this whole opening, like a panty. One time I read about something like it. I'll bet it hid the door to the room where slaves were concealed. That's the perfect answer for this. Add a ladder behind the shelves, and it would explain how they got the slaves into the room down below. Hey, I have to pee. Right back."

Abby pulled out several more jars of old fruit or tomatoes. One looked different from the rest, with a piece of paper instead of canned vegetables inside. She held the jar up to the light.

"Abigail … you found it." Silas materialized in the gloom of the space, solid and unwavering. His dark curls looked neat, tucked under the blue cap tilted on his head. The uniform fit him well, the brass buttons polished and shiny.

A deep sense of peace and calm overtook Abby. Silas looked whole, well, stronger, as if he had been infused with new life. "This?" She held up the jar.

Silas nodded.

Abby threw her arms around Silas and breathed him in. He now smelled of soap and fresh linen dried in the sun instead of smoldering fires and burnt coffee. "Does that mean you can stay with me? We can be together here— and you'll never leave me again?"

His arms tightened around her. He kissed the top of her head, down the side to her ear, and onward to her lips, gentle kisses that spoke of love. But not of passion. With a deep sigh he pulled back.

"You're leaving." Abby choked back a sob. "But I thought you loved me."

"Oh, Abigail, indeed I do love you. I been searching so long, and now things have been set right. I kin finally rest in peace."

"I don't understand." Abby clung to him, unwilling to let him go.

"You will." Silas released Abby and held her hand in the particular way he always had, his thumb gently stroking between her thumb and finger. "Remember this one thing: love is a river that flows without ceasing. Once the water leaves its source anything might happen. That ole river kin rush, flood, taint, or git clean. Don't matter none, 'cause it still keeps on flowing. The power of a mighty river won't never be denied. And neither will the power of love."

"Is this good-bye?" Abby held her breath, the whole of her being suspended in the moment.

Silas nodded. His smile lit the golden flecks in his eyes with an amber glow, like sunset over the river. "Sweet Abigail ..." He vanished.

Abby closed her eyes and held the jar to her chest. She had a sense of loss, but it held an aura of wonder. She didn't fully understand what he'd meant about love being a river, but expected that as all things with Silas, it would be revealed in time.

"So, you gonna hug that thing to death or open it?" Morton poked Abby in the arm.

Abby blinked and unscrewed the rusted lid. The metal top squeaked in protest, but she worked until she got it open. She turned over the jar, and the piece of paper fluttered to the floor.

She picked it up and scanned the faded writing, sucking in her breath. Her heart accelerated, and her hands trembled. "Morton, listen to this."

"Miss Leticia, she dun hid me reel good so's I can be free. My dear daughter Abigail, good Lord rest her sweet soul, could'a bin safe too. I s'pect she died of a broke heart when Mr. Silas got called off to war and leaved her here. Said he wud 'fite the good fite' for freedom, 'cause he loved her. Too much dyin' and now the good Lord 'bout ready to take Miss Leticia home wif him. I tol her I been a houseboy and dun learned my letters good. She sez wud I rite sumthin and hide it fer her. I jest be glad to hep this fine God-fearin' lady. Here is jest what she dun tol me:

My son Silas saved Pres'dent Lincoln's life. He wuz s'posed to be hid until the war wuz over then folks wud'a knowed he dun a brave deed. But that were not the Lord's will. Silas died with the typhoid fever a 'fore they cud move him from prison. My baby died wif no one to hold his hand.

I dun hid his di'ry in my Bible. His secrets got buried wif him in his grave marker. I hope sum kind soul finds this and makes things rite. Greaves me, he lies in shame when shud be hero. He is a hero to me. I, Leticia Jean Munroe, promise to the God I am about to meet this be the truth. I always keep my promises, 'specially to Him.'

I give my word this be what Miss Leticia dun tol me. Twones Allen, freeman."

"Now we know it all." Abby scanned the letter again. "Knowing is good, even if everything isn't the way I wanted it to be. Silas and Leticia should have lived long enough to see him become a hero after the war, and they didn't. But now the world will know what truly happened. I used to make up happy endings when things were sad. I guess I've learned it's more important to deal with what's real."

Abby kept silent on a certain part of the letter; Morton would ask too many unanswerable questions. It seemed clear that the first Abigail had been Silas' true love, and that he felt guilt after her death because he left her to fight against the South and slavery. Helping—and loving—Abby had provided a path for him to eternal rest. It had left her longing for the love that had gone on with him. She was his second love. He was her first.

"Abs, it's all too cool." Morton bounced on his toes. "This is a letter from a former slave; that's history right there. I bet everyone will be interested in Bikers' Rest. You have old letters and a diary, an Underground Railroad stop—Civil War stuff no one ever knew before."

"Let's put these other jars back where we found them." Abby looked up at the sound of a truck engine outside.

Before she could move the back door opened. "Abby?"

Abby ran across the room and enfolded Lisa in a hug. "*Mom.*"

FORTY-ONE

Abby pushed the porch swing with her toes, staring into the yard as an August shower drenched the rose bush. The floral fragrance, tinged with earthworms, wafted into the air; she breathed it in greedy gulps, inhaling memories of her dad, the old house—B.J.

Morton sat on the wicker chair opposite the swing. "What's going on up in that noggin of yours?"

"I think about my life as B.J., Before Jack, and A.J., After Jack. It's lame, but I had to do something to separate then and now. For a while everything got split up based on Dad being alive and—not—but these weeks since Jack— left—things changed. I miss him." She didn't share the sense of loss from Silas moving on. Love might have been a river for him, but for her it had reached a dam. "What's that look?"

"You miss the guy who would have killed you," Morton said with a snort. "It's twisted."

Abby rolled her eyes. "All right, maybe a little. But we have a connection I can't describe. No matter what, he's my brother. I blame his father for setting him up. The real Jack wouldn't have hurt anyone. I have to believe that." Footsteps sounded from the house.

Lisa walked onto the porch, the screen door slamming behind her. "Honey, I have to run into town for an appointment. There's a couple who want to get married here at Bikers' Rest, and we're going to talk about it. He's a history professor at Pitt, and loves the idea of having their ceremony at the site of a stop on the Underground Railroad. And listen to this; he wants to write a book about Silas Munroe."

"Awesome, Mom." Abby smiled. The professor would never believe her if she told him how handsome, kind, and gentle Silas had been. Or that ghosts had the capacity to love and to be loved.

"I like being called Mom." Lisa paused. "When the F.B.I. finally reached me and I heard about everything, I got mad because you might have been killed. I couldn't take that. But now you're okay—and we're okay—and even Jack is safe, so I have to thank you. I should be back in an hour or two at the most."

Abby waved as Lisa drove away.

"I get the feeling there's something you aren't telling me." Morton popped two M&M's into his mouth at the same time.

"Nope. You know what I know." Abby justified her statement with a silent, *you don't know what I feel.* She could never explain to anyone how it had been for her with Silas. Or how much she wished he could have stayed with her.

"Okey-dokey. Gotta go before it storms again." Morton gathered his empty candy wrappers and stuffed them into his pocket. "Let me know when the professor guy is coming. I want to meet him, you know, give him my scoop on local history. Maybe he'll put me in his book. And you."

"There are things I never did figure out."

"Yeah, but you solved the important parts of the puzzle," Morton said. "You even stopped Jack-the-Ripper."

"Don't call him that." Abby glared at Morton. "And

don't you ever tell anyone what my brother did."

Morton's face drooped. "Abs, I wouldn't do that. You can trust me. Besides, I don't mess with the F.B.I." He paused, started to speak, then stopped again. He popped a handful of M&M's into his mouth and crunched.

"What now?"

"I know the agents said not to talk about it," Morton said. "But I'm not sure why."

"The F.B.I. guy said the Secret Service and Homeland Security don't want to risk more danger to the president from other terrorists. They want this to go away because Jack and his father got too close to President Keller. You and I are the only ones who know the whole story, besides my mother. So I promised to keep the secret. And I always keep my promises."

"Abs, you gonna answer the phone?"

Abby started and picked up her cell. "Hello?"

"Miss Whitney?" a female voice asked. "Miss Abigail Whitney?"

"Yeah, and I don't buy things from telemarketers." Abby prepared to disconnect.

"Miss Whitney, this is the White House. Please hold for President Keller."

Abby clutched the phone.

"Abs, your face is white," Morton said. "Who is it?"

Abby shook her head and waited.

"Miss Whitney, this is Hartley Keller. May I call you Abigail?"

"Yes," Abby whispered, then stronger, "Sir."

"Abigail, I want to personally thank you for the role you played in thwarting the assassination plot against me—and for your discretion. It's a National Security matter."

"Yes, I understand," Abby said.

"I appreciate the sacrifice you're making for your country." President Keller cleared his throat. "I understand we have your promise on this."

"Sir, I always keep my promises. My father taught me

that."

"Then take care, Abigail. Good-bye." A click and silence.

Abby sat the phone on the padded seat and resumed swinging.

"What just happened?"

Abby smiled, but before she could answer him a white panel truck pulled up in front of Bikers' Rest. No logo or markings marred the smooth sides of the van. Two men in dark suits and sunglasses got out and unlatched the back doors.

"You getting a delivery?"

"I don't think so. And who delivers things in a suit?"

Abby picked up the phone and walked to the porch steps. One of the men appeared from behind the truck.

"Miss Abigail Whitney?"

"Who wants to know?"

The man held up one hand. "We're making a delivery, Miss."

"I told you." Morton smirked.

The slam of the truck door and the screech of a latch resonated in the misty air. The caress of warm drips from the trees barely registered as Abby walked toward the new, blue Cannondale bike being wheeled across the gravel. The man leaned it against the picket fence and returned to the truck.

"President Keller sends the regards of a grateful nation, and asks you to accept this token of his appreciation." The other man returned to the truck, and they drove away.

Abby ran her hands over the bike. The center bar had a Mt. Zefal air pump attached to it and a tool kit under the seat. A utility rack was mounted on the back, a water bottle on the front, and a can of dog repellent on the handlebars.

"It's just like Dad's bike." Abby got on, rode it around the yard, and then into the barn. She returned to the porch, where Kitty sat washing her fur.

"Cool. Happy for you." Loud rumbles of thunder

moved closer. Morton frowned. "See ya. You okay?"

Abby nodded and settled onto the porch swing waiting for the rain to begin again. Now that the excitement had ended, all she wanted was Silas. She yearned for the gentle touch of his hands, for his tender eyes gazing into hers, and for his singular focus on loving her. It would never happen again. The river still flowed past her door, but it had swept Silas's love away from her, not to her.

Through the mist a figure approached on foot. He seemed to be in no hurry, looking left and right as if taking in everything in his path. As he got closer, he studied Bikers' Rest, not appearing to notice Abby until he had climbed the steps and stood on the porch. He reached down and patted Kitty's head, setting her to purring.

His blue linen shirt and jeans were nondescript. In fact, nothing about him screamed to be noticed. Just an ordinary guy, maybe seventeen years old, taller than average, shoulders broad, and waist slim.

Abby didn't get up or speak. For some reason breathing had become difficult.

"Oh, sorry. I didn't see you there." He stared at Abby for several seconds.

She stared back. Because as unremarkable as he appeared to be in general terms, he sent Abby's heart into a spin. His dark brown curls dipped below one eye as if too independent to obey a comb. Expressive eyes—hazel with flecks of gold in them—bored into hers. He must not get much sun, because his pale skin showed little color except for a blush of heat high on his cheekbones.

With a big smile, he opened a dimple in his right cheek and revealed bright white teeth. "Hi there." He reached out to Abby.

She stood and grasped his hand. As they came together, he stroked the back of her hand between her thumb and finger before pulling away.

Abby worked to center her thoughts, to still her core, to believe what she plainly saw. Because this boy looked like Silas, right down to the handshake.

"I'm Abby."

His eyes opened wide, his deep voice almost a whisper. "Abigail ..."

"Yes. Abigail." She knew she would never use her nickname again.

"I'm Evan Munroe." He looked as flustered as Abby felt.

Abby swallowed hard. "Munroe?"

"Yes. Evan Silas Munroe. Supposedly this house belonged to some ancestors of mine a long time ago. I came to check it out." He paused. "This isn't a pick-up line, honest, but do I know you? Because you're familiar, like we're already ... friends."

Abby inhaled a hint of soap and fresh linen dried in the sun and knew, in the way that certainty comes with pure love. Silas had earned his rest. But he hadn't taken her heart with him. Instead, just as he had said, "Love is a river that flows without ceasing."

And that river had brought Evan Silas Munroe to her shore.

ACKNOWLEDGEMENTS

TO GOD BE THE GLORY!

Many thanks to those who have traveled this journey with me. My family—Erik, Heather, David, Evan, Aiden, Mischa, and Ben. My friends, Editor Yezanira Venecia, and Melissa Keir at Inkspell Publishing.

To my husband, Harry, more love and thanks than you can imagine.

Special kudos to photographer Sky Williams for his amazing portraiture, and Najla Qamber for the awesome cover art.

Love and thanks to Evan Wiesemann, perfect cover model.

Without the support and expertise of my writers' Group, Marcy, Cheryle, Helen, susan, and Linda—and SCBWI—this project would not be what it is today.

And thank you to my readers, for whom I am most grateful.

ABOUT THE AUTHOR

Laurel has been writing since the age of six, when Crawls the Caterpillar inched across her lined notebook paper propelled by a fat yellow pencil. She has published magazine and newspaper articles as well as blog posts with All The Way YA, SEAPC Magazine, and on her website. Her portfolio includes multiple children's stories in a variety of genres. She has two Young Adult novels—both paranormal romances—with Inkspell Publishing.

In addition to writing, her passion is for travel to exotic locations around the globe. The people she meets, the places she visits, and the quirky way she looks at life all inspire her work. She loves complex characters and intricate plots that mesh into multifaceted books, melding romance, mystery, adventure, and history.

Laurel was a chosen participant at Better Books, a

craft-based workshop near San Francisco. She is active in the Society of Children's Book Writers and Illustrators, and has been a presenter at their Fall SCBWI Conference in Pittsburgh.

When she's not deep into a writing project, Laurel is a medical missions' nurse, traveling for Southeast Asia Prayer Center, Hope in Haiti, Caring Hearts, and Convoy of Hope. She lives in Oakmont, Pennsylvania, with her husband and their fur baby, Mabel. All of that, plus she's the world's biggest fan of chocolate milkshakes and hugs.

Website: www.laurelhouckpages.com
Facebook: Laurel Houck
Twitter: @LaurelHouck
Instagram: laurelscottage